SLOW BOAT TO PURGATORY

By

Vernon Baker

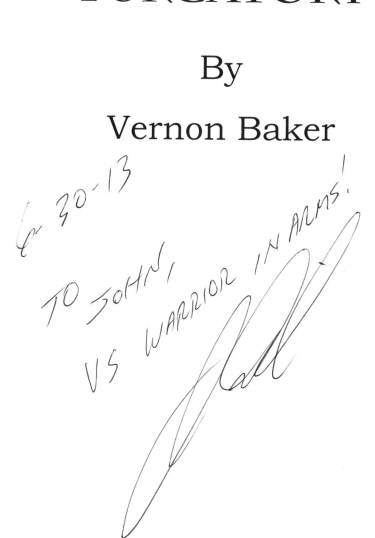

6-30-13

TO JOHN,

VS WARRIOR IN ARMS!

ACKNOWLEDGMENTS:

Special thanks to the following people who at one time or another found themselves in the Slow Boat, paddle in hand:

Terri Driver for being my first proofreader and Howie Cronin for buying the first book long before there was a book. Laura, Ricky, and Martin for being lab rats. Michael Garrett and Alan Rinzler for their lessons, candid observations, and suggestions. Terri Gibson for her keen eye. Harvey Ardman for being my first "editor" and Paige Pendleton for hours of reading, critiquing, encouragement, and for being one of the first believers. Dennis Driver...you know why.

DEDICATION:

For Ekco, my guardian angel.

PROLOGUE

Sweating, tossing and turning, lost in the dreams of another tormented night, I escape to find myself walking aimlessly down streets paved with five hundred year old cobblestones. Drifting under a full December moon, alongside canals full of the blackest water I've ever seen.

Nowhere to go and no one to see; just me, the moon, and a host of beings trailing along, unseen by most, but visible to me. Always just over my shoulder, wondering about me, plotting over me, coveting everything about me.

Low, almost unheard, music echoes down a rain and fog-soaked Venetian alley. I curse my existence wondering why it is I chose this life as waves of loneliness and remorse, so dank and dark, heavy to the point of being the final stone that crushes my very soul, weigh me down, slowing me to a dismal crawl.

I walk these alleys in the dead of night when mortals huddle beneath their covers, soaking up the essence of those lying next to them, and I can sense it, their comfort and peace, like an anchor pulling me into the inky blackness of the canals.

Night after night I prowl, waiting for the next call, the summons from the ultimate paymasters. When will it end, and have I done enough? Will I ever be able to do enough?

So I walk into the night as the music fades.

Into the dark until, half dead from the exhaustive burden of seven hundred years of walking the earth, I find myself back where I began my life in this city; in front of a small, almost forgotten church, hidden down a dark alley wedged in among stone piles called homes, apartments, and shops, a place forgotten after all these years by all of humanity save me.

The steps, time-worn in no small part from my own feet, do their duty bearing me up from the street into the overhanging darkness of a pillared portico sheltering the huge wooden door. A door locked to mortals, but less than a momentary obstacle to one like me. And then I'm in, among the stillness and reverence.

Only a few of the straggling horde who follow me dare to enter, those who claim to be on my side, but in fact could just as easily be my enemy someday. They hum and sway the closer I get to my destination, slowly falling under the spell of the place.

In my immortality, a wholly different state of being than the one enjoyed by those who now crowd around me, struggling to get close to the source of my veneration, I soon bask in the radiated grace emanating from the hollowed out space beneath my feet.

Finally, exhausted and worn beyond imagination, I fall face-down, fingers clawing at the spaces between the stones. My tears, laden with loneliness and pain, slip into the cracks, watering what lies unknown and unsuspected beneath the floor. Unknown and unsuspected by any mortal; known only to me and those who follow me through a dark and violent world.

In the end, all I am left with are my prayers. I hope someone is listening.

I am Gaspar de Rouse. I am immortal, and this is my life.

CHAPTER 1

France, February, 1944

He could taste the mud, blood and tears on his tongue; it was a mixture he'd gotten quite used to. Like the endless parade of dead bodies, screams and the ear-rending explosions of war, a war that had raged around and through him for close to three years now.

This was a bad day though, the worst yet. Lieutenant Randolph Donovan's body shook with the fear, rage and shock which possessed him.

A burst of phosphorus and shrapnel exploded to his right, two buildings down the street, sending a concussion of metal-laced air rampaging his way. He was thrown into the mud, water and who knew what else on the floor of the abandoned building.

After a moment, he pushed himself off the floor. He looked around the shattered remnants of the building. His platoon lay around him. Their bodies, as well as those of twenty dead Krauts, were scattered across the floor and into the street outside.

The Germans and his men had gone at it for a brutal half-hour. In the end, he'd been the only one left alive. The Krauts, a hardcore group of S.S. infantry, had been the better soldiers this day. More than thirty of his men lay dead at the hands of those Germans and at the climax of the orgy of screaming, dying men, he had faced three of the Germans armed with only a knife. He'd killed all three in a whirlwind of blood and gore.

Now, he was alone, a world away from his compatriots and directly in the path of the oncoming rush of counter-attacking Germans.

Peering over the edge of an empty window frame, in the direction of the German line, he could see movement. The guns had softened up the Allied positions for close to three hours. Now it was dark, and the sounds of artillery had slowly faded away. That could mean only one thing. They were coming.

He could see them now, silhouettes, wraiths really; death himself in a gray coat, metal helmet and mud-clogged boots, slogging his way across the killing fields, hungry for flesh and blood.

He cried then. Not from fear, but great wrenching sobs of self-pity, anger and remorse. Three years' worth of suppressed tears and angst welled up within him, hidden until now for the betterment of morale and discipline. But now, with those who needed him, who relied upon his stoic bearing and strength, spread out, torn, battered and bereft of life around him, composure seemed futile; unneeded.

He doubled over and expelled whatever was left of three days of rations and water onto the floor at his feet. Peering back out the window, he could see the massing Germans now only thirty yards or so from his position.

Well, if this was where it was supposed to end, so be it. Like a three year old child, he wiped tears and snot from his face. He checked the ammo pouch on his belt then worked the action on his Enfield, making sure the breach was clear of mud. Setting the rifle aside, he collected a death's head dagger and a potato masher from a dead German next to him.

He could hear the Germans yelling orders to one another. They were close, their voices echoing down the street.

He leaned back against the wall and closed his eyes for a moment. Taking a deep breath he turned, went out the door into the street and launched himself forward toward the approaching enemy.

He made no sound, he didn't fire. He just charged forward.

Cries and oaths of surprise drew his attention and the barrel of the Enfield. Slowing his advance to a steady, purposeful walk, he started firing at the shapes appearing out of the gloom around him. The action of the rifle felt smooth and hot in his hands. One, two, five, now ten fell at his feet as he waded into the mass of soldiers who hadn't expected this assault.

He dispatched fifteen souls before the Enfield clicked on an empty breach. Tossing the rifle aside without a second thought, he pulled the German grenade from his belt. He jerked the string and lobbed it some twenty feet forward through the doorway of another bombed-out structure. He pulled the dagger and dove to the ground just before the explosion of the grenade tore through a pocket of ten Germans inside the building.

After the explosion, he rose and crashed through the door into their midst, slashing and stabbing the writhing bodies carpeting the floor. As he slid the blade into the guts of a young soldier on the ground, locking eyes for a moment, he caught a glimpse of himself, wild-eyed, gray faced and haunted. A world away from the man he used to be.

A dark silhouette rushed him from the right and he found himself in a death clench with a badly injured soldier.

After a short struggle, which entailed gouging the man's eyes and jamming the blade into his throat, he looked out to the street to find himself in the middle of a charging horde of soldiers who seemed unaware he was amongst them. They were surging forward down the street toward the Allied line.

In a surreal world of death dealing, he stalked the Germans, picking one here, slitting his throat, and grabbing another there, knifing him in the gut. He dispatched another eight men in this way before he noticed that the flow of soldiers had turned and was coming back his way. He ducked into another bombed-out building and took up station next to a window that gave him a view of the street.

He felt it before he heard it, a rumbling vibration and then a sudden, *Whoosh!* as a geyser of flame exploded down the street.

As Randolph watched, the flames caught a group of four Germans who had stopped and were firing down the street. As the flames engulfed them, they began jerking and screaming as if they were spastic puppets at the end of some sadistic puppeteer's strings.

He knew what approached had to be an M-4 Zippo, a fire breathing American tank.

As if to confirm his suspicions, the barrel of a tank came into view and began spraying fire into the buildings along the street. He watched, mesmerized, as the flame-throwing barrel slowly moved his way until it was lined up on the doorway of the old building in which he was hiding.

Realizing he was about to be cooked by his own comrades, he turned and fled through the building, diving out a back door just as flames engulfed it.

He rolled to a stop in the middle of a muddy alley. Jumping up, he was confronted by a German soldier, coming out of a doorway into the alley, a wicked looking knife in his hand. His head was bare shaven, a nasty scalp wound oozing blood that flowed down his face. He looked like a caricature of the evil Hun in those recruiting posters stateside.

Randolph recognized the stripes on his tunic, a sergeant, and the twin lightning bolts on his collar. Staring at each other, neither seemed willing to make the first move.

Conjuring the words from somewhere Randolph said, "*Lauf, was du kannst*! Run for it!"

The German slowly shook his head, raised his knife and made a move toward Randolph.

Randolph reacted, moving to his right to avoid the onrushing German. Spinning, he kicked out with his right leg, catching the German flush on the back of the knee.

The big man staggered and grunted in pain, almost going down. Before he could regain his stance, Randolph was behind him, the S.S. dagger sliding deep into the man's back, just above the top of his trousers.

Randolph swung his left arm around the German's neck and jerked backwards. Withdrawing the knife from the man's back, he drew the blade across his now exposed neck, cutting deep into muscle and arteries.

It was over in less than twenty seconds. The big man struggled briefly before his gurgling breaths finally subsided. But it was those few seconds that cost Randolph everything.

The sound of an oath shouted in his direction made Randolph turn to look down the alley behind him. Two Germans crouched behind a pile of rubble and debris. As he watched, one of the soldiers raised a long tube to his shoulder, lining it up on Randolph. A *Panzerschrek*-a bazooka. The second soldier lifted his hand, middle finger raised in a universal salute.

Randolph was already moving to his left when he heard the explosion and the sound of the incoming rocket-propelled grenade from down the alley. He made it to an open doorway. It wasn't far enough.

The grenade struck the alley where he had been standing a moment ago and the explosion ripped through the walls of the old building, propelling Randolph through the room, slamming him into a stone wall.

Surprisingly, he didn't lose consciousness which allowed him to see the wall of flame flowing across the floor. In a moment, he was engulfed.

His body convulsed in pain and agony. He couldn't move to escape the flames which found their way into his mouth, eyes, ears and nose.

His whole body erupted in spasms that he couldn't control and his mind began to implode.

Then, in the moment before he began to lose conscious thought, he felt the fire consuming him begin to dissipate. His burning body seemed to cool and his mind, while tortured and cracking at the seams, registered the presence of someone standing over his convulsing body.

It was a man, a man in a dark coat the hem of which almost brushed the floor. In a moment of clarity, he realized the man stood amongst the flames, a pair of boots almost obscured by the fire.

Randolph felt hands sliding beneath him. They lifted him, and although amazed, he realized the man was carrying him across the floor and out through the flames into the street. At one point, he looked up attempting to see the man's face but all he could see was shadow cast by the brim of a wide, floppy hat.

"What's your name, soldier," the man asked.

Before he responded, Randolph realized his savior's voice was within his head.

"Randolph Donovan," he answered without speaking.

"Well, Randolph, I'm loath to see a warrior such as you fall prey to fire, so tonight, the Irish blood flowing hot within your veins brings you luck."

Randolph just stared. Was he dead? Was he having some sort of hallucination brought on by his injuries? What was happening to him?

A soft chuckle intruded on his thoughts, "The luck of the Irish, Randolph. These days, I walk these killing fields in wonder at man's capacity for evil and mayhem. But among all this carnage I never fail to find bravery, strength, and the occasional soul worth saving.

"Tonight has brought us together. Perhaps it will work to our mutual benefit, perhaps not."

Suddenly Randolph realized they were in a field outside the town. While they seemed to be standing still, he could tell time moved on. The sky above him was clear and, looking beyond the brim of the stranger's hat, he could see the heavens and a myriad of stars all moving across the night sky at speeds which left him dizzy.

The stranger lifted his head to the sky and in that moment, Randolph caught a glimpse of the man's face, dark, smooth, forbidding.

The last thing Randolph saw was the man's smile; he was smiling at the stars.

* * *

Randolph awoke three weeks later in an Army hospital in a suburb of Paris. Lungs scorched, skin as red as if he'd been left naked under the Saharan sun for days, but alive.

As they prodded and poked, drew copious amounts of blood and wondered at the way he was healing free of scars, the doctors kept telling him he shouldn't be alive.

He couldn't help them, he had no idea why he lived or how he'd arrived here.

It was only late at night, when he slept, that he dreamt of a man in a long, dark coat and droopy hat, who would come, sit next to his bed and with a wave of a hand, draw back the ceiling to reveal the night sky. They would sit together, the man telling him the names of the stars that whirled around their heads; the stars which seemed to be dancing only for them.

CHAPTER 2

The Coast of Maine, May, 2010

Alex Donovan coaxed his 1952 Jaguar XK-120 through the curves of Route One as he headed north to his grandfather's estate, Donovan's Acre. He'd just passed through the seaside town of Camden and to his right was able to catch sporadic views of the waters of Penobscot Bay through the occasional break in the trees. It was early May, and the roads had been mercifully devoid of congestion all the way up from Boston.

It was cold, but the top was down, and his brown curly hair was a windblown mess. A pair of black Ray-Bans shielded his eyes from the bright sunlight. A black scarf was wrapped tightly below his chin. He had to squeeze his six-foot, two-inch frame into the leather seat, but the all-encompassing feel of the car's timeless beauty and strength was worth the slight discomfort.

He was already five hours into the drive, taking longer than usual, due mostly to the fact the old Jag didn't like to exceed seventy miles per hour for any great length of time; that, and the need to stop occasionally to relieve his wrecked knee, a souvenir from a brief sojourn into the Hindu Kush. He'd decided to take the sports car because it had been his grandfather's gift to him upon his graduation from Annapolis. What he had to do over the next few days, at his grandfather's house, was a chore he wished he could avoid, so the rough-riding Jag fit his mood perfectly. He'd put off this day for two weeks and, as much as he'd loved his grandfather, the task before him left him with a deep sense of unease.

His grandfather, Randolph Donovan, had passed away three weeks ago at the ripe old age of ninety-six. He'd been in great health, and even at that age, his death had taken the family by surprise.

Alex had spent the weekend, before Randolph's death at the old man's house on the coast near the town of Northport. He'd helped his grandfather sail his 1945, thirty-eight foot Herrshoff across the bay from Islesboro, where he'd stored it for the winter, to his dock below the house.

Alex had complained and groused, as he had for the last twenty-five years, about launching the boat so early in the season. His grandfather, as he had for the last twenty-five years, proceeded to lambaste Alex for being a fair-weather sailor like all the other summer yachties who waited until June, sometimes later, to launch their boats.

He ridiculed the same "fair-weather pretenders," in late October, when Alex would again come up from Boston to help the old man put the boat up for the winter. He was always quick to point out his was one of the last boats to be hauled.

For forty-five years, the men at the boatyard, some of whom had been there for all those years, had worked on the boat and knew the old man's schedule. They knew better than to comment on it one way or the other.

Alex had weathered the tirades in silence just as he'd weathered the frigid April winds as they made their way from Islesboro.

After getting the boat to the dock, they had spent the weekend cleaning the vessel, checking the sails, rigging, and electronics. The men at the boatyard, as always, had done all this before they launched it, but it was a ritual of spring at Donovan's Acre. Alex, though he complained, loved these days and suspected his grandfather knew it.

He'd left Sunday, late in the day, after sharing lobsters, steamers, grilled Portuguese sausage, and two bottles of Montrachet from Randolph's cellar. As he'd driven up the long gravel driveway away from the house, he'd looked back in the rearview mirror to see his grandfather standing in the open front door. He'd put his arm out his window and waved. The old man raised his hand, turned, and disappeared into the old house.

It was the last time he ever saw him.

Now, as he turned the car off Route One towards the water, he thought about the events of the last three weeks since his grandfather's death.

The funeral service was to be a simple and brief affair aboard the sailboat. It had fallen to him, even though he was the youngest of the three grandchildren, to make the arrangements and see that their patriarch's wishes were followed.

Randolph Donovan had outlived his only son, Randolph Junior, by almost twenty years. Alex's mother, who had never quite succeeded in gaining her father-in-law's approval, had passed away ten years ago.

The three grandchildren, Alex, his brother Thomas, the eldest of the three, and his sister Ruth had been the only family at the service. Thomas' wife and two children had never had anything to do with Randolph and hadn't made the short trip from Manchester. Ruth, like Alex, had never married and had no children.

There had only been two other people there. Father Timothy Dugal, his grandfather's priest from Boston, and old Lucas Watson, who at ninety, had been Randolph's attorney for over sixty years.

His grandfather had decreed that he be cremated and his ashes spread from the deck of the boat into the bay in front of his house. So the five of them had piled onto the boat and Alex had motored out into the bay. While they were still in sight of the old house on the cliff, Alex dropped anchor.

After the requisite bitching from Thomas, who hated anything to do with the water and boats, Father Timothy had said a few words and led them in the Lord's Prayer, Alex noticing that Thomas abstained from even mouthing the words.

Alex took the small alabaster urn containing his grandfather's ashes and, removing the lid, had proceeded to dump the contents into the frigid water of the Bay. In his somewhat numb state, Alex failed to check the direction of the gentle breeze blowing across the deck of the boat and, to his amusement, some of the ashes blew across the boat straight into Thomas' face, which earned him a couple of barely suppressed oaths.

Alex had stood there for a few moments clutching the urn in one hand and a mast stay in the other. The tears had come then, and he'd mourned in silence. Mercifully, his brother remained silent. Father Timothy's hand on his shoulder had stirred him from his reverie.

"I think your grandfather loved you more than you know, son," said the priest. "I didn't see him much these last few years, but when I did, inevitably it was you he'd talk about. He thought the sun rose and fell with you."

"Thank you, Father," Alex said, gathering himself. "That means a lot to me."

Alex hoisted the anchor, moved back to the tiller, and turned the boat toward shore as they made the short trip back to the dock in silence.

Later, after Alex had secured the boat, they had shared a lunch of sandwiches he'd picked up at a local market and a bottle of 1991 Chappellett Cabernet he'd brought up from the old man's cellar. They'd made small talk for awhile until Father Timothy had said his goodbyes.

Then the three siblings, at a discreet prodding from Lucas, had gathered in the den of the old house.

Alex turned the Jag onto the road paralleling the water and downshifted through the little village of Temple Heights. The ancient cottages were packed almost one on top of each other, here and then gone as he quickly passed through the almost empty village. Even now, he could recall the dread as his two siblings had pulled up chairs, he in the giant wingback, in the den in front of his grandfather's old desk. Lucas had moved behind the desk and sat facing them.

What Thomas and Ruth didn't know was Alex was privy to what their grandfather Randolph's will had to say.

His grandfather had died a wealthy man. Not just comfortably wealthy, but some would say obscenely wealthy. Alex knew that his grandfather had inherited a modest fortune at just twenty-two, when his father, a Boston-based importer of fruit, timber, and other goods from Central America, had died. He'd been the only heir and the business had been sold just before the outbreak of World War Two.

Now, as they sat facing his grandfather's desk, Lucas nervously arranging various papers and files, he wondered how his siblings would react to what the attorney would have to say.

Lucas cleared his throat and took a drink from a glass of scotch Alex had poured for him.

"As you know, I've been your grandfather's lawyer for the majority of both of our lives. I've been with him these many years and have been privy to almost everything about his affairs. Everything in these documents he dictated to me personally, so I have no doubt these were his final wishes."

Alex could see his brother Thomas squirming in his seat in nervous anticipation. Ruth was completely still and appeared to be intently contemplating the pale lavender nail polish on her short fingernails.

"I'll now read the terms of the will," Lucas said.

"I, Randolph Donovan, being of sound mind and body, do state this to be my last will and testament."

Alex heard little of the legal mumbo jumbo.

"To my grandson, Thomas, I leave the sum of one million dollars."

Alex watched as a smile broke out on Thomas' face, and he thought for a moment Thomas might leap from the chair and dance a jig. Alex grimaced.

"To my granddaughter, Ruth," Lucas continued, "I leave one million dollars."

Ruth's only visible reaction was a clasping of her hands together. She flinched slightly when Thomas reached over, patting her on the back in some sort of congratulations.

Alex braced himself.

Lucas fidgeted nervously and shot him a glance; a glance he didn't acknowledge.

"To my grandson, Alexander..." He'd never been Alex, always Alexander. "I leave Donovan's Acre, all the contents contained therein, my boat, Crusader," and in what seemed to Alex an attempt at diversion, Lucas quickly added, "And any and all other assets in my name."

Alex stole a glance at Thomas, who was still smiling an idiotic grin that looked like it might flee his face and fly off to the moon.

"Good luck with the old house there, sport. Thank God he didn't leave me this money pit," he crowed.

Ruth sat silently.

Lucas then recited some rambling legalese Alex barely heard about contesting the will and having all rights revoked-blah, blah, blah.

"Well, that about does it, I think," stammered the old barrister as he gathered the papers in front of him in a harried manner which seemed lost on Thomas.

Not so Ruth. Alex felt her gaze and turned to find her smiling at him, but saying nothing.

"I'll have my secretary make up copies for all of you as soon as I get back to Boston. These things take some time to work out. I need to file some papers with the courts, do a little IRS housekeeping, etcetera, but we should have everything wrapped up and monies and titles dispersed in about a month.

"Any questions?" Lucas asked sheepishly.

Thomas was already standing and pacing the room. He was, no doubt, already trying to figure out ways to spend his new-found fortune.

"So about a month? That long? Can't we hurry this along?" Thomas asked, seeming quite giddy.

"These things take time, Thomas," Lucas responded. "You're lucky that it'll be that soon. Your grandfather had me set things up long ago in trusts and the like to avoid probate. A month is a short time to wait."

"Yes, yes, I suppose you're right," Thomas blurted out, but Alex could tell the money had already scorched a hole in his pocket and was quickly burning a path down his leg.

Lucas had gathered the paperwork, stuffing it into a worn and battered briefcase that looked as old as he did; all the papers except for a thick pile he placed on the corner of the desk closest to Alex, who wasn't the only one who eyed it. Ruth saw it as well.

"Now, if no one has any questions, I should be heading south. I have a four-hour drive back to the city, and my driver is almost as old as I am. He hates driving at night."

"Are you sure you don't want to stay here tonight, Lucas?" Alex asked. "There's plenty of room here for both of you."

"No, no. I have to get back or I'll never hear the end of it from Constance."

"How about you?" he asked his siblings. "We can get some lobsters from the lobster pound in Belfast and open a bottle from the cellar."

"Stay here?" Thomas asked, as if Alex had grown another head. "This place has always given me the creeps. This was always your place, sport. No, I'm heading back to Manchester. Watch out for ghosts."

"Ruth?" Alex turned to his sister.

"Thank you, Alex, but I'm going to head back with Thomas. I have an early morning flight back to California tomorrow," Ruth said.

Her eyes stayed locked on him for a moment, and she went on.

"I think it's great Grandfather left this house to you. I know how much it meant to you and how much you meant to him. You deserve everything he gave you."

A slight smile creased her face as she reached over and hugged him. As she did, she whispered in his ear, "And I do mean everything."

Alex looked at her, but said nothing as she released him and headed for the door.

"Yeah, me, too, little brother," Thomas said, coming across the room and holding out his hand. "I had nightmares the old man would leave me that old leaky boat just to spite me. Never mind this old fire trap."

Alex shook the outstretched hand for a moment before Thomas turned and hurried out the door after Ruth.

He stood there for a moment contemplating the empty doorway before turning to Lucas, who was now standing near the windows overlooking the bay. He was still nursing his scotch.

He turned from the window and looked at Alex. "I think that went rather painlessly," he said.

"Ruth knows," Alex mused.

"Yes, I believe you're right. But I would say she handled it rather gracefully. I'm not so sure Thomas would have been so disposed had he suspected.

"Won't he find out eventually?"

"Randolph had me set up an elaborate and costly array of trusts, offshore accounts, and various holding companies here and abroad with just this scenario in mind.

"He knew what each of you was like. He never liked Thomas. Oh, he loved him as his grandson, but he cared little for him, if that makes sense. He actually thought he was rather daft and never forgave him for the way he treated him. I blame your father for that, really, and he's very much his father's son.

"Ruth, he tolerated more, and he always had high hopes for her. But when she moved out to San Francisco and took up with the crowd she did, basically rejecting him and his money, he wrote her off.

"No, they'll be precluded from ever discovering the extent of your grandfather's wealth, now your wealth, I suppose. Your sister is smart enough to know two million dollars is but a pittance of what he possessed at his death.

"Still, it was a bit nerve-wracking for this ninety-year-old lawyer. Now, I think you and I have more than a few things to go over."

"Thought you had to get back to Boston?"

"Constance is positively ecstatic that my old bones are out of the house for the night. She mentioned something about Streisand or some other nonsense at the Hatch Shell. I have a room booked for me and one for my driver at the Camden Harbour Inn and will be enjoying Damariscotta oysters with champagne this evening."

"Well, let me see Thomas and Ruth off, then we can get on with it," Alex said as he moved to the door.

"Take your time. I know where Randolph keeps his scotch. Kept, I suppose. Your scotch, I imagine. Oh, hell," Lucas mumbled.

Alex headed toward the living room where he found Thomas and Ruth gathering their coats and heading for the front door.

"Are you sure you won't stay the night?" he asked, already knowing the answer.

"No way, sport. But thanks for the offer," Thomas said, going down the front steps and heading for his car. Ruth followed him down the steps. Thomas piled into the driver's seat as Alex opened the passenger door, holding it open for Ruth.

"It was good to see you, Ruth," he said.

"Likewise, little brother. You take care of yourself and this house. I'll stay in touch with you. I'm actually heading up a fundraiser next month for Greenpeace. We're hoping to buy some new high speed pursuit boats to send after the Japanese whaling fleet in the North Pacific. We need to raise a few hundred thousand dollars more. Maybe I'll send you some information and you can find it in your heart to donate a little something," Ruth said with a sly grin, then a wink.

"Ha, Greenpeace," Thomas said. "What a crock of crap."

Alex leaned down through the open window and gave his sister a peck on the cheek.

"Send me an e-mail with the details, and I'll see what I can do," he said with a grin. "Thank you, Ruth," he added sincerely.

"You better save your pennies, sport. You start sending money to your sister's charity of the month and you won't have enough to heat this old relic of a home," Thomas said as the car began pulling away.

Alex stepped back and raised his hand as the car headed up the drive. He stood watching until the car was out of sight.

Now, as he neared Donovan's Acre and the memories of the last few weeks faded away, he focused on the task ahead. He made his way along the last mile of twisting and turning shoreline road, the afternoon sun fighting through the dense foliage closing in on either side.

And then he was there.

He brought the car to a stop in front of the double wrought iron gates closed and padlocked across the drive. He got out and unlocked the padlock on the chain and swung both gates open. He returned to the car and drove down the curving gravel drive to the old house.

He stopped in the car park outside of the front door and shut off the Jaguar's engine with a turn of the key.

He sat there staring at the house, wondering again at all that had taken place.

CHAPTER 3

Maine

After Thomas and Ruth had left, Alex found Lucas back in the den, squatting in front of the fireplace, trying to get a sputtering flame to spread to some logs.

"I hope you don't mind," he said. "These old bones need warmth, and this house seems as cold as a meat locker."

"Here, let me get it going," Alex offered and proceeded within a few minutes to have a fast growing fire spreading its warmth into the room.

"Ah, much better already," the old barrister said, rubbing his hands before the flames. "This constant cold is just one of the many downfalls of attaining old age."

After a few minutes, Lucas moved to the large sofa in front of the fireplace and motioned for Alex to sit as well.

Alex noticed he'd set the large pile of folders on the coffee table before them.

"So, besides the house and everything in it, that wonderful boat, and the amazing stash of wine downstairs, here's what Randolph left you.

"I've prepared a series of files, much of which I won't go into detail now, laying out the various trusts, companies, and investments which are now yours.

"Many of these, especially the overseas trusts and companies, will require you dealing with the various attorneys and accountants in the countries in question. But I'll give you a brief overview.

"The first file outlines your grandfather's investments in various stocks, bonds, real estate, and cash here in this country. They're all listed by type and value. Most of these will be in trusts already naming you as successor trustee, meaning there's little to no paperwork needed. The value of these holdings as of yesterday was four hundred and forty-five million dollars. Give or take."

Alex stared at Lucas. "What?"

"I assumed you had some idea of the extent of all this."

"Well, he'd told me it was a large amount and he was leaving most of it to me. I just hadn't thought about that kind of number."

"We're by no means done yet, Alex," Lucas replied.

"The second file," Lucas placed another file almost as thick as the first in front of Alex, "is a summary of your holdings in fourteen different trusts, companies, and accounts based in Panama, the Cayman Islands and Belize. Again, you'll need to go to these countries and meet the different people who manage these holdings. I can make those arrangements as I assisted in setting up all of this. The value of these holdings, again as of yesterday, is two hundred and seventy-five million dollars."

"Holy shit, Lucas! Where did he get all this? Are you telling me I'm almost a billionaire?"

"We're not done yet, son. As to how your grandfather accumulated this wealth; remember, he sold his companies many years ago for what, at the time, was a massive fortune. He never spent a lot of money, relative to what he had, and over the years he invested wisely; almost preternaturally so. If the truth be known, your grandfather was one of the more savvy investors of the last sixty years. I'm lucky to have been able to ride his coattails for so many years, and I say that without any embarrassment."

"I had no idea. It's actually a bit overwhelming."

"You can handle it. I'll help as much as I can, and you have good people at every level of this to help you manage it, people he and I chose personally; whatever you decide to do with it."

Alex could see there were two more files left, both of which were much thinner than the first two.

Lucas opened the next to last folder and removed three sheets of paper, one of which appeared to be a legal document of some kind. Lucas placed the first document in front of him. It contained nothing but the name of a bank, Bergen and Cie, and a fifteen-digit number. Taped to the bottom of the document was a large, rather old looking key.

"This is a bank account in Zurich, Switzerland that belongs to you now. This number is the code required to access the account and to make any changes to the account.

"I have no idea how much is in the account. That was something Randolph never shared with me, nor do I know why he felt the need to have it. Remember, whoever has the code has the account. I imagine the key opens a safe deposit box of some kind.

"This next document is a deed. This is one of the few transactions I know of, which your grandfather never felt the need to share with me, so I know little about it. It is a deed to a piece of property in a town called Aux La Rouse. I went online when your grandfather gave this to me, and it appears to be a small village near the Pyrenees in the Languedoc region of France. I haven't researched the property the deed refers to. That's something I leave to you."

Lucas then placed the last item from the file in front of him. It was a piece of stationery from a law firm in Venice, Italy. The only thing written on the paper was the name "Vincente Brexiano" and below that a notation, in his grandfather's handwriting, which said, "Attorney ref. Palazzo."

Alex looked at it, puzzled.

"I have no idea what this is or what it means," Lucas offered. "I don't know the attorney either. I know Randolph traveled to Venice quite often. Other than that, I don't know why this is in this folder."

All of this was strange to Alex and, while the numbers surprised him, the secrecy did not. His grandfather had always been pretty tight-lipped about his finances, even with him, and rarely, if ever, talked about money.

"Last one." Lucas interrupted his thoughts and placed the last folder in front of him. He opened it and removed an envelope. "Your grandfather gave this to me about a month before he died. He said it was a letter to you, and it contained information of the utmost importance. He was quite circumspect; in fact, it was downright strange the way he acted when he gave it to you. It was as if, on one hand, he didn't want to give it to you. I started to ask him what could be so important, and for the only time in our relationship, he became cross with me."

With that, Lucas pushed the envelope across the space between them.

Alex stared at the envelope, his name written on the front in his grandfather's bold, elegant script, and felt a cold sweat wash over him. Something about the plain white blankness spooked him to his very core.

He stood and moved to the fire, staring down into the flames, wondering at the feeling of dread slithering down his spine, seeming to nest in the pit of his stomach. For a moment he thought he might be sick and, reaching out, he grabbed the mantle to steady himself.

"Are you alright, Alex?" Lucas asked, coming over to stand beside him.

"Yeah, I just feel a little queasy," he said.

"This is all a bit much, I'm sure. Perhaps we should have waited a few days for all of this. It's a lot to absorb, and the weight of it can be daunting. Why don't we call it a day? Let's share a couple of drinks and toast our friend, then you can join me for dinner. How about it, son?"

Alex seemed to be getting his feet back under him, and the cold sweat had dissipated. He felt a bit more like himself.

"You know what, Lucas? I think I'm going to take you up on that."

"Wonderful. I'll put the letter in the center drawer of the desk and, when you're up to it, you deal with it. You have plenty on your plate."

And so, after pouring himself a stiff scotch and sharing a toast--Alex rarely drank anything stronger than wine, but it was easier than delving into the cellar in his frame of mind--he tamped out the fire and closed up the house. He decided spending the night here wasn't in the cards, so he followed Lucas to Camden, where he booked a room in the Camden Harbour Inn and shared a great dinner with Lucas, after which he slept soundly all night. The next morning, he made his way back to Boston and his new and different life.

Now he was back, sitting in the old car wondering what awaited him.

He climbed out of the Jag, walked up the front steps to the old wooden door, unlocked it and, taking a deep breath, crossed the threshold.

CHAPTER 4

Maine

Alex entered the house and walked down the entry hall to the living room. He threw his overnight bag on the old leather sofa, which produced an eruption of dust motes which seemed to hang in the air.

He walked to the French doors looking out over the bay. The house was musty and quiet, already feeling as if it had been abandoned. But he could still smell his grandfather's presence, the unmistakable aroma of age and sameness.

He opened all three sets of doors and stepped out onto the porch. It was nearing the end of May, and it looked as if the notoriously fickle and uncompromising Maine weather was going to be benevolent by providing a rare, warm and rain-free weekend. The feeling of spring still lingered in the air but May weather here could go either way.

The open doors allowed a surprising amount of light and fresh air to invade the living areas of the old house. The kitchen, dining area, and living room all flowed together, sharing the same views out over the water.

A breeze, with just a hint of salt, carried the sounds of water and birds, seeming to wash the rooms of the aroma of decay. The rooms began to feel livable and fresh.

His grandfather's study would be another story. It seemed to exist on a separate plane of dark mystery as if in a different house, in an alternate world.

As a child, he would sneak down the hallway pretending to be some sort of moccasin-clad Indian attempting to sneak up on the occupant who always knew somehow of the approaching savage.

Now, steeling himself for what lay ahead, he crossed the living room and went down a set of stairs leading to the basement.

The basement was divided into two spaces; one, a storage area where the various and sundry detritus of a ninety-six-year-old man's accumulated leavings were piled and stacked in no apparent order. This would be a project eventually; one that didn't seem to exude as much foreboding as the one awaiting him in the study.

The other half was devoted to a state of the art wine cellar. Equipped with an expensive, professional grade, climate-controlled system, it housed his grandfather's collection of over forty-five thousand bottles of wine. Some were so obscure and prized, it was the only part of the house with an alarm system. Once a year, his grandfather paid an appraiser from Boston to spend a week inventorying and evaluating his collection for insurance purposes. Next to his collection of books, these were the only things Alex knew of that had been capable of engaging him and holding sway over his attention.

If his brother had known the wine collection in the cellar was worth more than his own inheritance, he would have most likely soiled himself. Of course, Thomas, had he inherited it, would have immediately called in the same wine expert in Boston to liquidate the collection, which his grandfather had spent a lifetime amassing.

He entered the cellar through an eighteenth-century carved wooden door which had been reclaimed from the Jewish quarter in Marrakech. His grandfather had bought it, as well as an assortment of rugs, and had them shipped home after one of several trips he'd made to North Africa and the Middle East.

The area had held a great interest to him, and he'd regaled a young Alex with tales of nights spent walking among the Pyramids, tent safaris to obscure parts of Africa, visits to chaotic kasbahs and descriptions of beautiful riads hidden behind non-descript walls of mud. When Alex would ask him why he kept going back, he would only smile and say "someday you'll understand."

He perused the bottles, knowing almost as well as his grandfather the locations and system he'd employed to manage his inventory. In his later years, Alex had become his wine steward as the old man, suddenly enfeebled it seemed by Alex's presence, would direct him on which bottles to pull. From memory, he would direct him to exact bins and slots, some of which contained wine that hadn't been tasted in decades.

Now he searched for something to fit his mood; dark, a little melancholy, but capable of fortifying his soul; an especially old wine in memory of the old man.

He took a look at several bottles, but nothing spoke to him, although some triggered evocative memories of past imbibings.

Just when he thought he might forget wine and make some coffee, his attention was drawn to the long oak table, hewn from a tree on the property which had blown over in a wind storm thirty years ago. He spied an old wooden wine box sitting right in the middle of the table, as if presenting itself to him.

Strange, he'd walked right past the box without seeing it. It was as if the old wine connoisseur had placed it there in anticipation of his arrival.

He pulled the rough-looking box closer and wiped a thick coat of dust off the top. Wherever it had been, it had sat years without attention.

The box was simple, with nothing but the words "Templier" burned into the wood. He tested the lid, finding it had been opened and, removing it, discovered the case full, less one bottle. The dark and obviously heavy bottles were still coated with a fine layer of dust, even though they had been stored in the box. He carefully lifted a bottle from the case and blew gently until he could see the details on the label: Domaine Templier, 1944 and above that, on the label, a simple drawing of a knight on horseback.

He'd never seen this wine before and had, over the years, he thought, inspected every inch of the cellar.

Something told him it would fit his mood.

He went back upstairs, bottle in hand, and from the kitchen grabbed one of the Reidel Bordeaux glasses he'd purchased for his grandfather's ninetieth birthday. Bottle and glass in hand, he walked down the hallway to the den and, with more than just a little trepidation, slid the door open.

Here the remnants of the old man's presence were at their most intense. He was assailed by a myriad of memories which seemed to roll over him like a wave. In a flash, he was an awestruck eight-year-old boy, sitting in the huge overstuffed wingback chair. With feet not even reaching the floor, he would listen intently as his grandfather read to him from one of the thousands of books lining the walls, as ever, enshrouded in the pleasing aroma of one of his fine Cuban cigars.

Alex flashed back to his grandfather reading Nabokov's *Lolita* to him from an old, leather-bound and signed first edition. He could remember understanding little to nothing of the words, but being entranced by their elegance and intricacy.

Buoyed by the memory, he walked across the room and drew back the ancient heavy curtains to let some light into the room. Even now, with a late afternoon's sunlight pouring in, the room seemed impervious to light and maintained the dark and mysterious mood of his childhood.

He went to a small antique liquor cabinet against one wall, found an old corkscrew, and gingerly opened the bottle of wine. He poured a small amount into the glass, swirled it expertly, and buried his nose in the glass. He closed his eyes and in a moment was reveling in layers of chocolate, anise, a hint of raspberries, the scent of some strange and unnamable flower, and a deep, comforting base of earthiness.

"Wow," he said out loud. He sipped it again, savoring the richness.

No wonder his grandfather had hidden this away. He poured a little more into his glass and moved back to the desk, setting the bottle down to breathe.

He contemplated the worn wingback and the simple utilitarian office chair pushed under his grandfather's side of the desk.

His grandfather's side.

He pulled the chair from under the desk and sat.

He ran his hand over the desk's scarred, scratched surface and marveled at the depth of his sentimentality, wondering what the old man would say if he could see him soaking up these moments.

He pulled open the middle drawer, extracting the envelope which Lucas had placed there two weeks before, setting it on the desk in front of him.

He ran his fingers over the envelope, marveling at the extravagant feel of it. He hefted it again and, turning it over, found a red wax seal embossed with a strange figure. He looked closer at the seal, then at the horseman on the label of the wine bottle. They looked eerily similar.

He'd never seen his grandfather use a wax seal before. It only heightened his state of suspense.

He opened the top right drawer, pushed around a collection of pens, paper clips, and various other things one would expect to find in a desk drawer and, near the back, he found a little leather case with the embossed words "Legatoria Piazzesi, Venice," on the top. He opened it to find a length of red wax and a small gold metal stamp.

He placed it back into the drawer, returning his attention to the envelope. He looked around for something to open the envelope until he found an old letter opener in the center drawer.

Placing the edge of the opener under the wax, he pried and chipped at it until it broke, freeing the back flap. He reached inside the envelope, removing what turned out to be several folded sheets of wonderfully soft, luxurious vellum.

He unfolded the sheets, placed them on the desktop, took a drink of the wine, and began to read the letter written in his grandfather's flowing script.

March 10th, 2010

Dearest Alexander,

If you are reading this letter, I am sure that you are sitting in your rightful place behind my desk. It is now yours as it should be. All those years when you were sitting in the old wingback in front of me, this is what I wanted.

Now you have it and, as you now know, a hell of a lot more.

I trust that old wily lawyer friend of mine, Lucas, handled the reading of the will with the aplomb which served me well these many years. As long as he stays on this earth, and chances are it will be longer than I did, you can, and I hope will, trust him as you would me. He will help you and can impart much I have not had the time nor the inclination, for whatever reason, to impart to you.

Except for this one thing.

I'm the only one who can burden you with this thing I have carried around for over fifty years. I do it only because someone must know what I know, because I have complete faith that you'll know what to do with this information. Even Lucas, my closest friend, knows nothing of this. He's too much the lawyer to have believed it had I tried to share it with him.

Even your grandmother knew nothing of it. Many times I think she felt I had a hidden paramour. Perhaps in a way she was right, though not the way she thought.

You, Alex, are the only one who has the intelligence and open mind. It is why I read to you all those years from the books which now surround you; Proust, Fitzgerald, Hemingway, and Tolstoy. All the greats and so many more we read. And it was for the great pleasure, insight, and inspiration, but also to prepare you for what lies ahead; to prepare your mind, to fertilize it and gird it to accept what you must.

Stand up now and go to the wall of bookshelves in front of you. When you get there, use the stool and find the second shelf down from the top. In the middle of that shelf you will find Nabokov's *Lolita*; That son of a bitch was a pervert, but his writing was angelic! Pull the book out, and behind it you'll see a brass lever. Push down on it. When you hear a click, pull out on the shelf. A section of it will slide out and down, and behind it you'll see a small niche. Inside are two books and a small jewelry box. Bring them back to the desk."

Alex looked up and could see the Nabokov--the same book he'd remembered his grandfather reading from when he was a kid.

He pulled the old wooden step stool over, climbed three rungs, and pulled the book from its place, setting it on a lower shelf.

There it was, protruding from the old mahogany, a brass knob in the shape of an elongated spoon. He reached out his right hand, pushing down on the lever, almost instantly hearing a sharp click that in his nervous state sounded like the crack of a rifle shot.

He grasped the shelf where the Nabokov had been and the shelf slid out, then down a few inches, soundlessly, with almost no effort.

There, in the shadowed depth of the shelf, was a small opening in the wall about two feet long and a foot high. He reached in and removed two books: one, a small, modern-looking leather-bound volume; the other a much larger and obviously older stack of parchments bound together with what appeared to be leather string. Next to the books was a small, black, velvet jewelry box.

He climbed down off the step ladder and returned to the desk, sitting down with the three items. He lifted the clamshell lid of the jewelry box and stared.

Inside was a beautiful piece of jewelry. Attached to a fine silver chain was an oblong gem stone. The charm, whatever it was made of, gave off a light which seemed to radiate and infuse the room with mesmerizing waves of light. As he looked closer, he could see, etched into the surface of the charm, a small cross.

He reached out, running a finger over the surface, and felt as if warm liquid energy had flowed up his arm to his elbow. It wasn't an unpleasant feeling at all.

Almost regretfully, he closed the lid and set the box aside.

He turned his attention to the two books. The smaller one looked fairly new and rather plain. Tooled into the brown leather cover was one word, *GASPAR*; a name perhaps?

He opened the book and flipped through a few pages. It was printed in English and throughout it referenced various chapters and pages apparently in another book. It made little sense to him.

He set it aside and pulled the larger, much older book toward him. Embossed into the cover, which was made of some sort of thick and durable leather, was the same strange word, *GASPAR*. He untied the straps holding it closed and lifted the heavy cover to reveal the first page.

Again, only this time in big bold and wonderful script, clearly ancient in origin, was the word GASPAR. Below that was a stunning illustration of a knight astride a huge, powerful horse.

The knight wore no helmet. His hair, a golden brown, flowed down to the middle of his shoulders. His face was clean shaven, and he wore a stern but almost mournful gaze.

It was his eyes which caught Alex's attention. They were dark, penetrating, and seemed to go right through him. They appeared to reflect some hidden knowledge or experience, and there was something about them which told him the man suffered from a great sadness, loss, or loneliness.

He was clothed in a long white surcoat over what looked to be armor or mail. A large red cross was emblazoned across his chest, and he wielded a sword that looked half as long as he was tall.

Alex looked closer and saw, under the horse's feet, being trampled in a most violent manner, were several strange, fantastic beasts and beings.

Suddenly Alex looked at the wine bottle again, comparing the drawing on the bottle with the illustration on the first page of the ancient manuscript. There seemed to be a theme emerging here, as they looked similar as well.

Alex turned the page, finding it covered with the same beautiful handwriting in a foreign language which might be Italian. He turned several more pages and found most contained more of the beautiful illustrations. Some were of strange beings, some seemingly part human-part beast, many disturbing.

What the hell had his grandfather left him?

He turned his attention back to the letter and began reading again...

I assume that by now you have found the books and the charm. What you have in front of you, my boy, is an amazing story. A story so impossible I know you will be tempted to believe I, in the end, was nothing more than a raving lunatic. Trust me when I say for some time I thought this myself. But I haven't lost my mind. I am not insane. Far from it. What you have in your hands is a translation, the smaller and newer book, of the ancient manuscript also in front of you, which I found in the depths of an old bookseller's shop in Rome in 1954. That ancient book tells a story; a fantastic and wonderful tale.

The charm: that was a gift.

The translation also tells my small part in this story, so I won't repeat it here. What I will tell you at this point is the story is true and real; all of it. How do I know this? I became obsessed with this ancient book. I would sit for hours before I had it translated, staring at the pictures, mesmerized by their beauty and by what they showed.

This book and the subsequent quest I embarked on consumed me for many years and took me all over the world. I became obsessed with proving that it was an actual account of a real man and his real world.

The translation tells that tale as the manuscript tells the tale of Gaspar; a real man, Alexander, a man who existed, who lived to tell his story and still lives.

Alex sat back and let out a breath he seemed to have been holding for a long time. What was his grandfather saying? This "Gaspar," a man who supposedly lived hundreds of years ago, was still alive somewhere? What kind of forgery or scam had his grandfather fallen for?

But something tickled at the back of his mind. The charm. His grandfather had said it was a gift.

He reached over and opened the jewelry box again and stared at the...what was it actually? He reached out and picked up the chain, lifting the charm into the air. He examined the surface of it closely, seeing again the cross etched into its surface. He turned back to the first page of the old book and to the illustration of the knight he assumed was Gaspar.

The cross was the same as the one on the knight's chest. He turned the charm over, inspecting the back. He held the piece as close as he could to his eye and could see something, perhaps writing, so tiny he couldn't make out what it was.

He searched around the top of the desk looking for his grandfather's old magnifying glass. As Randolph had gotten older, while his eyesight had remained relatively good, he did occasionally use an old fashioned, ivory-handled magnifying glass. Then he spied it, on a small side table next to the sofa, in front of the fireplace. He went over, picked up the glass and, holding the charm in front of it, tried to see what was on the back side.

They were indeed words, but even with the aid of the glass it was nearly impossible to make them out. He pressed the glass down until it was almost touching the charm and finally was able to make them out.

To my friend and confidant Randolph,

Sometimes the best stories are those never told.

Your friend forever,

Gaspar de Rouse

March 9th 2010

CHAPTER 5

Maine

Could this be true?

Had his grandfather found an ancient chronicle, complete with illustrations, written by some sort of immortal human?

Alex stared into the fire for a while, then returned the charm to the case, his fingers lightly brushing the luminescent face. Again, the touch brought a surging tingle to his hand. This time he left the lid open and positioned the box so the charm was in his peripheral vision, unwilling to let it out of his sight.

He returned to the letter, beginning where he'd left off:

As the story will show you, after several years of searching and following clues gleaned from the ancient book, I found the man; Gaspar.

Truth be told, it is more likely he allowed me to find him. He had known that I was searching for him. In the end, the most wonderful and soul quenching thing was, he became my friend.

He showed me things, Alexander, things even now I can scarcely believe. But believe I do.

And so will you. Because what I ultimately came to realize is that, while I thought it was only my destiny to find this man, it is in fact your destiny as well.

It is your destiny and your duty to find him now as I did so long ago. Your life and your future are tied to his, and you must not turn your back on this. I have left you the tools to fulfill this quest. It is now up to you.

Do not be afraid. He knows of you, and he awaits you. But he will not come for you. You must go to him.

Read the books and keep the charm close to you. It will keep you safe.

God be with you, my dearest Alexander, until we meet again.

Love,

Your Grandfather

He ran his fingers over the scrawled signature, feeling the rough, near the end, brittle flesh of the old man's hands.

A tear fell onto the signature, blurring the ink, marking it with his sorrow, a sorrow tinged with feelings of wonder and disbelief. He turned to the books and, opening the translation, began to read.

Alex awoke the next morning as an orange-red dawn peeked over the island, creeping into the room. He was still in the chair, his head resting on the desk in front of him. The first thing he saw as he opened his eyes was the charm in the still open box.

Sitting up, he discovered a painful crick in his neck. He'd slept for a few hours at the desk, not waking even once.

The overlapping narratives of his grandfather's story and that of the manuscript's author consumed him for most of the night until, exhausted, he laid his head down for what was supposed to be only a moment. He no longer doubted the story and, just as his grandfather before him, the more he read of the ancient manuscript, the more real the story became.

He was hooked, and there was no turning back.

Making his way to the kitchen, he realized the house was cold. He'd left all the doors to the deck open during the night.

He went through the motions of working an old French press until he had a steaming cup of coffee in hand. Making his way out to the deck, he sat in an Adirondack chair willing the caffeine and the heat into his bloodstream.

An osprey lazily glided across his field of vision in search of an early meal.

It's not an easy thing at forty-three years old to discover your future lies in the pursuit of an immortal man. It was even more unnerving to wonder exactly what that destiny entailed. What was it that awaited him if, in fact, he ever came face to face with this man? Strangely, though, he found he was much more at ease this morning. The doubts and disbelief of the previous evening had dissipated with each succeeding page of his grandfather's books.

Now, as he began to feel the stirrings of caffeine-fueled life, he recalled what he had read the night before.

He had discovered the translation contained his grandfather's narrative of how he had come to possess the ancient manuscript, which was written in an ancient form of Italian.

The story in his grandfather's book had begun in 1954.

CHAPTER 6

Rome, June, 1954

I was alone, having left my wife in Boston for this trip. When she had asked why I wanted to go to Rome and more particularly why I wasn't taking her, I said I'd felt a calling, something I couldn't explain.

And so I left, booking an extravagant passage on the Queen Mary out of New York, and landing in Southampton. Then I made my way to Rome via ferry and train, without exiting the train once. I wanted to be in Rome as soon as possible, and had no idea why. I didn't even know how long I was going to stay. When asked at the hotel, I had said two weeks. That had been four weeks ago.

The day I discovered the book of *GASPAR* I had made my way through the city, lazily traversing the ancient stones lining the sidewalks. I was meandering aimlessly, finding little shops filled with various knick-knacks, food, wine, and books. I stopped at a sidewalk café for a light lunch of grilled sardines, bread, and a not inexpensive bottle of Chianti.

I let the warm summer sun and the noise of a Roman afternoon lull me into a peaceful state.

After my lunch I resumed my wandering, dodging housewives finishing their shopping, children making their way home from school, and the ever-present dogs roaming the streets for handouts, until I realized I was in a steadily deteriorating neighborhood.

I stopped at the door of a coffee shop, looked in and, deciding it looked safe enough, entered. I ordered a cup of black coffee and sat on a rickety chair by the large front window.

I sipped the almost syrupy brew, letting my gaze travel the street outside. My eyes were drawn to a storefront across the street three doors down. An old man slowly swept the sidewalk in front of the store in some sort of vain attempt at imposing his measure of cleanliness and order. The sign stenciled onto the brick above his head read "Pastorini, Book Seller."

I was surprised when the old man paused and turned his head, staring in my direction. The man stood there for more than a minute, broom suspended mid-stroke above the sidewalk, with his head cocked to one side as if trying to see through the glass.

I was somewhat unnerved by his staring and almost moved away from the window. But the man suddenly turned away and, setting his broom against the wall, disappeared through the door of the shop.

I put down my cup of coffee, pondering the book shop down the street. I've always had a weakness for books, and Rome had proved to be full of shops overflowing with manuscripts and volumes calling out to me. Like a moth to flame, I found myself exiting the coffee house working my way to the door of the bookseller.

As I crossed the street and approached the entrance to the shop, I suddenly felt like I was being watched. I could sense it as strongly as I could smell the musty age and timeworn essence of the books emanating from the doorway. I stopped and looked around, but not seeing anyone who appeared to be taking undue interest in me, shrugged off the feeling and entered the bookshop.

It was dark and quiet, the sounds of the street seeming to fade away, dissipating as my eyes took in the walls and tables overflowing with all manner of volumes. I moved deeper into the shop, running my fingers over the stacks, stopping occasionally to pick up one or two that grabbed my fancy.

"What is it you seek, friend?" came a voice from the even darker recesses of the shop.

I peered into the gloom, trying to make out who was speaking to me.

"Well, I'm just shopping, I suppose. I don't have anything in particular I'm looking for. I just love old books."

"Perhaps I can help you."

At that, the old man who had been sweeping the sidewalk shuffled out into the relative brightness, in my direction. He extended a hand, which I took, startled by the strength in the aged hand.

"My name is Antony. Antony Pastorini. This is my shop, at least for now. And you must be an American?"

"Yes, I am. Randolph Donovan is my name."

"I could tell by the way you drank your coffee."

"You could tell from that distance."

"When you've been on this street for as long as I have, nothing escapes your notice. We don't get many tourists in this area anymore, which is part of the reason that bastard Sicilian landlord of mine is close to throwing me on the street after selling my books here for fifty years."

"You speak English very well," I observed.

"That's a result of spending the majority of my life surrounded by books from all over the world. If I wanted to read them, I had to learn the languages. I can speak eight different languages beside my mother tongue. It comes in handy when that son of a goat comes looking for rent. I can curse him in Arabic, and he thinks I'm speaking gibberish."

I smiled at the thought of the old man lambasting the landlord and found I was instantly growing to like the old bookseller.

"So you're about to be kicked out of here? What are you going to do with all of these books?"

"That's a question that I have no answer for, my American friend. Not only is this home to my books, but it's my home as well. The *testa di merda* has no heart. I'm only three months behind, but he wants this space to turn it into some sort of restaurant for his little *una bella fica. Bastardo!*"

"Can't you have some sort of sale? Maybe find a bookseller in another area who might want some of your books?"

"Vultures! All of them. They know if they wait until he tosses me in the street they can swoop in and take them for virtually nothing. No, I'm truly in, how do you say? Deep shit!"

"Well, maybe I can help you. I could buy some books and maybe you'd gain some time with this landlord of yours. Lord knows I'm shipping back half of the books in Rome it seems. What's a few more?"

The old man eyed me shrewdly for a moment, then, turning and heading for the depths of the shop, beckoned me to follow, "Come with me, young man. I doubt anything out here would interest you but if, as you say, it's books you seek, then perhaps we can find something that will serve us both in the back."

I followed him past stacks of books, weaving this way and that, actually struggling to keep up with the old man. The walls were lined from floor to ceiling with rows of books, but we were moving so quickly I had no time to see the titles. The shop had to be huge because I realized I'd been following the little bookseller for what seemed like quite some time. The volumes here seemed different as well. No longer dingy, dark, and worn--here they looked bright and in impeccable shape.

I slowed to look closer at some of the books stacked haphazardly on the tables to find that many looked positively ancient and written in languages I didn't recognize.

"Come on, American! I think I have what you're looking for," said the still moving old man, not even glancing over his shoulder.

I hurried after him, heading deeper into the seemingly never ending depths of the shop. I could hear the shuffling steps ahead of me and occasionally caught glimpses of the book seller as he dodged around tables and boxes.

Finally, winded and amazed at the size of the place, I turned a corner around a tall stack of books and found myself facing the old man.

He was standing in a rather large space cleared out of the midst of thousands of books. In the center was a long, low table, behind which the old man stood. The table was lit from above by a large and beautiful chandelier which looked to hold more than a hundred brightly burning candles. On the otherwise empty table was a book.

"How big is this place, Antony?" I asked as I approached the table. "From the outside it looks much smaller."

"Oh, it's quite large. As you can see, my collection is quite vast."

I stopped in front of the table and examined the book on the table. I could see it was old, the cover made from some sort of leather, the bindings lengths of leather cord.

Tooled into the cover was one word, *GASPAR*.

I looked at the old man again, "What is this?"

"It's what you're searching for," he replied.

I stared at the fellow, as a feeling of some confusion came over me. What was this man talking about? Did he know I had felt compelled to visit Rome, but didn't know why?

Antony pulled two chairs from the shadows and placed one on each side of the table. He sat gesturing for me to do the same. We sat there for a moment staring at each other, the book lying between us.

"I've been waiting for someone like you to come into this shop for many years," Antony said. "A man capable of appreciating this book."

"What kind of man is that, Antony?"

"A searcher."

"And you think it's this book for which I search? Unknowingly, I might add."

Antony smiled. "Perhaps we should look at this book and see if I'm correct."

With that he leaned forward and ran his hand over the cover. His gnarled and twisted hands came to rest on the tooled letters, which I could now see were inlaid with gold.

"It was forty years ago this week, Randolph, that I came to possess this manuscript. It's without a doubt my most treasured volume. It's a masterpiece, and the story it tells is beyond compare."

I studied his face as he spoke and, from the almost religious fervor that seemed to pass over his visage, I could tell this wasn't some sort of sales pitch.

"I'll tell you how it came into my possession," Antony began. "It was late on a Friday afternoon, and I was in the process of closing my doors when an old priest barged in clutching something wrapped in cloth under his arm.

"In those days, this wasn't the rundown neighborhood it is now, and it wasn't uncommon to be visited by members of the higher strata of the Roman citizenry. I wasn't surprised by the priest's presence. Many of the clergy would come here from time to time looking for books. What did surprise me was his obvious state of agitation. He seemed frightened, in fact terrified, and not quite sane.

'Do you buy books here?' he asked.

"I told him I did and asked if he had something to sell."

'I do,' he replied. 'But I'll only sell it under one condition, that you never tell anyone where you got it. I'm a worker in the Vatican archives, and I can't be connected to this manuscript.'

"I was instantly on edge, for while I'm not averse to trafficking in books of, shall we say, cloudy provenance, dealing in books stolen from the Vatican archives is another matter altogether.

"I began to object and actually tried to push him from the store. He became almost hysterical with fear.

'Please, friend, please! I can't bear to see this book destroyed, and I don't know what else to do with it. It must be saved and the story within it preserved. My superiors want it burned. I'd sooner die than see that happen. Please, just look at it and see for yourself,' he said.

"Against my better judgment, I gave in to my curiosity and, after closing and locking the front door, at his insistence, I led him to this very table to examine his book. I unwrapped the cloths he had used to hide the volume, and there it was; the story of *Gaspar*.

"I was, as I still am today, mesmerized by what I found; an ancient manuscript hundreds of years old and of a workmanship the likes of which I had never seen. But it was the story and the illustrations which instantly possessed me, and to this day they still do.

"Obviously I bought the book. I would have paid anything for it, but in the end I paid some ridiculously small amount the old priest insisted I give to a charity. He was adamant he hadn't stolen it for personal gain, but to conceal it from someone within the Vatican who wished it destroyed. I never saw the old priest again."

By this point I was listening in rapt attention to the story of the book's acquisition. I couldn't take my eyes off the manuscript in front of me. The old man's hands still rested on the cover, and his fingers had continued to caress the letters as he spoke.

"Here, take it. Open the cover and see what you've found." The old man pushed the book toward me with quivering hands.

I ran my hands over the cover much like the bookseller had, reveling in the feel of the leather cover and the finely tooled letters. I carefully lifted the cover and examined the first page. The name *GASPAR* appeared again, now in beautiful red flowing script. Below that was an illustration of such beauty and detail that I felt I was looking at a living, breathing painting.

The illustration was of a knight on horseback trampling a host of strange and what I felt were demonic beings.

I began turning the pages, finding page after page of script I couldn't read and more of the beautiful illustrations.

"How old is this book, Antony?"

"As close as I can tell, it was produced in the late 1500's, perhaps early 1600's."

"I can't read it. What language is this?"

"Italian, but the Italian of those days was much different than the language we speak today. It took me some time to learn to read it."

I continued turning pages in rapt fascination for several minutes, until when about halfway through, the old man reached over and gently pulled the book back to the center of the table and closed it.

I was surprised by the pang of regret washing over me as the book was drawn away.

"See? Does it not possess you?" Antony whispered.

"How much do you want for it?"

"Ha! That's the question, isn't it? What is something like this worth? What is it about this book that so easily consumes us and led to a priest stealing it from the most secretive archive in the world to save it from fire?

Why would anyone want to burn such a thing? All good questions and all things that I suppose make it almost priceless."

The bookseller paused, then said, "Perhaps the question I should ask is, what would you pay?"

"I have no idea what I would pay. I'm not in the habit of paying for things I can't even read. What's the story this book tells?"

"That, I think, will remain a secret for now. But believe me, you wouldn't believe it if I told you."

I knew the man needed money to save his business and asked, "How much do you owe to your landlord?"

"About three-hundred and fifteen-thousand lire," the bookseller responded.

I quickly did the conversion to dollars in my head and said, "Then I'll pay you three-hundred-thousand lire plus another one-hundred-thousand to help you get back on your feet."

"Done!" exclaimed Antony.

I was surprised by the instant acceptance of his offer. Was I being conned? Was the wily old bookseller in fact selling me a fraud? Regardless, I reached into my wallet and handed over the bills.

As if reading my thoughts, the old man whispered, "I would have sold it to you for a single American dollar, my friend, for within this book lies your future and the future of one who comes after you."

The old man's eyes bored into mine, unblinking for a moment, before he stood and shuffled into the shadows, returning shortly with a dusty wine bottle and two glasses. I pondered his enigmatic words for a moment, completely baffled by what he'd said.

"Now we'll drink a toast to your acquisition and my salvation," Antony said as he poured a generous measure of red wine into the glasses.

We raised our glasses and drank. I was amazed at what I tasted. It was the most incredible wine I'd had in Italy.

"Besides your destiny, it appears that you've found your perfect bottle of wine as well," said the old man, eyes twinkling in mirth. "It comes from a small winery in the south of France in the foothills of the Pyrenees. I get it from a friend, an old friend."

The bookseller put down his glass, again disappearing into the shadows momentarily before returning with a canvas satchel. Reaching down, he caressed the worn leather cover one last time, his fingers hesitating lightly on the letters before lifting it carefully and placing it within the satchel.

"Go now, my American friend. Take your book and embrace your future. You've helped me more than you know, and I owe you a debt of gratitude I'll someday repay."

And with that, the old man, now moving much slower, led me through the vast and cavernous book shop until we arrived at the front door. He opened it, standing aside as I exited. I turned and, taking the old man's outstretched hand, shook it.

"Learn to read the book, Randolph. Learn the secrets it contains and follow its clues. Now you must go where the book leads and to what awaits you. Good luck, my American friend, and be safe."

The old man ducked back into the shop and closed the door.

I stood alone in the dark street. Night had fallen. I held the satchel close to my chest in a protective embrace. As I walked down the street in the direction of my hotel, I felt like a different man. I felt as if something within me had been completed and fulfilled. This was why I had come to Rome.

CHAPTER 7

Castel Gondolfo, Italy, May 2010

The sound of a ringing phone echoed down the halls of the villa. It was just past three a.m. and the sole occupant of the palatial home slept soundly in his bed.

Two bottles of Montepulciano had numbed his brain and it took twenty rings before, fumbling, he reached out to the night stand to find the handset.

After his hand closed on the phone, he pressed the answer button. "*Prego.*"

"Excellency?"

The sound of the voice cleared away the foggy remnants of the man's stupor. It had been years since he had heard this voice.

"Dominicus?"

"No names!"

"One moment," the old man said. He sat up in bed and switched on a lamp. He ran a hand over his bald pate trying to gather himself.

"It's been a long time, old friend," the now fully awake man said. "I wondered if you still lived."

"Oh I live, perhaps not as well as you with your villa, limousine and exalted title."

"Ah, it is you. How could a person not recognize your venomous wit?"

The man on the other end of the line went silent.

"Are you there?" asked the old man.

"I'm here. We need to talk and not on the phone."

"I'll be back in Rome in two days. We can meet then."

"We need to meet now."

"It's three in the morning and my eyesight doesn't allow me to operate my car anymore. I sent my driver home after he dropped me here."

"I know. I'm standing outside your front door."

The old man felt a strange fluttering in his chest at the caller's words. What was he doing here? How did he even know about this place? He had purchased it, with cash, through a Bahamian corporation two years ago. No one was supposed to know he owned it.

"Did you hear me, Excellency?"

"Yes, I did. I was just surprised. Give me one moment to dress."

The caller hung up without a word.

Cardinal Salvador Rocha rose and picked up a robe lying across the foot of his bed. He shrugged it on tying it off at the waist, over his protruding belly. Going back to the night-stand, he opened the drawer. Reaching in, he pulled out a small, chrome-plated, semi-automatic pistol. He checked the clip and made sure a round was chambered, the movements coming naturally even after all these years. The simple act of arming himself stiffened his spine. Dropping the pistol into the right hand pocket of the robe he exited his bedroom. He padded barefoot down the tiled hallway toward the front door.

He went through a lavishly furnished great room and headed for the massive front door. He had almost reached it when a voice from behind stopped him instantly.

"You didn't think you could hide this wonderful place did you, Salvi?"

Turning slowly toward the voice he could make out a man sitting in one of his antique parlor chairs. The man's face was in shadow but his hands were visible. In his left hand was a wine glass half filled with red wine, an open bottle on a side table next to the chair. In the man's right hand, its barrel lined up somewhere around his eyeballs, was an evil looking black pistol fitted with a silencer.

"You look well fed, Salvi. Vatican life agrees with you."

"It's been a long time, Dominicus. Why the pistol?" the cardinal asked.

"You may have moved on from my world, old friend, but I have not forgotten your skill with a pistol.

"By the way, your cellar is phenomenal. I hope you don't mind, I helped myself to a bottle of '62 *Petrus*. I must say though, you go on drinking two bottles of the nectar every night, all your skills with the pistol will fade away like your trim physique."

"Why are you baiting me, Dominicus?" Salvador asked. "And more importantly why are you here? I've heard nothing from you or the rest of the Order for years."

"You weren't supposed to hear from us. You were however supposed to manage our funds, not enrich yourself at our expense."

Salvador felt a cold sweat break out on the back of his neck. There was no way they could know. He had covered his tracks meticulously. Every euro he had transferred had been assigned to some sort of legitimate, if ephemeral, expense buried in the reams of financial data generated by the billions of dollars, at their disposal. Yet here was Dominicus. His mind worked furiously. How had he tripped up?

A taunting laugh interrupted his thoughts. "Salvi, you of all people should have known you couldn't get away with this. Sooner or later somebody was going to discover your hidden lifestyle; the villa, the wine, the trips to exotic environs...the little girls."

What had been a trickle of cold sweat was now a river running down the middle of his back. They knew it all.

"Things were quiet, Salvi. Over the hundreds of years of our existence, the Order has had these times of quiet. For twenty years we didn't have a clue, a trace of evidence, a hint of our quarry. You of all people know that. We worked side-by-side for years. Did you think we went away? You were entrusted with safeguarding our assets and you abused that trust. You were so good, almost as good as me."

"Listen, Dominicus. I can explain all this and I can undo it. I hadn't heard from anyone for so long, it was almost as if everyone had disappeared. It was a mistake; I realize that. Give me some time and I will make it right. Please, tell the others they can trust me to make this right."

The whole time he was talking, trying to inflect his words with fear, something he didn't have to try very hard to do, he was analyzing the situation. Domincius was right. He had once been almost as good, perhaps as good as the man sitting before him. The pistol in his pocket called to him.

He moved slowly away from the door, toward the shadows where Dominicus sat. He nonchalantly dropped his hands into the pockets of the robe, his right hand closing over the pistol.

"They will listen to you, Dominicus. They trust you. You and I were always friends. We did so much together. I, like you, have given my entire adult life to the cause. That must be worth something."

Dominicus was silent and that scared Salvador. As he moved to the chair across from where Dominicus sat, the pistol in his friend's hand slowly followed him.

Now, he could see his face; a face that looked little different now than it had all those years ago. The hair still jet black, the jaw line hard and without sag. The eyes were as hard as they had ever been. Only a webbing of crows feet, at the corners of his eyes, gave tell to the passage of time.

It was when Salvador began to sit, that Dominicus fired. Two quick shots from the silenced pistol and the bullets struck, one in his right hand, the other in the left. He cried out in agony, his hands flying out of the pockets, the pistol ending up on the floor at his feet. Two more bullets, one in each kneecap, drove the old man out of the chair to the floor.

Salvador Rocha had been a killer once, and now he realized his time had come. A spinning montage of victims flashed through his mind. As he lay on his tile floor he saw a parade of faces; the faces of those he had killed.

He looked up at Dominicus, who hadn't moved from the chair, his face a blank and empty slate. He had seen that face many times, always right before Dominicus ended someone's life.

"You betrayed us, Salvador," Dominicus whispered. "You betrayed me. There is no redemption for you here. Take your chances with someone on the other side."

He saw Dominicus' finger tense and closed his eyes.

Dominicus Bureau took a sip of wine and grimaced. The wine had turned. A shame really, it should have been a great bottle.

He stared at his old friend lying dead on the floor before him, two ugly black holes in his forehead. This, too, was a shame. Dominicus had never had very many friends in his life. Actually, he had only had two, his mother--did that count?--and Salvador "Salvi" Rocha.

They had traveled the length and breadth of Europe, and a goodly part of the rest of the world in search of their quarry, coming close several times. They had faced death on numerous occasions, dealing it out too many times to remember.

Now it had come to this. Greed, sloth, perversion and age had taken its toll on Salvi. It had failed to touch Dominicus. There was too much to do. Whispers and tell-tale rumors had again begun to filter through his sources and spies. The Arimathean was on the move. What Dominicus searched for, what they and those before them had searched for over hundreds of years, would be found, if not by him, then by someone after him. Someday they would find it and the world would be changed. He had no time for traitors or thieves.

He stood up and slipped the pistol under his coat into a holster under his arm. Taking a cloth out of his pocket he wiped the wine glass and the bottle.

Without glancing at his friend he moved to the front door thinking, *What a shame, a bottle of '62 Petrus.*

CHAPTER 8

Paris, France, May 2010

Dominicus Bureau sat outside a café on the Boulevard Saint-Germain, sipping espresso and reading a copy of Le Figaro.

He hated Paris. He hated all of France if truth be known. The fact he was French did not temper the intensity of his hate.

It wasn't the people. He had no trouble with them. He had mastered the art, and it was an art, of being able to look at someone and send them scurrying for safety. He'd had this ability since he was a young man. It worked well with most Frenchmen and even better with Parisians. It had driven him from the pulpit and the confessional very early on in his life as a priest. It had driven him straight into the arms of those who needed a man of the cloth, so committed to God that he would do anything they asked. Anything.

No, he had a more visceral and ingrained hatred of France that pre-dated anything you could see, touch or feel in this modern version. His hate went back much further, which was the reason he was here now.

He had left Italy after cleaning up the mess that was Salvador Rocha. A new custodian of the Order's assets had been elevated to replace the traitor.

Still, Rocha's betrayal and his subsequent termination was a setback. It had taken many years to work him into his position in the Vatican.

In the end, Rocha was only one of several members of the Vatican hierarchy who belonged to the Order. It was a shame to lose one of such high rank but they would go on as they always had. For over eight hundred years they had existed. One Salvador Rocha would not spell their end.

Dominicus put down the paper and tossed a few euros on the table. He stood and stepping off the sidewalk, crossed the street to a small boutique down a side street. Entering, he paused for a moment. Two Japanese women were trying on dresses while a sales girl feverishly dashed this way and that, piling up new dresses and re-hanging others that didn't meet some sort of test only the women could decipher.

He nodded to the woman behind the counter as he drifted past her into the back of the shop. He made his way around several racks of clothing until he reached a stairway leading down into the dark.

Without light, he made his way down the steps until he had reached the basement. He made his way to the far wall, as his eyes quickly adjusted to the dark. Kneeling, he ran his hand along the joint where the masonry met the floor. He found a brick with an indentation along one edge. He pressed and a small section of the wall, perhaps three feet high and two feet wide, slid inwards.

Dominicus ducked through the opening and once through, pushed the section of wall back into place.

He was in a narrow passageway lit by the occasional light bulb hanging from a single strand wire, running off into the distance.

Dominicus headed down the passageway until, three minutes later, he came to a wooden ladder which led up into the dark. Without hesitating, he climbed the ladder until he reached a trap door. Raising a hand above his head, he pushed up and slid through the opening, then, quietly, he lowered the door back into place.

He was inside a storage room. Boxes and crates were stacked in no apparent order and, in fact, looked as if no one had touched them for some time.

He moved through the room until he reached a door set into the wall. Knocking three times, he stood back from the door and waited. He looked at the ceiling where he saw a small video camera staring back at him. He glanced away from the camera just as the door opened.

A man in a dark suit stood to one side holding the door open. Dominicus went through the door into a large room with stone walls and stone floor. It was stark in its lack of ornamentation or furnishing. Only a round table with chairs spaced evenly around its circumference occupied the space.

At the far end of the room, a raging fire burned within an enormous fireplace. Six men stood in front of the fire talking among themselves. Each man had a glass in hand and the smell of fine cigars reached Dominicus' nose. He made his way across the room drawing the attention of the men in front of the fire.

"Ah, Dominicus. There you are. I guess we can begin as you are the last to arrive. As usual I might add," said a tall thin man with an unkempt bush of white hair and a hook nose.

"Someone has to be last, Jonathon. I prefer it be me so I know there is no one taking undue interest in our gathering," Dominicus said.

"Knowing Dominicus is out there watching my back is something I find very comforting," said another man who entered the room from a door near the fireplace. He raised his glass in a salute to Dominicus.

"Welcome Dominicus. It's good to see you," the man said. He was short, maybe five feet tall, slender and obviously fit. At seventy years old, a year younger than Dominicus, his hair was jet black, but unlike the priest's it required a bi-monthly dye job to maintain its color. His face was that of a studious man. If a person was to guess his occupation and said banker, they would be right, although technically he owned a controlling interest in eight European banks. His name was Phillip Gotier. He was the current Grand Master of the Order.

Waving his hand in the direction of the table and eight chairs in the center of the room he said, "Let's begin, shall we, gentlemen. We have much to discuss."

The men made their way to the table taking chairs in no apparent order. The table was heavy and obviously old. It was bare other than a strange ornamentation carved into the center. It was a cross with a sword thrust through the middle cutting the cross in half. The detail was exquisite and was outlined in gold leaf.

Gotier remained standing after all the others had taken their seats. He looked around the table for a moment before speaking, "Welcome to my home once more, Gentlemen. As you know it has been over twenty years since we last met as a full council. In that time we have lost three of our members, one within the last two days."

At that, Gotier glanced at Dominicus and gave a slight nod. "Salvador betrayed our trust by stealing from us and using funds for his own purposes. It was something we could not allow to stand. The fact he was our highest ranking Vatican plant could not justify his betrayal. Brother Dominicus took care of this problem two days ago. Brother Schmidt," here he nodded to a rotund, red faced man to his left, "has assumed the position of controller of the Order's finances."

"Is there any chance of exposure due to Salvador's betrayal?" the man named Jonathon asked.

"No. Dominicus has assured me that our internal controls were never violated in a way that could expose us. It was only Salvador stealing from us," Phillip answered.

"Do we know the extent of the theft?" asked a dark skinned man who had the look of a Spaniard or perhaps Portuguese.

"Apparently, Juan, several million dollars was removed, most of which is gone. Dominicus feels we can recover some of it. But this is not why I called you all together today. I called you here today because we have news of the Arimathean."

At this, the men began talking among themselves excitedly. Gotier held up his hand and the men went silent. "I will let Dominicus tell us what he has learned of late."

Gotier sat and nodded to Dominicus. The old priest remained seated and began to speak, "Randolph Donovan has died." This elicited another round of excited murmurs from the assembled men. "It was a month ago. I received word from America a week after it happened. I immediately alerted all of our contacts and spies around the world, instructing them to be extra vigilant for signs of movement or information."

Dominicus paused for a moment letting the suspense in the room build for a moment. "I have received a second piece of information in the last week which indicates to me the Arimathean is on the move. It is obviously related to the death of Donovan who, as you all know, we suspected of being the Arimathean's facilitator and friend.

"Two days ago our Zurich contact observed what he felt was a strange security drill at Bergen en Cie. We have known for sometime that this is one of many store houses used by our quarry. The drill was strange in that all of the security personnel left the building and apparently the bank was left without any of its security apparatus in place.

"This is similar to what happened in late 1948, right after we indentified Bergen en Cie as a possible storehouse. At that time, we had one of our last confirmed sightings of the Arimathean. I have ordered additional surveillance in Zurich as well as other potential repositories we suspect belong to him."

"Dominicus, I hate to interrupt but why did we never move on Donovan?" Jonathon asked. "I believe I advocated for that exact thing over twenty years ago. If you believed he was working with the Arimathean, why didn't we take him and extract the information. It seems to me we have lost our best opportunity in the last few hundred years."

Dominicus shook his head as if he was speaking with a child before answering, "Our goal is what the Arimathean protects. We need him, not his lackeys. Did we learn nothing from the pogroms of the past, the heavy handed inquisitions of his past acquaintances? I would have loved to have walked into Donovan's house in Maine and introduced him to real pain and fear, extracting whatever it was I could from the old fool. But in the end, his master would never leave himself so vulnerable as to be caught by such juvenile tactics.

"We need to trap him. We need something that will draw him to us, out into the open. When we can overwhelm him, catch him unawares, we will succeed."

"So you say, Dominicus. But as long as I have been a member of this council we have failed to get any closer to our goal and we know nothing more today than we did twenty years ago," Jonathon said. "You seem to have all the answers but nothing to show for your efforts. I personally am beginning to wonder if this Arimathean actually exists, and if he does, if we have the right people spearheading our field efforts."

This elicited a nervous shifting of feet and hands from the other members of the council and one of Dominicus' patented stares.

"Do you have doubts, Brother Jonathon, really?" the Grand Master asked in a quiet voice.

Silence filled the room. To a man, every other member either stared at the table top or risked furtive glances around the table. Expressing a disbelief in the very essence for the reason of their existence as an organization was something never uttered out loud. Certainly many of them had wondered and felt similar doubts, but in the end, their history and the awesome potential of what it was they pursued inevitably dispelled those doubts. But no one had ever voiced those doubts out loud. Not here.

Jonathon was silent, his eyes going from the Grand Master to Dominicus. "No, I don't doubt our mission. I believe in it with all my soul. Like many of you, my father and my grandfather, and for some of us several generations of our forefathers, have been committed to this crusade. I am still committed, but I am tired of waiting. I am tired of waiting for this mythical man, the Arimathean, to show himself. We react, we never attack. I say we go on the attack now. If you believe he is on the move than let's attack every one of those places we suspect. I am tired of waiting. I want it found, brought before our enemies, and our rightful place established."

The murmurs of quiet agreement rose from several members of the council. Others were silent. Dominicus said nothing.

"How long have you been a member of the Order, Jonathon?" Gotier asked.

"My father brought me into the Order over fifty years ago."

"Fifty years, most of your life in fact. We have been here together, Jonathon, all those years. Rising up within the ranks, paying our dues," Gotier said. "Fifty years is nothing, nothing! What of all those who went before us who fought, died, searched and paved the way for us? You grow tired of waiting? What of our quarry? Seven hundred years he has been guarding what we crave. Seven hundred years one man, made immortal by the devil's own hand, has eluded us and all those who have gone before. If you are tired, Jonathon, perhaps it's time you step down and allow one with more stamina to take your place."

Silence filled the room. No one moved. This was a moment none of them had ever experienced. Would it slip into insurrection?

Finally, Jonathon spoke, "I have given my whole life to the Order. I will not give up now."

Gotier stared hard into the man's eyes before responding, "I expected nothing less, my friend. We all have our moments of doubt."

Turning to Dominicus the Grand Master said, "What do you plan to do now?"

"I am monitoring all of our intelligence networks and, as I said, I have ordered additional surveillance on prime targets. I have extra assets moving into place all over the world. The key is to be able to react, with force and speed, if we catch his scent. I know how he moves and how he operates. If he comes out into the open, we will attack. We will be ready."

"Good. I think we can adjourn until we have further information. We will need to elevate three members from the Order to replace those we have lost. I will be contacting each of you for nominations. We will reconvene to elect the replacements. Now, stand with me."

All of the men stood and as one pulled up the right sleeves of their shirts and held their arms up, fists clenched, in a sort of salute. A tattoo, an exact replica of the ornamentation carved into the table adorned each man's arm.

"Once more we pledge our commitment and our honor to the Order of the Broken Cross, the real Templars, and to our quest," Gotier chanted and then as one they all said, "So we pledge, one and all, until death."

Thirty minutes later Dominicus sat in front of the fire sipping a glass of wine. Gotier, sitting across from him in another chair, was the only other person left in the room.

"Do you think we have an opportunity now to find him?" Gotier asked.

"As good a chance as any in the last thirty years," Dominicus said while staring into the flames.

"I want nothing more than to see it before I die, Dominicus. To actually put my hands on it and realize its power is my greatest wish. Time grows short for us, my friend."

"Our mission is to find it or to ensure the survival of the Order so that those who come after us have the chance to do what we have not. I believe there are some who don't have the commitment necessary anymore," Dominicus said quietly.

"You speak of Jonathon, which is why I wanted you to stay behind until the others left. I think he falters... fatally."

Dominicus looked from the fire to the Grand Master, their eyes locking. Nothing was said. No further words passed between them. Dominicus stood, walked to the table, and put down his glass.

"You're a good man, Dominicus. Perhaps the greatest hunter the Order has ever had," Gotier said from in front of the fire.

"And still he evades us. Still it evades us... me."

Gotier stood and turning smiled at Dominicus, "Go find him old friend. Something tells me it is our time."

CHAPTER 9

The Coast of Maine, May 2010

Alex felt excitement coursing through his veins as he read the story of how his grandfather had discovered the ancient book. That it seemed almost pre-ordained was a thought that had struck him at several points in Randolph's narrative. Coupled with his assertion that Alex was now destined to find this Gaspar character, feelings of impending events began to germinate in the recesses of his mind.

It had been a long time since he had felt this kind of excitement. The kind of excitement brought about by the anticipation of action. The feelings took him back in time.

Alex had graduated from Annapolis at the age of twenty-two, the love of the sea imbued in him by his grandfather. After graduation and upon entering the Navy, he'd been posted for a time to a guided missile frigate stationed out of Japan. Quickly, he realized the life of a shipboard lieutenant held little attraction for him. While he was lauded for his attention to detail and dogged adherence to his duties, boredom set in rather quickly. And so, over the objections of his commander, who didn't want to lose an officer of his caliber, he volunteered for Naval Special Warfare training; the Seals.

It didn't take long to discover that he'd found his calling and, for the next eight years he was assigned to Seal Team One in Coronado, California, the last few years as a platoon leader. His time in the Seals found him in the Persian Gulf during the first Gulf War and took him throughout Asia and other parts of the world on various missions, some known, most never talked about.

He established a reputation as a fearless but meticulously prepared leader who wouldn't hesitate to lead his men on the most dangerous missions. Over the years and the missions, he had lost several members of his teams, and he'd suffered grievous injuries on two separate occasions. The last one had ended his career. There was little room for a Seal Team operator with a shattered knee courtesy of a 7.62 round.

And so he had left the Navy at 32 years of age with a modest pension and a host of skills now seemingly unusable in the civilian world. He'd moved back to Boston where his life revolved around doing little but prowling book stores, attending a couple of Red Sox games a week during the season, punishing his stubbornly noncompliant knee at a local gym, and tending to the old brownstone on Commonwealth Avenue he and his siblings had inherited from his mother. She'd passed away just before his retirement, leaving the old building to the three of them.

Alex occupied one of the four apartments in the building. He'd convinced his siblings to keep the building and allow him to manage it. He sent off a small check to his brother and sister every month, and his share, along with his pension, gave him just enough money to avoid employment.

For ten years now that had been his life.

Occasionally, he received a call from an old comrade checking up on him or offering him some sort of work for the various military contractors that seemed overly populated with former special operators like him. He'd avoided the offers like the plague, unwilling to subject himself to a desk job while others traipsed around to far off corners of the world's most violent shit-holes doing the work he could no longer do.

His only respites, from the monotony of his new life, were his sojourns to Maine and his grandfather's home. The trips had become more frequent over the last few years and had provided him with a certain solace he found nowhere else.

Surprisingly, his grandfather had rarely talked with him about his Navy days. Alex knew his grandfather had fought in World War Two but he never talked about his experiences. Alex had respected his silence. Alex had, through the years, kept Randolph up to date on his life through letters and visits when on leave. The old man seemed content to ignore the history, only once inquiring as to the state of his knee. His only comment, "Someday your knee will be good as new," had baffled Alex at the time.

Now, as he sat pondering the books before him and the stories contained within, that growing sense of excitement stoking a fire within him, he wondered where to start. What would it take to prove this story true or expose it as a fraud?

He retrieved the stack of folders containing the details of his new wealth; the files given him by Lucas two weeks ago. He hadn't touched them again and had only spoken to Lucas once since their meeting. The lawyer had called him to see how he was doing. He'd told Alex he was willing and able to help him when he was ready. Perhaps now was the time to start.

He dialed Lucas' number and, after a few moments on hold, listening to some vapid Barry Manilow tune, Lucas picked up the line.

"Alex. How are you? I see you're calling from Maine."

"Hi, Lucas. Yes, I'm up at Grandfather's place."

"Your place now."

"Ah, yes."

"What can I do for you, Alex?

"Well, I have some questions about a couple of the files you left; the one with the Swiss bank info in particular."

"Yes?" Lucas answered.

"Well, how would I go about finding out what's in that account?"

"Pretty straightforward stuff, really," Lucas said. "You simply need to go to the bank, present yourself, and give them the account code and the key. They'll then provide you with whatever information they have."

"That's what I thought. I have to physically go to Switzerland to find out." Alex said.

"Yes. They would never give out any information over the phone," Lucas said. "That's one of the downsides of an account like this; private, but not the easiest to access."

"I think I'm going to go there and see what's in the account. Do I have a bank account with any money in it I can use? I'm a little short on cash."

Lucas laughed. "Alex, you're going to have to get used to the fact that you're a wealthy man now. I have everything here at the office. Your grandfather had an account he used for day to day expenses. We can sweep money into it from a variety of sources as you need it. Just come by the office and I'll give you the check-book and all the pertinent information. There's also a debit card linked to the account so you can get money from it anywhere in the world. There's currently just over two million dollars in it."

Alex chuckled. "I guess I'm not as short as I thought. I'll come by in a couple of days and pick up the card. Thanks, Lucas."

"You're quite welcome, my boy. Come by at noon and we'll go to Abe and Louie's for lunch. I'll even let you buy."

Alex hung up the phone and shook his head at the strangeness of it all. He was about to go off on an expedition to find out the true source and reality of his grandfather's ancient Italian book. Apparently, his search would begin in Switzerland. In the meantime, the sounds of the water, the birds, and a gentle breeze blowing off the water beckoned him.

He stood, made his way to the window and looked down at his grandfather's boat berthed alongside the dock below him. Turning to the desk, he picked up the two books and headed for the kitchen. He threw some bread, an assortment of cheeses, some prosciutto and a couple of apples into a small cooler. He went down to the cellar and retrieved a bottle of '68 Bollinger and after locking up the house, made his way down the path to the stairway leading to the dock. After stowing his meager provisions, he made sure he had some linens and blankets on board and working quickly, he cast off, sailing into the bay.

The wind was coming straight up from the south and it wasn't long before he was making eight knots across the bay, tacking back and forth, getting the feel of the old boat once more. He made his way around Turtle Head and, five hours later, he was anchored in a quiet and deserted inlet just south of Buck's Harbor. As dusk spread its pinkish glow in the west, he settled into the cockpit with his champagne, cheese and bread, and by the light of an old lantern, he began to read his grandfather's narrative once more.

CHAPTER 10

Boston, July, 1954

I returned to Boston with a growing sense of purpose. The book, written in the old Italian and completely unreadable, held my attention completely. I spent almost every waking hour on the trip home mesmerized by the pictures. Even though I couldn't read the text, the pictures began to form a narrative in my mind. What was strange was that every picture contained the knight who appeared in the very first picture. Over the course of the book, his style of dress, the cut of his hair, and his locations changed, as if keeping pace with history's passing. What never changed was his face.

When I reached Boston, I began a search for a translator who could read the book and create a complete translation. I had a keen sense of the need for secrecy. This story was too incredible, too supernatural and I didn't want to be thought a crazy fool. I also wanted to get it done as quickly as possible. So I got in touch with the Italian departments at Harvard, Tufts, Boston College, and Boston University and hired four separate translators, all of them unknown to the others. I would give one translator a chapter, then skip several chapters and have him begin on another.

In the end, none of the two men and two women had seen the whole book or read all the chapters.

Finally, the translators were finished. Still, I put off reading the translation. I wanted it bound and printed into an easy to read volume. Taking the train to New York, I contracted with a small printer to produce one volume. I told him I was a frustrated novelist who had failed to find a commercial book publisher so was going to have one printed for posterity.

The small volume and the non-descript leather cover were quickly finished, and on a stormy January night, I sat down in my small office and began to read. It began this way.

Alex continued to read his grandfather's translation of Gaspar de Rouse's story as night closed in. The silence of the Maine coast created an atmosphere of peace, seclusion and mystery. He quickly realized that the translation began with a narrative written not by Gaspar himself, but by the Venetian painter who had illustrated Gaspar's book. Filling his glass and settling in under a Swans Island blanket, he lost himself in the unfolding story.

Venice, 1575

My name is Bartholomew Delcorso. I am a painter. I am writing this story in Venice, in the year of our lord 1575, about an incredible event in my life that happened to me ten years ago when I met Gaspar de Rouse; a man who became my friend and confidant. Every word of this story, while fantastic, is true.

Venice, 1565

I first met him in a small but festive taverna off one of Venice's hidden alleys. It was the kind of place known only to a select few and frequented by a mix of the Venetian population who, for the most part, rarely mingled. The entrance was hidden down a set of stairs leading into the cellar of an ancient merchant's home, well below the level of the canal that ran by the front.

It was dark, musty, and more than a bit damp, but it enveloped you in an embrace which made it hard to resist. It was called, "The Vizier's."

It was owned and operated by a dark-eyed Byzantine woman whose name I had never heard. She had inherited it from her Venetian husband who, rumor had it, had found her in a Constantinople whore house and convinced her to accompany him to Venice.

He bought the old taverna and, after a few years of establishing it as a place to meet, connive, and conspire without too many prying eyes, died of some sudden, unexplained malady. He died screaming incoherently, and holding his guts as he chased his wife brandishing a meat cleaver. He fell like a stone before he could get to her, which led to just a bit of speculation she had introduced him to some sort of poison or Byzantine concoction unknown to the local doctors.

Regardless, it was just dark enough, loud enough, and she was just attractive enough that I was drawn back to it almost nightly. I would sit and order a good bottle of wine, and she would cook me some spicy concoction of lamb and saffron or mussels with some sort of seasoning I could never identify.

I had a few acquaintances there, but for the most part, it was a place I would frequent for the coolness of the stone walls in the summer and the heat from the fireplace and liquor in the winter.

I first noticed him on one of those cold, damp Venice nights sitting at a table near the fire. He was sitting quietly, staring into the flames, nursing a glass of brownish liquid the Byzantine woman would pour for him out of a bottle hidden behind the bar. It had no markings or label, and it took both of her obviously strong hands to hold it when she poured. I never saw her pour him anything else or pour for any other patron from that bottle.

The first night he sat there for what seemed like hours, never looking anywhere but into the fire and occasionally lifting the glass to his lips.

Many a night I would sit and watch him, trying to get up the courage to approach him. Why I was scared to do so, I didn't quite know, until finally the woman would come and tell me she was closing and I would leave him still by the fire.

I actually began to leave my patrons earlier and earlier, neglecting their commissions, to find myself rushing down alleys, laying wagers with myself on whether I could beat him to his spot by the fire and what would happen if I did. But I never did. I never could beat him there.

So it went until, a cold and blustery December night. I was sitting across the room from the fire when I sensed a presence close to me. Looking up from my plate of mussels, I found myself staring at the man who had been sitting every night by the fire. He was taller than I had guessed. As always, he was simply dressed in a long dark coat he never removed, simple, rough-looking pants, and leather boots which almost reached his knees.

I was so shocked to find him at my table that we both stared at each other for what seemed like a lifetime, then his face broke into a bemused smile and he said, "Care to share a drink, friend? I feel I've come to know you over the last two months."

I stammered something about him being welcome, at which point he sat across from me, gesturing to the woman.

She came across the room and placing two glasses before us, poured from the strange bottle, which he asked her to leave at the table. He held out the glass in a gesture of salute, and I raised my glass in return, briefly touching his. He threw back the glass, drinking the full measure of the liquid in one swallow.

That was when I made my first mistake. I took my glass and, emulating him, I drained it in one giant gulp.

I almost sprang to my feet as the liquid scalded a path down my throat. It was as if the devil himself had decided to brew a liquid produced from the smoldering embers of the fires of Hades. I felt as if my guts were being wrenched from my body, and I gripped the table with both hands so forcefully, it shook.

The whole time he said nothing until, after several moments of dire pain in which I thought I was in fact making my way to the Promised Land, he began to laugh. It was as if every fiber of his being was feeling it, in a way so infectious, despite my seeming dire condition, I began to laugh as well, and for some time we laughed as if old friends.

Amazingly, he then took the bottle from between us and, holding it to his lips, he drank a draught from the bottle. I swear he emptied a goodly half of it. He slammed it down and, reaching across the table, held out his hand. I took it, shaking his hand, finding a grip that was solid, firm and warm.

"I am Gaspar de Rouse," he said.

"Bartholomew Delcorso," I replied.

"I began to believe you would spend the next twenty years watching me, and I am sure your patrons want their paintings finished sometime before they leave this earth. I decided I had better just get the introductions over with."

I felt a sense of embarrassment at the obviousness of my curiosity, which gave way to a sense of concern that this man whom I knew nothing about seemed to know things about me.

As if sensing my concern, he winked and said, "Do not worry, friend. I make it my business to know who inhabits the space around me."

"How did you know I was a friend?" I asked.

"It's a gift. One which has served me well for a long time," he said with a smile.

Now that I was sitting across from the stranger, I had a chance to take the full measure of the man. What struck me most was an almost overwhelming sense of age which seemed to radiate from him. It was as if I were looking at an ancient painting that had somehow come to life. At the time, it seemed strange as he didn't appear physically to be that old. In fact, I would have placed his age at closer to thirty years than forty. Perhaps it was his eyes; dark and seemingly bottomless pools flashing in the dim light of the bar, speaking to me instantly of a great and wrenching sadness.

His face, while devoid of the creases and wear of age, was deeply tanned as if he'd spent a good part of his life in the sun.

His name sounded French, but he seemed more like the men of the Levant who frequented Venice's harbors.

He reached across the table and lifted my bottle, smelling the contents. He murmured his approval and filled my glass.

"Your taste in wine is good, my friend. I think it best you stick with your wine. Perhaps we'll share mine another time."

"What in God's name is that concoction?" I asked.

He laughed lightly. "In God's name? If only you knew the irony of your statement, *Signore Pittore*."

That was the second time he had referred to my profession. So he knew I was a painter. It seemed he knew a lot about me while I knew nothing about him. I was about to inquire when he held up his hand in a quieting gesture.

"There will be plenty of time for questions, my friend. I'll share with you the answers to whatever you ask and to many things you can't even now begin to imagine. But now the smell of those mussels is working its magic on my stomach, and I haven't eaten a good meal all day. Let us eat, drink, and enjoy the hospitality of this wonderful place."

He gestured to the woman who seemingly appeared out of nowhere with a heaping plate of shellfish he immediately attacked with ravenous gusto.

I was watching him eat when I realized I was feeling quite drunk. I looked at my bottle and found it was still half full, but there was no doubt my head was attempting to separate from my body and take flight to the upper reaches of the ceiling.

I tried steadying myself by placing my hands on the table, but it was clear I was inebriated beyond reason. I glanced at the stranger and found him staring at me with a somewhat bemused look on his face.

"Like I said, I think you should stick to your own wine for a while. It takes some time to fortify one's self against my special blend. Did I tell you I make it myself? No? Indeed, I do. And this batch had a provenance that imbued it with a little extra strength."

Nothing he was saying to me made sense. While I felt the overwhelming desire to lay my head on the table and just go to sleep, I sensed I should quickly head back to the safety of my home, so I began to stand, even as the room began spinning around me at a frightening speed.

I had almost made it to my feet when the room suddenly stopped spinning. I fell backwards into the chair and found no matter what I did, I couldn't move from my seat.

I looked around the room, amazed at the number of people who had packed themselves into the bar. I didn't recall seeing any of these people enter. There had, in fact, been only two or three other patrons in the place when the stranger had sat down.

Now there looked to be thirty or more. Some were seated at tables, some were standing, and to my obviously enfeebled mind, some were sitting on the wooden beams holding up the ceiling.

I gaped up at the spectacle of seven or eight people sitting there swinging their legs back and forth drinking from giant mugs staring directly at me.

I looked around the room again and realized everyone in the place was staring right at me. Who were these people? I didn't recognize them, but every one of them was staring at me, everyone except the stranger who had gone back to filling his face from his bowl of mussels.

"What? What are you all looking at? Do I know you people?" I shouted. No one responded. Silence.

"They won't talk to you."

I looked at the stranger. He was leaning back in his chair staring at me, his arms folded across his chest. He looked around the room, then back to me.

"What do you see?"

"People; rude and annoying people who think it's okay to stare at a man trying to eat his food in peace," I said loud enough for all to hear.

"Really? Are you sure that's what you see?" And then he raised his left hand and snapped his fingers.

It was as if by snapping his fingers he had conjured up a scene straight out of some hellish nightmare.

All around me were various creatures and beings which immediately assaulted my very sanity. Beings with wings jutting from their backs stood by the fire. Two animals, at least I think that's what they were, of a species I had never seen before, with the heads of lions atop the bodies of voluptuous women, stared at me from the bar.

The people sitting on the beams in the ceiling had morphed into the most hideous looking creatures, appearing to be half bat and half snake, with long reptilian legs and snouts like those of swine.

Everywhere I looked were the most unbelievable monstrosities of malformed, seemingly cobbled together beings that in my wildest nightmares I would never have imagined.

I looked back to the stranger to find him stern faced and pensive. Panic gripped me down to my very soul, and just when I felt I'd begin screaming in terror, he slowly raised his right hand, nonchalantly snapped his fingers, and the vision was gone.

And so was I.

CHAPTER 11

Venice, 1565

I t was still morning, although the sun was well on its way to the middle of the sky. The pounding on my door surprised me as I rarely had visitors at my home. Usually I received friends, patrons, or students at my shop, but here at home, it was an unexpected disturbance at what was, for me, an early hour of the morning.

I was still nursing the after-effects of my encounter with the stranger from the night before. My plan had been to not leave my bed until the infernal pounding in my head ceased creating explosions of brain-numbing pain behind my eyeballs. But whoever was beating on my door was obviously not aware of my plan.

I staggered from my bed in the back of the apartment and shuffled to the door, twice being helped along by the providential placement of furniture by which to steady myself. In an ever-quickening pace to stop what sounded like the imminent destruction of my centuries-old front door, I pushed my debilitated self toward the noise.

I reached for the door prepared to eviscerate the fool who was dismantling it with his pounding. Opening it, I found myself staring down at the smallest man I'd ever encountered, staring up at me, his fist, mid-pound.

Before I could commence with the aforementioned vivisection of this interloper, he broke into a smile whose radiance only served to further blind my already severely diminished, alcohol-debilitated eyesight and stuck out his miniature hand in greeting.

"Good morning, kind sir! I hope I didn't awaken you at this late hour of the morning."

The little man looked as if he'd been dressed by one of Venice's finest clothiers. From his head, which was topped by a gemstone encrusted skullcap, to the red velvet, fur-trimmed jacket and pants, down to a pair of incredibly small but obviously expensive knee-high boots, he was the picture of Venetian high fashion. He had skin which appeared almost translucent, it was so white. His features and limbs were of a perfect proportion to his size.

"What in God's name do you want and who are you?" I asked, ignoring the outstretched hand. The croaking emanating from my mouth sounded as if it belonged to some long dead creature of demonic origins.

"My name is Sabatticus, kind sir. I've been sent by my master, Gaspar de Rouse, to escort you to your appointment at his palazzo. I'm to bring you to him right away, and his personal gondola awaits in the canal, a short walk from here."

"Your master is the man I met last night who plied me with that infernal liquor which has left me in this state of near death?"

"Indeed he is, sir, although perhaps you speak just a bit harshly about my master's favorite wine. He did tell me you might be feeling a tad worn this morning, so I brought along an elixir to fix you right up."

And with that he pushed by me into the foyer heading down the hall toward the tiny kitchen near the back of my hovel.

I stood open-mouthed and staring in the doorway for some seconds before the little man, still heading away into my home, called over his shoulder, "Come along now. I'll fix you the best cup of morning tea you've ever had." He disappeared around the corner and into my kitchen, the sounds of banging pots prodding me into action.

I closed the door and headed toward the kitchen, now thinking about this man Gaspar whose little minion had roused me from my bed.

Gaspar.

I now remembered the name, but in fact could recall little about last night other than drinking some of the man's vile wine, and having the most frightening nightmare of my life. I did not, now that I thought about it, remember how I'd gotten back to my home. Nor did I remember arranging to meet my new friend this morning.

"My master made sure you got home safely last night and that no harm came to you," the little voice from my kitchen called out.

I turned the corner to find the tiny man standing over an already flaring cook fire on top of which my tea-pot was set. Into the pot, the little man was dumping the contents of a small leather pouch he'd pulled out from inside his jacket.

I instantly had grave misgivings about drinking anything from the pot after my experience the night before.

Again, as if reading my mind, he turned to me and said, "Now don't be afraid, kind sir. I've brought along one of my family's finest teas. I assure you it will restore your good health and clear your mind in just a matter of minutes."

I sat at my wooden table and watched the little man work, stirring the mixture in the pot and stoking the now fully raging fire for a few minutes until he pronounced, "Ah, here we are!"

He proceeded to pour a full measure of the now steaming liquid into my only tea-cup, handing it to me with a flourish that made me feel as if I was being served in one of the Doge's finest parlors. He stepped back, folding his hands in front of him, and waited for me to drink.

I looked down into my cup, with not a small amount of trepidation, at what was a dark brown, not quite clear liquid of unknown provenance. I looked back to my tea maker, who only smiled more broadly, his face beaming with obvious pride.

"You say this is an old family recipe?"

"Very old."

"What is it exactly?"

"Tea, sir."

"Ah. That helps so much."

Putting my nose down to the cup, I took a tentative smell of the liquid's aroma. It actually smelled wonderful, instantly evoking memories of childhood mornings on my father's farm in the hills outside Florence.

It smelled of fresh mown hay, sunflowers, honey, and milk. I had visions of my mother in the kitchen of our tiny farmhouse, singing quietly as she made biscuits and cakes, smothering them with honey and milk, as my sisters and I waited patiently at the long wooden table of my childhood.

I almost began to cry.

"What kind of tea did you say it was?"

"I didn't. What kind would you like it to be?"

This morning was shaping up like none other, so raising the cup to my lips, I prepared to taste the concoction when he interrupted me and said, "You're perceptive, though. It has all of those things in it."

"What things?"

"Freshly mown hay, sunflowers, honey, and milk."

I stared dumbfounded at this strange, mind-reading midget of a man for a moment. Then, wondering just a bit at my sanity, I drank.

It was without a doubt the most wonderful thing which had ever passed my lips and, with eyes closed, my mind reveling in the sensuous flavors and smells, I drank the entire mixture.

"My Master awaits us, and would be most upset if I failed to bring you to him at once," said the tea maker.

I opened my eyes and, to my amazement, every bit of the loathsome aftermath of the previous night had faded away as if it had never happened. I was fully awake, refreshed in a way I had never felt. The demons banging on the anvil in my head only moments ago had ceased their torture. It was as if every bit of my being had been cleansed and purified by one cup of tea.

"I don't know what you gave me . . . what was your name again?"

"Sabatticus, sir."

"Yes, right. Sabatticus. Well, I don't know what that was, but it was fantastic. You could make a fortune selling it. Have you ever thought about that? I could introduce you to merchants I know who could help you sell it. It's amazing. What kind of name is Sabatticus anyway?"

The little man just smiled. "I could never do that, sir. It's too precious, and it's only for relieving the effects of certain things. Like my Master's special wine. As to my name, it's Greek. I come from an old and famous family. Perhaps you've heard of them? No? Well, no matter. But now you must dress, sir, for we must depart for Palazzo Vertichelli."

"Yes, right. I suppose I can go for a little while, but it must be a brief visit as I have much work to do today. Give me one moment and I'll dress."

And so, after cleaning up as best I could on short notice and dressing in something not splattered with paint, I found myself following the little man out of my apartment down a series of passageways leading off the alley in front of my home.

What a sight I'm sure we made, the tiny little man dressed up as if for a royal ball, with me actually struggling to keep up with his rapidly churning little legs until we reached a canal landing about five minutes' walk from my door.

Waiting for us, bobbing gently in the water, was an elaborate gondola of immaculately varnished wood. It looked as if it were made from dozens of individual exotic species and, unlike many of the most elaborate gondolas of the day, it wasn't painted. The varnished sides were so highly polished, it was like looking into the finest Venetian mirror. It also had a fully enclosed compartment, with windows down the sides, covered in a canvas of the deepest, most vibrant color blue.

But while the boat was awe-inspiring, what drew my attention most was the person standing with one sandal-clad foot on the landing, the other on the boat.

He was the complete opposite of my new-found friend Sabatticus. In fact, he was the largest human being I had ever seen. He was robed from head to foot in what appeared to be the dress of a desert nomad, and his skin, what was visible through the openings in the bright white cloth that almost completely obscured his face, was a sun-burnished bronze which mirrored the color of the wooden boat he straddled.

"This is Malamek," said Sabatticus as he leapt easily onto the boat. Disappearing into the compartment, he added, "He'll be taking us to our Master."

I was rooted to the landing, staring at the giant. He in turn was staring back at me with an unwavering gaze. I actually sensed nothing which spoke of danger, but the very fact that in one morning I had come across both the smallest person and the largest person I'd ever seen, left me with a sense of general unease I couldn't shake.

"What kind of name is Malamek?" I asked in a rather shaky voice.

"It's Arabic, sir" Sabatticus responded. "He comes from an old and famous family. Have you heard of them?" came the little voice from inside the boat.

I felt as if I'd awoken into a Venice I'd never before encountered, one populated by midgets, giants, and fantastic boats that lay hidden behind some curtain never before parted. I had lived in this city for thirty-five years, many of them spent on the canals and quays while painting and observing everything passing by. I had never seen these two beings nor this boat, which gave me pause.

"Come, sir. The giant can paddle faster than any man alive, but even he won't be above reproach if I don't get you to my Master quickly."

The giant held out his hand to assist my boarding and, when I reached out my hand, he took it gently, his touch as light as a feather. Before I ducked my head and entered the cabin, I glanced back to find the giant wielding a paddle the size of a tree trunk which he was using to propel us along the canal at a speed which almost took my breath away.

Sabatticus sat on a luxuriously padded bench on one side of the cabin with his feet not even reaching the floor of the boat. I took a seat opposite, sinking into a mixture of plush silk pillows and extravagantly padded bench.

The little man just gazed at me with his radiant smile.

"I'm amazed I've never seen you, this boat, or your giant friend in all my years in Venice. I've lived and worked here for over thirty-five years. It's most strange, Sabatticus."

"Our Master doesn't require the use of the gondola much during the day, sir. I'm not surprised you haven't seen it or us before. My Master spends little time out of the palazzo when he's in Venice, preferring to enjoy his home."

"You say when he's in Venice. Does your Master hail from somewhere else?"

"These questions I'm sure my Master will answer for you, sir, but it's not my place to do so."

I looked out the windows of the cabin pondering Sabatticus' enigmatic statement to see we had reached the Grand Canal and were traveling through the masses of floating traffic that plied the waterway during the day.

The canal was clogged with traffic heading in both directions; gondolas laden with construction goods, produce, and anything else the waterlogged city needed. Taxis and private gondolas sped this way and that in a chaotic race up and down along Venice's most famous canal. Amazingly, no one seemed to be startled by or even acknowledge our presence. The giant seemed to have no difficulty navigating us through the mass of humanity clogging the waterway at a speed which continued to astound me.

"Is your Master's palazzo on the Grand Canal?" I asked.

"It is, sir. It's just a short distance away now."

"What did you say the name of it was? I've actually done paintings of a large number of the palazzos along the Grand Canal for my patrons."

"It's Palazzo Vertichelli."

I had never heard of this palazzo. "And he owns it?"

"Yes."

I was surprised by this development, as the Palazzos along the Grand Canal, were, in general, fabulously expensive and most had been in the hands of their owners, an assortment of royalty and wealthy merchants, for generations. The stranger I had met last night had given me absolutely no indication he was of that circle of Venice. In fact, I wouldn't have been a bit surprised if he'd been of the artist class to which I belonged.

While I made a decent enough living and had enough patrons to insure I didn't want for just about anything, I certainly wasn't in the same league as the owners of the palazzos on the Grand Canal, and I didn't know any other artists in Venice who were.

"We've arrived," said Sabatticus, jumping off the bench and climbing out of the compartment.

I looked out the window to see we were approaching a large, bright white, but plainly decorated palazzo that had, until now, escaped my notice. It was three stories high and had one long balcony above the canal on what appeared to be the third level. Above the balcony, almost at the roof line, I observed an ornamentation, something most, if not all, of the palazzos were famous for. Most were either family crests or variations of the same, but this one was different.

I found myself transfixed by it. It was a skull, mouth gaping open in what looked like an unholy scream, and below the skull were two crossed bones. Beneath that was a carved banner inscribed with a string of words I couldn't make out.

The chill that traversed my spine began at the base and ended at my hairline. The symbol evoked a feeling of dread and unease, and I began to seriously wonder if I had been a fool to take this boat ride.

Just before the gondola floated through the two huge open canal doors, I saw a brief movement on the balcony above me and could see a man, both hands resting on the railing, looking down at me. Our eyes met, and the man raised his hand in greeting just as the gondola floated into the darkness under the palazzo.

It was Gaspar.

CHAPTER 12

Somewhere over the Atlantic between Boston and Zurich, May 2010

A lex settled into the leather seat in the first class section of Swiss Air Flight 53 from Boston to Zurich.

He took a sip of his champagne, kicked off his shoes, and ran his hand over the knapsack in the seat next to him. It contained the two books and the charm, still ensconced in its box.

The plane had leveled out at thirty-five thousand feet, the nose pointed north over the Atlantic. Alex had watched the sun race to the horizon and fade away like his old life, one moment here and the next gone.

Now, as the stewards and stewardesses busied themselves with making their passengers comfortable, Alex pondered what he was doing. His hand snaked into the knapsack and retrieved his grandfather's translation.

He'd left Maine early in the morning before dawn and had lunched with Lucas at Abe and Louie's. They had made small talk, all the while Alex feeling like Lucas was studiously avoiding asking Alex about his plans. Alex just as studiously avoided volunteering anything.

After lunch, they had returned to Lucas' office where he'd received the check-book and debit card for what was now his own account, signed a few papers requiring his signature, and he had said goodbye.

A car and driver Lucas had arranged took him to the brownstone where he'd hurriedly packed a bag. After a stop at an ATM, where he'd tried out the debit card and retrieved a wad of twenty dollar bills, he'd been dropped off at the Swiss Air check-in at Logan Airport.

As a Seal, he'd learned all about the intricacy of money laundering and secretive banking. He had, in fact, had occasion to use the services of several banks in Panama for just such purposes. But those had been operational situations. Now he was jetting to a bank, for what, he had no idea. What awaited him he didn't know. All he knew was his grandfather had said the book held all the clues.

He retrieved his grandfather's translation and opened it to where he'd left off...

Palazzo Vertichelli, Venice, 1565

The gondola floated to a stop within a large gallery under the palazzo, next to a landing lit by flaming torches. The giant stepped off the boat and secured the gondola.

Sabatticus then leapt off the boat and bounded up the stairs as I followed. For such a little man, he was quick, and I had to hurry to keep up with him. We went up a flight of stairs until we reached a large wooden door that Sabatticus pushed open. I followed him through the door and found myself in a large courtyard contained within the walls of the palazzo.

I felt as if I'd stepped out of Venice, straight into an emir's palace. The courtyard was full of urns and planters filled with exotic palms and flowers. The floors, which were laid with marble, were covered by dozens of carpets which would have been the envy of a Turkish prince. In the middle of the courtyard, surrounded by all this luxury, was a large pool of crystal clear water flowing like a stream from one end to the other.

I wandered the courtyard in awe, taking in more detail. Besides all of the plants and trees, which gave me the feeling of being in some fantastic botanical garden, as I examined the pool, I noticed beneath the surface brightly colored fish lazily swimming its length.

The walls of the courtyard were plastered in finely muted pastels with beautiful mosaics sporadically spaced along the walls. The mosaics displayed various scenes with knights on foot and on horseback in battle with what appeared to be Moslem soldiers. Every one of the knights was clad in armor over which they wore white cloaks with a large red cross on the chest.

I had never been to the Holy Land, but it was easy to see it held a special place for the owner of this palazzo. I had completely forgotten Sabatticus and turned to find him smiling his smile and watching me intently.

"This has to be without a doubt the most beautiful courtyard in all of Venice."

"It is, sir. The master spends many hours in meditation here. It is in fact, his favorite place in the home."

"Ask him if he'd like to know why that is," said a voice from behind me.

Coming down a wide marble staircase, at the far end of the courtyard, was my new friend whom I now knew as Gaspar. I recognized him immediately, even though, instead of his long coat and somewhat plain appearance the night before, today he was dressed in a long one-piece robe of pure white. Instead of boots, he now wore plain brown sandals.

"It's my favorite spot, which is saying something in this house. Do you like it, Bartholomew?"

I moved toward the stairs to greet him and said "I can fully understand why anyone would want to linger here."

"Perhaps this is where you'll paint for me, my friend. I can think of few places where a painter of your stature would be more at peace."

We met near the bottom of the steps. He grasped my hand, and then hugged me as if we were long lost friends.

Before I could inquire as to what he wanted me to paint, he asked, "Did my favorite tea maker alleviate any discomfort you might have felt after last night's frivolity?"

"He did, indeed. In fact, he should start selling the concoction. He'd be rich almost immediately."

Gaspar laughed, and I was again struck by its depth and richness. It was as if he rarely laughed and, when he did, he savored it like a fine wine, not knowing when it would come his way again.

"I think Sabatticus would find himself with some angry family members on his trail if he ever tried that. Besides, sometimes special and hidden things are best left that way. It's what makes them priceless and keeps them safe.

"Now, how was your ride here? What did you think of the gondola and my boatman? And be careful because Malamek is sensitive about his size, and he's standing right behind you."

I whirled around to indeed find the giant standing silently three steps behind me, holding a silver tray on which he carried two small, fine crystal goblets and a crystal carafe of what appeared to be red wine, although with this man, who knew what it contained?

"It's a beautiful boat, and he's a masterful gondolier. I'm perplexed, though. How is it such a unique gondola and such an unusual boatman are unknown in this city? I know many of the wealthiest people in Venice, and I've spent countless hours on its canals and waterfronts, yet I've never seen nor heard tell of either Malamek or your gondola."

Gaspar, now holding my hand, pulled me along with him toward a small table next to the pool set beneath the fronds of some exotic palm.

The giant silently followed us and, as we sat, he placed the silver tray between us. Then, with amazing grace and delicacy for a man with such enormous hands, he poured two full glasses, one for each of us. After pouring, he moved away, positioning himself a short distance away from us against the wall.

"You have questions about me, which is understandable. Last night I purposely avoided going into too much detail as I wanted to simply get to know you better. Let's say I wanted to take your measure in person. I rarely use the gondola. I have everything I desire in this home and seldom leave it. I have house-maids who go out to the markets and, if I need something I usually have it brought to me whether it's clothes, books, or painters. I have no need for Venice's night life or festivities. I rather like it that virtually no one seems to know that I exist."

In the light of day I noticed that both Gaspar's face and hands carried scars, most of them small, although just above the top of his robe and below his chin I could see the beginnings of what appeared to be a vivid and jagged scar disappearing beneath his robe.

He took one of the glasses and held it up in a toast. I reached out, took the other glass, and with great trepidation, I peered into it to ascertain whether I was once again faced with the evil brew from the night before.

Gaspar chuckled. "I promise you, I won't subject you to my favorite wine again until you're ready. This is some of the finest wine from the countryside outside of Florence. I'm sure you'll love it."

With that he touched his glass to mine and drank. I did the same, reveling in the taste.

"I really am confused, Gaspar, as to why I'm here and why you sought me out. I'm also perplexed having lived in Venice most of my life, I'm ignorant of your family name or this beautiful palazzo."

"Well, my friend, my family name is de Rouse. I was born in France, in the foothills of the Languedoc and grew up in the Holy Land. I've owned this place for some time, but as I said, I don't move in the circles of Venice's high society.

"As to why I've sought you out, I want you to paint for me. You are a painter, no? In fact, I hear tell that currently you're Venice's most popular painter, even though you find it hard to finish your commissions in a timely manner. As a result, you don't have the wealth a painter of your talent should.

"I want you to paint a series of portraits of me. And to ensure you finish them in a timely manner, I propose you move here, into my palazzo, until they're done. Of course, I'll pay your normal fee and in addition, a large bonus upon completion. That's why I've sought you out and why you're here. Now, how about we have a nice lunch of fish, some cheese, bread, and more of this wonderful wine?"

I stared at Gaspar, unsure how to respond to his proposal. I was in the midst of several commissions and, as he'd correctly surmised, I was having trouble finishing them. I had been spending more time at the taverna watching him than painting. More than a few of my current patrons were getting annoyed at the pace of my progress.

Now this enigma of a man was proposing I should drop all my previous commitments to not only paint several portraits of him, but to move out of my home into his palazzo with a Greek midget, a giant Arab, and who knows what else?

Gaspar seemed oblivious to my consternation as he gave instructions to the giant, who glided off silently into the palazzo.

"I know what I propose is somewhat unusual and that it comes as a bit of a shock, but I promise you, beyond it being your most financially rewarding commission to date, you'll find your stay here to be enlightening in many ways."

I hesitated. I still had the nagging feeling Gaspar was hiding something from me.

"I don't see how I could do that, sir. You're correct in your assessment regarding my current commissions. I have, in fact, been lax in my discipline of late. But if I were to abandon my current paintings and take up your offer, I would incur the wrath of a goodly number of the city's elite which would do my reputation irreparable damage. I beg your forgiveness, but I must respectfully decline your generous offer."

Gaspar appeared to disregard my comments as if he hadn't even heard them.

"This old house is a special place, and I'm looking forward to having someone new around to talk with. Not that Sabatticus and Malamek are unwelcome members of the house, but conversationalists, they're not."

I started to voice my objection when the giant came out of an alcove beneath the stairs carrying two enormous trays, one in each hand, laden with plates of food and bottles of wine. He set them on a serving table next to us, and I was instantly overcome by the amazing smells of cooked fish, assorted cheeses, fruits, and exotic spices.

"Not only is he Venice's finest gondolier, he's without a doubt one of her best cooks as well," said Gaspar.

The giant began serving up plates heaped with fish and rice. These were followed by stacks of warm flat breads and an array of cheeses and fruits, some of which I had never seen before.

Gaspar was pouring wine from one of the new bottles into a glass in front of me. "This is a wine I recently acquired from Spain. The Spaniards are amazing wine makers, even though they tend to be a hotheaded sort. Try it, Bartholomew. It compliments the fish perfectly."

And so it went throughout the afternoon as we ate, talked, and drank. I would protest his proposal and beg to be excused from it, and he would ignore my pleadings as if he hadn't even heard them.

Slowly, and not just because of the copious amounts of wine we drank, I began to fall under the spell of this strange man. As the afternoon wore on, I found myself telling him my life story; from my younger days in the countryside outside Florence, to my days of tutelage in the city's hallowed schools of art.

He exhibited an amazing knowledge of the art world, talking at length of the great masters as if he knew them and had met them. When I would question him on this, he would smile and ask me to continue my story.

Finally I told him of how I had come to Venice, lured by the great wealth of the merchant families and their penchant for commissioning painters to paint their portraits.

The sun had passed over the courtyard, and long shadows now fell across the floor. Malamek cleared the remnants of our meal and placed a giant Narguileh between us. After he had lit it, Gaspar took one of the pipes and began to smoke from it, gesturing for me to do the same.

The pleasing tastes of apple wood and spices conspired with the wondrous lunch, and soon had me leaning back into the cushions in a state of extreme relaxation.

"I've admired many of your paintings, Bartholomew," Gaspar said. "I think of all the painters I've seen and met in my days, you're without a doubt one of the most talented. That's in part why I ask for your help. You see not only do I want you to paint my portrait, there's something else I require of you."

Intrigued, I listened as he continued.

"I have a story I wish to tell. I want this story to be chronicled in words and in paintings. What I want is for you to write a book, a book about my life."

"I've never written a book," I responded. "While I can draw and paint, the written word has never been my forte."

"This is not a problem, for what I want you to chronicle is so extraordinary the words will flow from you like the rivers of spring."

"I mean no offense, but what is so extraordinary about your life? Why is it you seem so intent on having me abandon all of my other work to do this task for you?"

He was quiet for some time, and I thought I had offended him, but after a moment of contemplation he looked into my eyes and said, "Because, someone needs to know the truth. Someone needs to know why I am immortal."

CHAPTER 13

Palazzo Vertichelli, Venice, 1565

I stared across the table through the smoke rising from the Narguileh. "Did you say immortal?" I asked, not sure I had heard him right.

Gaspar gave a gentle laugh. "That's what I said. I am three-hundred and nine years old."

I was about to laugh at the absurdity of his statement when I suddenly realized Gaspar was no longer smiling. His eyes, now locked on mine, were so intensely serious, I realized either this man was completely mad or he was in fact telling me the truth.

"How am I to believe such a thing?" I responded.

"I swear to you it's true," he said. "Do you think you know everything there is to know about this world and the worlds beyond this one? What makes you so sure such a thing is not possible; your faith perhaps?"

"My faith? There's nothing in my faith which could ever lead me to believe such a thing."

At this, he chuckled and shook his head sadly. "I was very much like you once, Bartholomew. I had my faith, and it told me what to believe and what not to believe. Now I know differently. Now I've seen the truth of what this world is, what lies beyond, what we are and what we can become. Are you so afraid you'd walk from here never to be given this chance again?"

Confused, I asked, "A chance for what?"

"A chance to see what no mortal has ever seen before and lived to talk about, a chance to see for yourself the real world," Gaspar said quietly.

And then he said something that chilled me to the bone.

"Don't you really want to know the truth about heaven and hell, angels and demons?" he asked.

Did I? Did I really want to know if everything I believed, everything I'd been taught from birth, was perhaps a lie? Or maybe he would confirm what I believed to be true.

I could see him watching, waiting. His inscrutable face betrayed nothing, not a hint of what secrets he harbored or what things he'd seen.

I had to know. I had to know what this compelling and possibly immortal man knew.

Slowly, like a gently forming ripple on the surface of a fathomless pool, a smile formed on his face. "You have to know, don't you? Does it scare you what you might hear? Like what you saw the first time we met; will you believe it?"

"I don't think I'm afraid as much as I wonder if I'll ever be the same. What will I become if I embark on this journey with you?"

He paused for a moment, thinking, then said, "I can't answer that for you. But let me ask you this; are you the same man today as you were yesterday? Have you not become a different man this week than last? Have you become some sort of statue whose very being is carved from stone which, while able to move, always returns to its former shape no matter what forces it encounters?

"Is it not possible with every breath you take you become a different man, as if some unseen artist, wielding chisel and hammer, continues a never-ending sculpting of who and what you are?

"If it's change you fear, perhaps I've chosen the wrong painter."

I pondered his words and thought about the changes which had indeed occurred just in the hours since I had made his acquaintance.

I had left my home and neglected my patrons. I had said not a word to my friends or students, nor told anyone where I had gone. I had allowed myself to be ensconced in a palazzo of incomparable beauty and extravagance with a mysterious stranger who claimed to be immortal, a midget who could read my mind, and a giant who could render himself and the gondola he piloted invisible to all.

No, I wasn't afraid of change, and he was right; I had to know.

I didn't have to say it. He knew. He raised his hand slightly, and the giant appeared from the shadows carrying a bottle that looked disturbingly similar to the infamous bottle from our first meeting. The giant poured a small amount into my glass which still contained some of the wine we'd been sharing.

"I'm going to give you just a touch of my wine," Gaspar said. "It'll be just enough to help loosen the ties which shackle your mind, but not enough to render you incoherent. An amount which will allow the full import of what I'm about to share with you to penetrate the fog of your preconceived notions."

Now I was scared. I didn't fancy a repeat of my last experience with this man's brew.

The giant, who had disappeared with the bottle, now returned with a small, intricately carved vessel, a brazier. It appeared to be made from some kind of stone, and the workmanship was exquisite.

He set it between us, removing the lid. From under his cloak, he produced what looked to be a small piece of incense the length of my ring finger. On closer examination, it was obviously a small piece of bone. He broke the bone in two and, to my wonder, a small flame appeared at the broken ends of both pieces. He placed them both into the brazier and closed the lid, disappearing back into the shadows.

I looked closer at the brazier. It was round in shape, and carved into the surface was an assortment of beings not unlike those I had witnessed in the taverna the night of our first encounter.

Spaced at regular intervals around its circumference were carvings of strange symbols, and in the middle of each symbol was a small hole from which whispering tendrils of white smoke were now rising.

"Come," Gaspar said. "Take a drink of my wine."

I took a tentative taste and, while I could taste the fire of his brew, I experienced none of the pain of my first exposure.

"Now lean forward and breathe in the incense from the brazier."

I leaned forward and took a deep breath. As I did so, Gaspar slowly waved his hand through the smoke, gently pushing it into my face.

The smell of spices, flowers and earth invaded my senses. Almost instantly, a feeling of calm enveloped me. I felt as if the space around me was expanding. It seemed as if I'd been set free from an enclosed and suffocating confinement into a wide open, endless expanse of space.

I leaned back, looking at Gaspar. He was leaning forward into the smoke, eyes closed, slowly and methodically breathing in the incense. His eyes opened as he sat back, his gaze settling on mine. I felt as if he were looking into my mind, probing and exploring every nook and corner, searching for the remnants of something, I knew not what.

Apparently satisfied at what he'd found, he began to speak.

"I always had my beliefs about God. Beliefs imparted to me by my parents, teachers, and my priests. When I became a Templar, those beliefs were expanded, refined, but always they were basically the same. I believed what I was told and what I learned. I studied, questioned, and made up my own mind, or so I thought, about God, the devil, heaven and hell. I felt I understood what awaited me in the life after, and I had no reason to doubt my beliefs. I was perfectly ready to go to my grave believing as I did.

"I was an ignorant fool!

"Tell me, Bartholomew, do you believe in God and the devil? Do you believe in a heaven and a hell?"

"Of course. I was born and raised in the church like you. I've lived my life believing and have tried to live in accordance with those beliefs."

"Good, because trust me when I say this, it all exists. All of it! God, heaven, the devil and hell.

"Angels and demons are as real as you and I, but there's more, so much more. While all of it exists, it's so much different than you can possibly imagine. You must see it to believe it.

"So, let us talk of demons and angels, what I've come to learn. Let me show you what I've seen."

He slowly stood from his seat and came around the table to stand beside me. He grasped my hands, slowly helping me to my feet until I was standing directly in front of him.

Then, in a move I didn't resist, he enveloped me in his arms, pulling me close against him. Leaning down, he placed his forehead on mine, our eyes locked in an unbreakable gaze, then he whispered, "Don't be frightened. Close your eyes."

CHAPTER 14

Palazzo Vertichelli, Venice, 1565

arkness enveloped my mind, darkness of a depth and substance the likes of which I had never experienced before. How could one feel darkness? I don't know, other than I felt it like a weight upon my very soul.

"The darkness will lift in a moment," came Gaspar's voice; a voice which seemed to come from inside my head.

I could see nothing nor could I feel anything other than the weight of the darkness and Gaspar's embrace. I couldn't even speak. No words would come to my mouth, which wouldn't move. I began to struggle against the panic welling up inside me.

"Easy, I'm here," Gaspar whispered. "Soon the darkness will begin to abate, and we'll arrive at our destination. Whatever you do, whatever you see, whatever you think is happening, don't panic. Stay by my side. You'll be safe with me."

And as he said it would, slowly the dark began to lighten until I could make out the shape of Gaspar still embracing me. His features began to come into relief, and I could see he was watching me intently. He released me, and

I found I could move. I took a step back from him, instantly assailed by a wave of dizziness.

"How do you feel?" he asked.

"How should I feel? I feel a little sick actually."

And with that I began retching, and in a moment was gripped by a violent spasm of vomiting I swore might never end.

Just when I thought I might never be able to take another breath, the spasms stopped. I found myself on my knees face-down in sandy soil, staring at Gaspar's sandal clad feet.

"Here, drink this," Gaspar said as he reached under his cloak and retrieved a leather flask. I drank as he held it to my lips, embarrassed by my sickness. I drank the liquid thinking it tasted similar to the tea the midget, Sabatticus, had made for me.

"I had Sabatticus make this tea just for this trip. You needn't be embarrassed by your sickness. This always happens the first time you make this journey."

I rose to my feet, with the help of Gaspar, as the tea's magic surged through me. I gathered myself and began to examine my surroundings.

We were standing atop what appeared to be a small knoll. The light around us was a light not unlike that just before dawn. Not dark, but not fully bright. As my eyes adjusted to the twilight, I began to make out our surroundings. The ground upon which we stood was like a hard packed sand, more pebbly than fine, devoid of vegetation.

"Look to the plain below us," Gaspar said quietly.

I looked out in the direction of his gaze. As far as I could see a smoky haze seemed to envelop the sky. Here and there columns of smoke were rising slowly, twisting upwards, dissipating into the haze.

It was then I caught a faint smell of something rank and foul. It was a smell so sickening, I instantly began to feel the spasms overtake me once more.

"Take another drink from the flask," Gaspar said.

I sipped at the flask, and the spasms were once again, tamped down.

"Is this hell?" I asked.

Gaspar chuckled. "This is hell. Just not the one you imagine. This is something altogether different. Come, I want you to see this," and he slowly began walking down the slope, pulling me gently by the hand.

We made our way down the side of the knoll, the stench of what lay below us growing stronger as we descended. I began to make out shapes and forms lying on the ground. Everywhere I looked, the ground undulated with what I began to suspect were bodies.

But whose bodies?

As my eyes adjusted to the light, we neared the bottom of the slope, and the scene before me was laid out in all its hellish glory. For what I was seeing was almost beyond comprehension. I had stopped where I was, forcing Gaspar to come up short as I still grasped his hand.

Before me, corpses were scattered and piled everywhere I looked. It seemed barely a space existed, not a clear piece of ground which wasn't covered by bodies.

"What is this place? What happened here?" I asked, barely able to speak.

Gaspar was silent for a moment before he spoke. "This is a battlefield. The aftermath of one of the many, sometimes, it seems, constant, battles between what you call angels and demons. This is what it looks like when these beings come together on the fields of death."

Gently, he pulled me forward as we entered the killing ground. Picking and choosing our way carefully, he led me through the maze of bodies which I could now examine clearly.

I saw the most bizarre forms among the bodies. Over there was an almost skeletal form with bat-like wings, but with a not quite human skull. Next to that was a wolf-like creature the size of a small horse with fangs as long as my hand.

Farther along, a tiny form the size of a small child lay atop a pile of bodies, clutching a sword longer than his body. I stopped to examine the child and dropped Gaspar's hand. The body, while small, was heavily muscled, with hair that would have flowed almost to the ground.

"A cherub," Gaspar said. "This is a particularly nasty variety, not at all like those fanciful babies you paint. No, these are warriors of the first rank. I've seen them take on a hundred of the fallen and come away unscathed. See the beings under it?"

I looked closer, seeing at least a dozen creatures that looked like giant snakes, dead and mangled beneath the cherub. They had dozens of arms down the sides of their bodies, each hand clutching an evil-looking blade.

"Those lovely beasts, while not quite as deadly as hell hounds, are one of hell's more vile creations. If you let one get close enough, you'll have quite the time fending off those blades."

"Hell hounds?" I asked. "They actually exist?"

Gaspar laughed a mirthless laugh. "Unfortunately, yes. Come over this way. There are a few of the wretched things that met their end here."

I followed him a short distance to a pile of corpses larger than most of the others. Here were scores of the beasts I had noticed earlier; huge wolfish creatures which should only exist in a nightmare.

"What could have killed all these beasts?" I asked.

"Look there, under those dead hounds," Gaspar said, pointing a short distance away from us.

I walked over to where he pointed and saw a creature with the head of a lion atop the body of a woman. I remembered I had seen two of these beings in the bar the first night I had met Gaspar.

"I saw beings like this the night we met," I said.

"Yes. That's an angel, or at least the closest thing you'll find to what you imagine them to look like. They even have wings, although this one's were lost in the battle."

I could see Gaspar was right, for on the angel's back, where I would imagine wings would be, were two jagged, bloody stumps.

"I'm actually a bit surprised to find an angel here, apparently taken down by hell hounds," Gaspar mused. "Something else must have been here as well."

Gaspar headed off, intensely examining the various corpses as if he was looking for something in particular. I wandered after him in silence, contemplating what I was seeing.

With almost every step, I was faced with new, bizarre creatures all arrayed in the pose of violent death. My mind was reeling from the spectacle when I realized I'd wandered away from Gaspar. I turned frantically this way and that, searching for him as panic rose within me.

Suddenly a call of "This way, brother" reached my ears from my right. I hurried in the direction of the voice to find Gaspar kneeling over something on the ground.

"Stay close to me. It's not guaranteed that everything on this field no longer lives," Gaspar scolded.

Suitably chastised, I knelt next to him to see what he was examining.

What I saw was a creature of such absolute beauty that I stared open-mouthed and speechless. It looked like a bird the size of a large man. The body was covered with scales of the most brilliant iridescent colors. Even in death, they gleamed like dozens of rainbows. The face was that of a hawk, but the eyes, staring open and lifeless, looked as human as mine.

"This is no human," Gaspar whispered.

"What is it? It's beautiful."

"That's a demon. A fallen angel. He's an important one as well. His name is Andras. I would imagine he was the one who killed the angel we found, but not before taking a mortal blow." Gaspar pointed to an ugly wound in the demon's side.

"That's a demon? How do you know his name?"

"Look, around his neck. The charm carries his name and quite a bit more."

He reached down and jerked the charm, which was suspended from a heavy gold chain from the demon's neck. He slid the necklace under his cloak while I watched, transfixed.

"He was the master of thirty legions, most of whom I would guess are scattered across this plain. We never crossed paths, but I've heard tell of him. A fearsome warrior and one I'm glad I never came across."

Gaspar must have felt my eyes upon him as he turned, our eyes locking.

"This is insane. I'm sitting in a field covered with the most amazing, grotesque beasts and beings, some of whom you claim are angels and demons. I'm seeing death and mayhem on a scale I could never imagine. And here I sit as you rob a demon corpse of its jewelry."

Gaspar laughed. "What? Do you not approve? Look here at the demon's talons."

He reached down, grasping one of the demon's feet. A small blade suddenly appeared in his other hand, and in a deft motion he severed the dead being's talon from the foot.

"This little piece of our dead friend Andras," He held it up for me to see, "Mixed with the proper ingredients contains more power than you can imagine. Things like this and the amulet on his neck could very well save my life someday."

He stood and began to walk away. I knelt, still transfixed by the thing at my feet, the weight of what I was seeing almost suffocating.

"Let's sit here awhile," came Gaspar's voice.

I rose and walked over to where he was seated on a large, flat rock a little distance from the carnage. I sat next to him, and he passed me the flask.

"Drink a little more tea," Gaspar said.

I took a drink and handed it back to him. He drank from it as well and gazed over the ravaged landscape.

"I'm more than perplexed, Gaspar," I said. "This place is not hell, but you said it was a type of hell. Why did you bring me here?"

"I can sense a seed of disbelief still residing within you. Perhaps you think I've drugged you or maybe this drink clouds your mind. I'm real, Bartholomew. And so is all this.

"This place, to the beings which lie here now, is hell. They'll never leave here because their souls, those which had them, have died here. Angel and demon alike lie here for eternity. There is no afterlife for these creatures. They gathered on this field, died, and it's here they'll stay. This realm, the way you see it now, will be only a field of death and nothing else forever. There are many, many others like it. So many, a being such as I would never be able to see them all. This is a hell, and it's one of many."

"What were they fighting over?" I asked.

Gaspar gave a derisive snort. "Who knows? It takes little to draw these foes into battle. It's in a constant state of war these two adversaries dwell.

"Perhaps it was simply a soul that drew them here. A soul one side coveted and the other didn't wish to part with. Perhaps it was an ancient quarrel between former brothers."

"Former brothers?" I queried.

"Of course. Don't forget many of these beings, at one time or another, lived together in the place you call heaven. Some left in the first revolt. Others in later ones."

"Later ones?" I interrupted. "I know the story of the original revolt of angels against God and their casting out from heaven. There were more?"

Gaspar shook his head. "Do you believe heaven exists in some sort of perpetual state of peace? Do you believe revolution can only happen once or that there has only ever been one like Lucifer?

"There are as many warriors in heaven as poets and minstrels. There are as many capable of unbelievable destruction as there are those who know only angelic peace. It's an ongoing war; one that seems at times to rage continually.

"And it's not just heaven where revolution takes place," Gaspar continued. "Demons, those who reside in the realms of the fallen, sometimes rebel and foment revolution against their masters. Do you think that demons, once fallen, never mourn their choice or wish to return from whence they came? Demons are aware of their better side and are capable of deeds of honor. I've experienced that unexpected occurrence and, in fact, was saved once, early in this life, by a reluctant and remorseful demon. But that's a tale for another time."

I thought of what Gaspar had said and pondered the depth of the infinite universe that he described. It was so fantastic and bizarre I could barely summon any sort of rational thought.

We sat there for a while sharing the flask, both of us apparently lost in our thoughts.

I looked at this amazing man beside me and wondered at all he'd seen and done. Sitting here with him, I realized I knew nothing of his true soul or what he truly was. I was lost in the desire to know more and like the wretched souls in the hashish dens of Venice, trapped in a web of desire, unable to escape, I felt a craving.

Gaspar turned to me, and with a sadness which seemed to age him before my eyes, whispered, "There's such a thing, dear Bartholomew, as too much knowledge. A mortal man can see too much and feel things he has no way of comprehending. Trust me when I say this, I'll only show you so much. I don't wish to see my friend reduced to the depths of madness I've touched."

He stood and reached down to help me up.

"Let's leave this place. You've seen more than enough for this day."

We stood, and as he turned reaching for me, as he had in the moments before we'd traveled here, I saw him tense. In a whirlwind of speed and violent motion, he wrenched me into the air, propelling me behind him onto the rocky soil.

After rolling and tumbling to a stop a few feet behind him, I looked up to find him with a broad sword in one hand and the short-bladed knife in the other. He stood, facing away from me, as if ready to charge. When I saw what loomed before him I shrank into the ground in abject terror.

Standing before him, just feet away, was a being much like the dead demon, which Gaspar had been pillaging sometime before. The multi-colored scales of this very much alive demon gave off brilliantly cascading waves of light in an aura around it.

While beautiful and awesome in its appearance, it gave off a palpable evil which seemed to permeate my soul.

As I watched, the being began to shimmer and oscillate as if fading in and out of substance. In utter amazement, I watched as the bird-like demon morphed into the unmistakable figure of a human.

It turned his eyes from Gaspar, stared straight at me, and began to laugh.

"Well, well. What have we here, Gaspar, a mortal traversing this hallowed ground? Surely you know the danger you place this wretch in. He might happen across something here that would find his flesh a perfect prelude to a delectable soul-devouring mid-day snack, something like me perhaps."

The demon turned his attention back to Gaspar, whom I saw hadn't altered his state of readiness one bit.

"Easy, Gaspar," the demon whispered in a quiet but menacing voice, "I've already fed today, and my hunger is sated. No need for us to dance today."

I stared at the demon, now in human form, and marveled at his appearance. If I had been attending a ball at the Doge's palace, this thing would have never earned a second glance. He was dressed as if he was a Venetian noble in the finest clothes, wearing a hat with a large ostrich feather perched in the peak, something all the rage these days. He was handsome, but not stunningly so, his skin the color of alabaster. His voice was smooth and soothing, but with a hint of underlying malice.

He turned his gaze back to me and spoke, "I do so love Venice, and the fashions of the day are quite stunning. It's a place I love to visit. I've spent many a night strolling the quiet streets, mingling in the palaces of some of the more prominent inhabitants. I also adore your paintings. They're so life-like and--"

At that Gaspar interrupted "Silence, fallen one. This mortal is off limits to you, and I won't suffer your tired games. We're leaving this place now. Don't get in our way."

The demon hadn't taken his eyes off mine, and I couldn't tear them from his gaze. I was scared to the depths of my soul, and the now smiling fallen angel apparently knew it.

"Don't be scared, Bartholomew," he said. "Even though you're fair game, here in this realm, you're in the hands of one of the greatest warriors in the history of mankind. Gaspar is more than capable of protecting you from me. Although, we each have our weaknesses and we always have our better somewhere out there waiting and watching for that perfect moment. Isn't that right, Gaspar?"

The demon had shifted his gaze back to Gaspar, whom I saw had eased back toward me a few feet.

"You're right, Caym," Gaspar said. "Frankly, I'd love to pursue that question, but today is not the day for us to decide if you or I are the better."

"No, I suppose not, although I wonder what is in this mortal that has piqued your interest. Why are you so taken with him you would breach all manner of rules to bring him here? Are you so lonely in your current state you need the friendship of mortals to assuage you? If so, perhaps you're weaker than I thought."

Caym had moved forward toward Gaspar, and I suddenly realized the danger we were in. This demon, who it seemed had done battle with Gaspar before, sensed I was an impediment to Gaspar and apparently was trying to decide whether to take advantage.

Gaspar was now within a foot of where I lay on the ground. I lifted myself slightly, preparing for what I did not know.

"Don't move, Bartholomew," Gaspar said. "We're leaving this place now. Perhaps on another day, Caym, you can try your luck with me, but today you'll stand down and give us leave."

I wondered what restrained the demon. His form began to shimmer and undulate as if he would revert back to his true form. After some moments he relaxed and stepped back a bit from Gaspar.

"Leave this place, Templar, and take your pitiful painter with you. But be warned. Next time I find you in this realm, we'll dance our dance of death. If you're so foolish as to be accompanied by this mortal, I'll enjoy his flesh almost as much as yours."

At those words, the demon turned his gaze to mine and smiled a smile of such abject evil I thought my heart would exit my mouth.

And then he was gone.

I watched as Gaspar visibly relaxed, sheathing his sword. He slipped the dagger back under his shirt and turned to me.

"Well, that was fun. Now what do you say we get home and drink a bit too much wine?"

He helped me to my feet and, embracing me as he had before, we fell into the darkness which now seemed to promise safety and relief.

Moments later, we were standing in the courtyard of Gaspar's palazzo where I proceeded to faint dead away.

CHAPTER 15

Somewhere over the Atlantic between Boston and Zurich, May 2010

Alex awoke with a start. The book lay open on his lap clutched in his hands. The soft drone of the jet's engines reminded him in an instant where he was. He'd fallen asleep, but something had awoken him from a deep sleep.

He sensed a presence to his left and, turning, found someone seated next to him. He was surprised as the seats beside him had been empty when they had taken off from Boston and had remained empty until he'd dozed off. But what was most disturbing was the person, a man, was staring laser-like right into his eyes. A thin smile creased the man's face.

"Where are you going?" the man asked.

The question, while straight-forward, confused Alex for a moment before he responded, "To Zurich."

"That's not what I asked. Where are you going?" the man asked again.

By now Alex had regained his composure and, no longer groggy from his sleep, he replied, "Who are you and what are you doing in this seat?"

The man gave a derisive laugh before responding, "It's always the same, names, names, and more names; as if that somehow makes it easier."

Alex took a closer look at the man who was dressed in an expensive looking suit which spoke of custom tailoring and no expenses spared. The French cuffs of his shirt were studded with cuff links which looked as if they were hewn from single diamonds, and his tie, a shimmering almost iridescent blue, was knotted so perfectly, images of razor blades flashed through Alex's mind.

The man's skin was the color of the mahogany on his grandfather's boat. His hair was jet black, falling well past his immaculate collar.

"You have no idea, do you?" the man whispered.

"Listen to me. I don't know who you are or why you've snuck up here to sit next to me, but I think perhaps for the good of both of us, you might want to go back to your seat," Alex replied.

The man laughed, a deep resonating, sneering laugh which made Alex shift his weight away from the stranger. He finally turned his gaze from Alex and summoned a steward.

"I'll take a glass of champagne, please, and one for my good friend, Alex," he said.

"How do you know my name?" Alex asked.

The man didn't respond to Alex's question and seemed to forget Alex was beside him for a moment until the steward returned with two glasses of champagne.

Only then did the stranger turn back to Alex and, passing him a glass, raised it in a toast and said, "You may call me Mr. Arusmus if you like. I not only know your name, I know everything about you. Even things you yourself don't know. Would it shock you if I said I even know when you will die?"

Alex started to rise to get away from this deranged individual. But when he was halfway out of his seat, the man laid his hand gently on Alex's and suddenly he couldn't move. He felt a slow, slithering, cold sensation, starting at his feet, working up his body, into his chest, forcing him back into his seat. The champagne glass in his hand fell to the floor silently.

"Relax, Alex. I only want to see you and get a sense of who you are. I mean you no harm, at least not now. A shame you wasted the champagne. It's quite good. So, back to my original question; where are you going? Wait, don't answer that. Let me tell you where you're going. In fact, let me show you," said the stranger, who was now leaning across the seat and had relocked his eyes on Alex's.

Alex couldn't look away, even though something told him he had to. An overwhelming sense of fear and the need for flight, mixed with white hot anger to fight this man, coursed through his veins, but he couldn't move. He was paralyzed.

The stranger's ever-present half smile grew larger, the first flash of brilliant white teeth showing through the full deep red of his lips. The smile continued to grow, the man's mouth gaping open, slowly transforming and distending wider and wider. Alex found himself looking into a dark cavern without a bottom, only the man's eyes giving off a hint of light.

A feeling of entrapment began to grip him and, as if being drawn into the man's gaping maw, Alex felt himself being pulled from his seat toward the depths which seemed to lurk beyond those now bloody lips.

Alex resisted. He dug his fingernails into the seat in an attempt to counteract the magnetic pull. Every muscle and tendon in his body seemed to be separating from the bone. Just when he thought he'd be torn from his seat and swallowed whole, he felt a hand gently touch his from his right side.

In an instant, the man on his left returned to normal, the gaping mouth disappearing back into the sneering smile which now seemed to be tinged with just a bit of anger.

Alex found he could move and, turning to his right, he found an elderly man clad in a simple cardigan sweater, corduroy pants, and brown loafers smiling gently at him. His smile was as full of safety and friendship as the one on his left was devoid of it. He looked like an Ivy League professor with the air of great knowledge and understanding. Unlike the man on his left, Alex knew instantly this man was his friend.

The man said nothing for a moment, his hand still gently resting on Alex's, then spoke quietly, "Hello, Alex. I've waited a long time for this moment. I thought now was as good a time as any to say hello. My name is Boniface."

The old man smiled an even wider smile and, leaning forward, whispered in his ear, "'Til we meet again."

Then, raising his hand, he gently ran his fingertips over Alex's eyes closing them.

Alex awoke with a start, feverishly hot and sweating, his hands cramping and stiff. He looked around the cabin of the jet. Everything was quiet, and the few other passengers slept or quietly read. No one sat beside him on either side. He flexed his fingers and hands and looked at the arm rests where he could see the clear indentations of his fingers in the leather.

A faint odor of expensive cologne mixed with a musty time-worn scent of something pleasing, permeated the space around him.

The book lay closed on the seat to his right.

The nightmare, for surely that's what it was, was as vivid in his mind as if it had actually happened. He took a deep breath and tried to clear his mind. Stretching his legs, his foot kicked something on the floor. He reached down and retrieved an empty champagne glass.

What the hell was happening to him?

Trying to calm his nerves, he reached for the book and opening it lost himself in the story once more.

CHAPTER 16

Palazzo Vertichelli, Venice, 1565

I awoke the next morning upon a luxurious bed, covered by soft blankets. I was in a beautiful chamber, the walls of which were decorated with plaster reliefs of stunning detail and paintings, many of which I recognized as works painted by some of history's greatest painters.

I slipped from the bed, dazzled by the room, slowly turning in circles contemplating the brilliance that surrounded me.

"This is one of my favorite rooms in the whole palazzo," came a voice from behind me.

I turned to find Gaspar leaning against a balustrade on a balcony outside a set of huge double doors.

I walked through the doors to find myself overlooking the Grand Canal, the sun not quite in the middle of the sky.

"How was your rest?" he asked.

"Actually, I don't remember a thing after we returned from that infernal place. I remember coming back to your courtyard, then everything went blank," I said.

"That happens on occasion. Even to me it still happens. Do you remember what you saw last night?"

"How could I forget? I've never seen such things. And that demon, what did you call him?"

"Caym."

"Yes, Caym. I've never felt such evil in all my life."

Both of us were silent for awhile before I spoke again.

"You're telling me the truth, aren't you? That was no trick played on a weak mind under the influence of some strange narcotic. You really are what you say you are. And what is that actually?"

"It's all true, Bartholomew," Gaspar said. "And there's much more. As to what I am, that will be revealed to you in due course. Can I assume you'll be staying here with me and you'll take up the task I asked of you?"

"How could I not?" I said.

"Exactly. Then let us partake of Malamek's breakfast and we can discuss how best to begin our adventure."

We ate our breakfast among the palms and solitude of the courtyard in almost total silence. The only sound was the whispering shuffle of the giant as he served us and the gentle sounds of the slowly moving stream.

I was lost in the memories of our trip to the angelic battlefield and all I had seen there. Gaspar seemed content to allow me this time of reflective silence as he ate, but said nothing.

Finally, I put down my fork and set aside my tea. Looking at Gaspar, I said, "People will think I've lost my mind for taking up your offer. Can you imagine the reactions of my priest to your story?"

Gaspar smiled. "I never said I'd ask you to publicly disclose my true nature or to make my story public. I only said I wanted someone to know the truth. For now, that someone is you. Perhaps in some other time, when the world is a different place than it is now, my story can be told, perhaps when I'm gone. For now, it's enough to share it with you and know there will be a mortal record of my time here."

"Caym was right, wasn't he," I asked. "You're a lonely man."

"You have no idea the depths of the pain which comes from living this long," Gaspar said. "The weight of watching those around you, many whom you come to love and cherish, succumb to nature's normal course, is one that at times I can hardly bear. Caym was right about my loneliness. Demons like him feed on that loneliness and rejoice when they see mortals wallowing in it. I suppose it makes them feel a little better that other beings are tormented by it just as they are."

A thought entered my mind and, before I could stop myself, it exited my mouth, "Have you ever had a wife, Gaspar?"

I instantly regretted asking the question, for the look on his face nearly brought me to tears. After a moment, a stray tear did in fact fall from the corner of one of his eyes.

"That's something I'll never have. I once loved a woman, but this life I lead, a life I chose, leaves little room for such things. Now I make sure to avoid that particular pain," he said.

"You said you chose this life. What did you mean by that?" I asked, changing the subject.

"Are you so eager to start? Well then, follow me, and perhaps we'll begin the task before us," he said.

He led me to the far end of the courtyard where two massive wooden doors were set into the palazzo walls. Malamek stood to one side and, at a gesture from Gaspar's hand, the giant, with a gargantuan effort, pulled open the doors. I followed Gaspar into what appeared to be a small chapel, dark save for the light from several lanterns hanging from the walls and a few candles on a small, but intricately carved wooden altar at the far end.

The space was cool, quiet, and full of a reverence which enveloped me in a comforting embrace. The walls were covered with a myriad of icons, many of such stunning beauty that, as an artist, I felt I had entered a dream world. On the two side walls, barely a space existed which wasn't covered with the amazing paintings. Some seemed familiar in style, while others were like nothing I'd ever seen. I recognized the Byzantine style of Constantinople and the refined brilliance of some of Europe's greatest artists. Others looked as if they came from the far reaches of the north. Many were obviously ancient; the oldest appeared Jewish in style.

I moved slowly along the walls, immersed in the tiny paintings, some smaller than my hand. I turned to find Gaspar standing just inside the doors which the giant had silently closed behind us.

"My God, Gaspar, there must be hundreds of these paintings," I whispered.

Gaspar moved along the walls, his fingers gently running along the frames, barely touching them, but seeming to search out particular ones as if rediscovering them anew.

He made his way to the altar, turning to face me. There was a quiet, a peacefulness emanating from him I hadn't sensed before and, when he spoke, it was in a low, mesmerizing voice, almost hypnotic in its pace.

"This is my sanctuary. No mortal in all the years of my life has ever seen this room before you. This is where I come to cleanse my soul and restore my sanity. I can stay here for days sometimes, fasting, praying; trying to make sense of all I've seen and done. It's the only place where I ever feel truly alone, free from the prying eyes of the mundane and the divine.

"These paintings you see are my most prized possessions. In fact, possessions is probably the wrong word for them; I'm their caretaker, their protector. I've gathered them from the farthest reaches of the earth, some I rescued from certain destruction. There are over one thousand of them, each unique in its own way.

"Some were painted by great masters, some of whom you can identify. Others were painted by the hands of the untrained and unskilled. Even those possess a certain beauty and soul, invested with the spirit of the painters, if not artistic skill. Some of those simple, rudimentary ones are my favorites because they were painted not for money or fame, but from some inner joy and need for expression."

I continued to watch him as he spoke, struck by the contrast between the man before me now and the warrior who had been prepared to go to battle with a demon such a short time ago.

"I'm the same man, Bartholomew, warrior and priest. The day I became a Templar, so many years ago, I became that dual man. It's the same today, though my foe has changed. Come over here beside me. I want to show you the mirror of this room."

Gaspar gestured for me to stand beside him and, looking down, I found we were standing on a large red cross carved into a block of pure white marble set into the floor. The cross looked to be made from some sort of translucent material which seemed to collect the candlelight around us. I watched as Gaspar knelt on one knee and placed his right hand directly in the center of the cross. He held it there for a moment before standing again and, turning to me, said, "Here we go."

Almost before I realized it, we were slowly sinking into the floor of the chapel, the marble stone with the luminescent cross sliding downward into the dark.

The movement was soundless and smooth, and I looked across to Gaspar as the chapel faded away above us to find a mischievous grin on his face.

"I love this little trick, don't you?" he said.

"How does this work?" I asked.

"Complicated, to say the least, but trust me when I say it took a long time to perfect," he replied.

As we were gently lowered into the stone-walled shaft, the light above us gave way to almost total darkness, but only briefly, as we began to enter a space below which was filled with light. Slowly, the room came into view until we came to a stop, the marble platform now recessed into the floor of this lower level of the palazzo.

This room was indeed the opposite of the one above us. Where that room had been dimly lit, full of peace and tranquility, this room was filled with bright light. But it was what was arranged along the walls and on long tables running down the center of the room that set this room apart, and there was nothing peaceful about this place.

Gaspar had stepped off the cross and was moving down one side of a long table in the center of the room. As I watched, he repeated his movements from the room above, gently running his fingers over the objects arranged precisely down the length of the table.

What he ran his fingers over was a mass of weapons, the scope and breadth of which left me breathless. Every kind of sword, knife, club, or spear was displayed on the walls and on the table. I couldn't fathom how some of the weapons were used, they were so fantastic. While I didn't know how they were used, that they were designed to kill was in no doubt.

This was in fact an armory, a warehouse of killing tools which could have outfitted a small army. Some of the weapons were clearly foreign in provenance while others were more identifiable. Others still were so bizarre that I had little doubt they were not of this world.

"You're perceptive," Gaspar said, as he hefted a small stone jar which fit neatly into the palm of his hand. "Many of these weapons came from realms beyond ours, like the killing field we visited last night. I learned a long time ago scavenging those fields after the battles are over can yield weapons of immense power. Like this little trinket. It's full of a substance which, when you throw it and it hits the target or the ground, it explodes with a force which could kill ten men, or ten demons.

"Or this one here," he said, reaching up and pulling down a wicked looking weapon from the wall. It looked like a scythe, but this one had at least ten long blades arranged down the shaft to just above a leather-clad grip. "This was something I found many years ago in the hands of a dead angel. He had over fifty demons and hellhounds piled around him he'd shredded to pieces with this weapon. To this day I've yet to master it. Almost took off my head the first time I tried it."

I followed Gaspar as he walked along the walls and the table, listening as he described the various weapons. Not being a warrior; in fact, I had never owned a sword or knife in my life, I was mesmerized and slightly terrified at the arsenal confronting me. While terrifying, there was something beautiful and alluring about these instruments of death, and I found myself hefting a particularly beautiful curved sword. The weight seemed perfectly balanced in my hand and natural to hold.

"For not being a warrior, you have a keen eye for weapons, Bartholomew," Gaspar said. "That's a sword made of Damascus steel which came into my possession early in this life. It in fact almost took my life. It gave me this." Gaspar pulled his cloak open to reveal the jagged scar which barely showed itself beneath his chin. The scar, a vivid purple welt, ran down his chest, disappearing below his stomach. I couldn't understand how someone could have survived such a blow.

"Again, another story for another day. Suffice it to say the demon who wielded that sword met his end at my hand and that sword has served me well on more than one occasion since."

We continued walking along the table until we had reached the far end of the room and, like the space above us, this room had a small altar against the wall. The altar was made of some sort of silver metal embossed with all kinds of fantastic figures and faces. The craftsmanship was of a style and type I could not place, and I was at a loss to determine how it had been made. On the top of the altar lay a single sword, a long and heavy broadsword whose edges were scarred and chipped, obviously from years of battle. The blade ended above a plain but heavy haft with a leather-wrapped handle, and engraved into the blade just above the handle was a single rose.

"This was my father's sword. He died when I was a fairly young man fighting Saracens in the Holy Land. It was brought back from the battle by survivors who gave it to me. It was lost to me at the beginning of my current life, but I found it, with the help of an angelic friend. It's all I have left of him," Gaspar whispered.

He lifted the sword from the table, holding it in his hands for a moment before moving to a small stool against the wall where he sat. He gestured for me to sit before him on a thick Persian rug and, with the sword laid across his lap, he looked me in the eye and said, "I'll tell you the story of how I came to be. You'll retell this story as if seen through my eyes. My story begins in Acre in the year of our lord 1291."

CHAPTER 17

Acre, the Holy Land, 1291

Gaspar had worked his way through Acre's smoke-filled alleys for six solid hours, a trek which, in better times would have taken thirty minutes, at times knee-deep in the blood and gore of Saracen and Christian alike.

He had, for the most part, avoided the major battles, occasionally encountering smaller skirmishes and knots of fighting and dying men, women, and children. When he'd found himself in the middle of these frenzied orgies of humans tearing each other to pieces, he had claimed his share of souls in self-defense. At least twenty Saracens and a group of twelve Genovese deserters, trying to take advantage of the chaos of the moment, had felt the taste of his blade as he made his way back to the fortress.

His heart ached at the sight of his beloved Acre in the throes of death. The city was falling, and its fall was accelerating with every passing minute as more and more of Kahlil's troops swarmed the walls, overwhelming the few remaining defenders who still possessed the will to fight.

He'd been sent to assess the situation on the front lines. What he'd seen left him with a feeling of anguished dread and barely suppressed rage.

He'd witnessed much in his thirty-five years, but what was occurring now in the streets and alleys of the burning city was like nothing he'd seen before. It was as if the Saracens, knowing the last stronghold of the Christian kingdom in the Holy Land was falling, were going insane with a bloodlust which seemed unquenchable. The soon to be victorious Saracens were sparing no one, even slaughtering many of the women and children whom they normally would capture to be sold as slaves.

He'd passed by, avoiding many a scene of brutality which, in not so desperate times, he would have charged into, creating a whirlwind of death and destruction only a battle-hardened warrior such as himself could impart.

In the end, all of it had been unnecessary. In the run up to this day, they had been presented with many opportunities to avoid this end. It had been the hubris, greed, and stupidity of Venetians, Genovese, Franks, Popes and yes, even Templars, which had led them to this.

Today, he'd only killed when his way was blocked, and he had done so with speed and, when possible, stealth, in his attempt to regain the fortress. He would have preferred to have stood on the walls above the Gate of St. Anthony and died with scores of his enemies around him, but he'd been given a reconnaissance mission for the Order, and he wouldn't fail in its completion.

On the ground level of the fortress, he'd waded through the mass of commoners, men, women, and children who had managed to make their way to the sea wall, taking refuge within the Templar walls as they fled the oncoming Saracen tide. Many had tried to stop him, grabbing his tunic, women thrusting wailing babies or small children into his arms in the hope somehow he could save them. He'd brushed them aside in frustration at his own impotence and in the tormented knowledge of what awaited them outside the walls.

The Grand Master William of Beaujeu had taken as many as he could into what the knight now knew was only the temporary safety of the fortress.

He'd ordered the gates closed and barricaded when they could no longer fit anymore within the walls. William himself had died on the walls several days ago. Gaspar, who had been fighting nearby, had helped carry the Grand Master's body back to the fortress.

He had gained the secret entrance to the sewers hidden within a grotto beneath the seaward wall of the fortress and was now striding up the steps of the eastern tower to the battlements where the remnants of the Templar leadership awaited his report.

As he made his way up the stairs, he passed many of his brothers in arms whose faces begged questions, but he stopped for no one, and no one dared stop him until he stepped onto the battlements. He approached the small group of knights peering out over the city in the direction of the approaching wave of death.

Sensing his approach, they turned toward him and, to a man, though he knew they were besieged with questions, said not a word. He could see as he approached the new Master of the Temple, Theobald Gaudin, and Peter de Severy the commander of the Templars, weren't among them. Before he could ask their whereabouts, one of the brothers pointed to the seaward side of the tower. There he could see both men staring out over the harbor into the horizon.

He left his questioning brothers and made his way around the battlements until he was standing next to the men. Neither man said anything for some time, and Gaspar looked out over the walls to the ocean below. What he saw there filled him with a rage he couldn't contain, and in a momentary lapse of his legendary stoic demeanor, he let fly a stream of curses which would have normally drawn a sharp rebuke from the men standing beside him.

Below him and stretching far out to sea, into the setting sun, was a tableau of cowardice and shame. Boat after boat was streaming from the quay out to sea, away from the soon to be conquered city. What infuriated him was the boats weren't full of escaping citizens of the city, the defenseless women and children, the old and infirm; no, they were standing twenty and thirty deep along the shoreline, many wading into the waves trying to climb aboard the departing vessels.

The ships were filled to the brim with men at arms, the cream of the city's aristocracy and the more prosperous merchants, escaping the burning shores with pendants and flags flying high in haughty disdain for those left to die. To a man, he cursed them with every epithet he could muster until, verbally spent, he simply stared at the spectacle of cowardly retreat and swore to remember every banner sailing into the west.

A few moments later, he felt a hand resting on his shoulder and, remembering he was standing next to the two leaders of the order, he turned to face them finding Peter de Severy wearing a bemused, but sad smile.

"I'd wager that was the most impressive and creative bout of swearing which has ever fallen upon these ears, brother, which is saying something for a man of my years," said de Severy in a quiet voice.

"Look at them," Gaspar responded. "They flee like common cowards, not nobles and warriors. With those men we could forestall the Saracens and at least try to dictate some sort of terms which would save some of the people within these walls."

"Well, that may be," replied the older knight, "assuming the Saracen has a shred of willingness to spare any of us. At this point, I highly doubt that's the case. Forget all that for the moment. Tell us what you saw on your foray to the outer walls. Leave nothing out and give us your sincere assessment of how much time we have before we're besieged here in our own fortress."

And so Gaspar related what he'd seen during his mission into the city and out to the front lines of what was left of the battle. When he was done, the Grand Master said, "I would think we have a day, perhaps a day and a half, before Kahlil launches an all-out assault on our garrison which means we have much work to do."

"Yes," said de Severy, "time is short. Come, brother, let's gather the commanders and set about planning our defense. We have much work to do. If Kahlil will still listen to our entreaties of truce, we'll attempt to save as many of these lambs as we can."

They had gathered in a room which had windows and a small balcony looking to the east toward the approach of Khalil's hordes. Gaspar hadn't seen his fellow warriors, almost all of them veterans of years of vicious battles with the Saracens, so despondent.

He understood their pain, for while he hadn't been born in the Holy Land like many of these men, he'd been born in the foothills of the Pyrenees in the Languedoc region of France, he had in fact spent much of his childhood, from the age of ten, growing up in this very city. The fact they, the current defenders of Christendom's last major outpost in the Holy Land, would actually fail in their duty weighed heavily on all their hearts. To a man, they felt they had failed and now wanted nothing more than to die, taking as many of the enemy with them as possible.

De Severy stood in the center of the room, hands tightly clasped behind his back, the commanders arranged around him. He cleared his throat and began to speak. "As some of you know, last night I sent brother Gaspar on a mission to ascertain the situation along the outer walls and within the city proper. I did so because most of our normal lines of communication have broken down. We're unable to tell from one moment to the next the state of the battle. Gaspar has returned with news of a dire nature.

"I won't attempt to put a good face on this situation. We are without doubt facing the loss of Acre. We have three choices. One, we can fight to the death, and death it will be, for we won't be able to stop the Saracens in the end. Two, we can attempt to sue for some sort of peace with terms which would allow us to save as many of the people we've sheltered within these walls as possible. The third option is for us to make our way to our fleet of ships which, as you know, lies anchored in the port, and flee the city."

At the mention of the third option, several of the commanders began to angrily object. Gaspar, still seething in anger at witnessing the fleeing ships earlier, remained silent.

Their voices were stayed by de Severy's raised hand. After regaining their silence, he continued.

"The third option is not the option I will choose. It may be the option I demand some of you to take. The Order has many things of great value within these walls I won't allow to fall into the hands of the Saracens. Many of these items are artifacts, manuscripts or icons which have been collected over the many years our order has been in the Holy Land. They've been moved here for safekeeping over time as our lands have fallen to the Saracens. These must not fall into their hands. I'll be tasking some of you with the job of ensuring these items make it to our fortress in Sidon.

"As for the rest of us, we must choose between the first two options. If it was only us who faced the Saracens here, then I would say without question I'd rather die in the Holy Land than to flee the Saracen horde. But that's not the case, for within our walls we now have hundreds of men, women, children, and the infirm who will most certainly die along with us. I can't damn them to that hell. So, we must at this moment, at least, choose the second option which is to sue for peace and attempt to save those in our care. The Holy Land is lost, brothers. We must do what we can for our flock."

There was an uneasy silence among the brothers as they contemplated de Severy's words. Gaspar knew while most of them would rather die than surrender, they saw the wisdom of his words and would stand behind him wherever their destiny led.

Later that evening, de Severy summoned Gaspar to his private Chamber. He climbed the stone steps from the dining room where he and many of the other knights had assembled to partake of some sort of watery gruel. The stew had been tasteless, but for the occasional chunk of meat, he strongly suspected were the remains of some knight's beloved steed.

He knocked on the heavy wooden door of the commander's chamber and heard a muffled, "Come." He entered, seeing de Severy seated at a small desk near the only window in the room. A small sputtering lamp gave off the only light, casting undulating shadows across the walls. He closed the door behind him, striding forward, stopping before the desk.

"You summoned me?" Gaspar said.

"Yes, brother. How was your meal?"

"It was mercifully shortened by your summons."

De Severy chuckled. "Yes, I attempted a bowl of that horrid stew myself. I thought the horse meat might at least provide some flavor to the cook's mash. Alas, I was wrong. What I would give for a plate of figs and dates or maybe some of that wonderful goat cheese from those Bedouin herders of the Negev."

At the mention of the food, Gaspar's stomach did a gentle somersault. The Grand Master had ordered the majority of the fortresses' remaining food stores rationed out to the hundreds of refugees now crowding the lower levels of the fortress. Other than an occasional piece of meat, now solely gleaned from the slaughter of the Templar's horses, the fighting men weren't getting much to eat. It was a telling sign of the precarious state of the Christian fortress.

"But I didn't ask you here to listen to my laments on our lack of culinary options," de Severy said sadly. "I asked for you because I know our dear departed brother, William, believed you to be the most trustworthy and committed of the brethren left in the Holy Land. He trusted you completely, and so shall I. You've grown up in this land, have you not, brother?"

"I have. My father brought both myself and my brother from France when I was a boy of ten years. I've lived in and around Acre for the majority of my life. My father had many lands here; farms, orchards, vineyards."

"I never knew your father or your brother."

"They both died in 1271, when I was fifteen, fighting with the armies of King Edward.

"My father, though he wasn't a Templar, had always wanted his sons to become Knights of the Order. My brother was nineteen when he died. He never had the chance to fulfill our father's wishes."

"After they died what happened?"

"At the time I was studying here in Acre with the brothers of the Templar Order. He had left instructions with them, should something ever befall him, I was to be cared for and trained until such time as I was accepted into the Order. At the age of eighteen I was initiated into the temple. All of my father's holdings were given to the Order at that time."

The thought of those days so long ago had transported Gaspar back in time to his days at the monastery. He could remember the feelings of sadness and abandonment upon the death of his father and brother. He remembered, as if it were only yesterday, his acceptance into the Templar Order, the feeling of family and communal brotherhood he'd embraced upon his acceptance. He'd wanted nothing else for as long as he could remember, and the donning of the white surcoat, with its brilliant red cross sewn on its center, had ignited a fervor of commitment and service which had never abated, but had in fact grown stronger with every passing year.

"It's somewhat unusual a boy of ten would be brought here from Europe. I understand your father was a wealthy Lord in France with many lands. What of your mother? Did you have other family?"

"I did. My father believed strongly in the idea that this land shouldn't be in the hands of the Saracens. He was a religious man. He wanted both of his sons to grow up to be protectors of the Holy Land. My mother was not so disposed. She believed it to be a fool's errand. I remember my brother and me sneaking out of our room on many a night to listen to them arguing over his plans. She pleaded with him to leave us with her. Obviously, she didn't prevail upon him and we left France in 1266. I never saw her again."

"Does she still live?" de Severy asked.

"She died some twelve years ago."

"And what of your family's lands in France?"

"I have a sister who's two years younger than I. She's still in France. She manages the lands with the help of my mother's brother."

"As your father's only surviving son, shouldn't those lands have been yours by inheritance?"

"When I took my vows, I renounced all claim to my inheritance."

De Severy was quiet for a few moments, and it seemed to Gaspar he was choosing his next words carefully.

"Your father sounds like a pious man, brother. These days I find myself wondering at the wisdom of popes, kings, and pious men."

Gaspar was surprised by this statement, but said nothing. His face must have given him away.

"You're troubled by my words? Don't be. We find ourselves on the precipice of complete and utter failure in the mission your father and so many, including myself, have committed our lives to," de Severy said with obvious bitterness in his voice.

"Popes and kings have squandered everything men such as you and I, martyrs like your father and brother, have fought and died for. Greed and avarice have clouded their judgment, and our own Order bears much blame for where we are tonight.

"The Holy Land is lost, Gaspar, and I fear we'll never again see this kingdom in the hands of Christians."

"But, Sir," Gaspar implored, "we can't give up. The infidels may win this battle, but men after us will come and reclaim this land. They must! It's why we ourselves exist!"

"There was a time when that was true. Now the kings of Europe busy themselves with wars and intrigues at home. Popes have more interest in their own kingdoms, and they forfeit their duties to secure this land, to petty and devious machinations at home. Even our own Order seems more interested in amassing great wealth and playing bankers to kings than to fulfilling our solemn commitments."

"No, Gaspar. Our days here are done. That doesn't mean we don't have our sacred trust. It doesn't mean we're absolved of the duties of our Order, and it doesn't mean we're without our own destiny, which brings me to why I asked you here tonight."

Gaspar's thoughts were a whirlwind of turmoil. He agreed with much of what de Severy had said. He knew he was right about where the blame lay for their current situation. He himself had felt the frustration and anger at the steady losses of the last many years, the majority of which could have been avoided.

But he wasn't ready, as de Severy seemed to be, to give up and declare that all was lost. It went against everything he held to be true and the cause which he'd sworn to uphold.

De Severy had stood and moved to a small alcove in the corner of the room. Gaspar watched as he drew a knife from his cloak and began prying at the stone in the wall. After he'd removed three small blocks of stone, he retrieved something from the dark space behind the stones.

He returned to the desk and placed a small piece of rolled-up parchment in front of him. On top of that he placed a large, old looking, metal key.

"No, Gaspar. We each have our duties to perform in the coming days. Some of us will die here defending this land to the end. You, brother, will not. Your destiny lies elsewhere."

CHAPTER 18

Acre, the Holy Land, 1291

"What I'm about to give you, Gaspar, is something our martyred former Master, William, gave to me. It's something which has been handed down from one caretaker to another since its discovery over one hundred and fifty years ago. I need your solemn oath as a Templar and as a man of God you'll accept this duty and fulfill it as best you can. You must do this knowing it may cost you your life. It's possible I am going to die in this city, and there is no other man with whom I would entrust this secret. Will you accept this mission?"

Gaspar was a Templar. He'd committed his life to the Order and to God. He didn't hesitate.

"I will do whatever you wish me to do."

"Good. Then follow me. We're going to take a walk," de Severy said.

He collected the items on the desk and bade Gaspar follow as he exited the room. They went down the hallway a short distance before they turned into a small alcove which housed a small altar with a Christ on the cross. It was an old relic Gaspar had never seen before as he hadn't spent much time on this level of the fort.

De Severy slipped behind the altar and pushed open a small door hidden from view.

The commander went through the doorway which Gaspar could see led to a set of steps descending into the dark.

"Come, follow me carefully. There's no light in the stairway. Just step slowly and carefully. We'll be at our destination shortly."

Gaspar began heading down the stairs, slowly feeling his way from step to step, hearing de Severy ahead of him doing the same.

The darkness was total and the space just wide enough to accommodate his shoulders. The steps continued to lead downward in a circular manner, and after quite some time, Gaspar realized they had to be well below the lowest levels of the fortress.

Finally he heard de Severy whisper, "Here we are. Stand still for a moment."

He listened to the sounds of the commander shuffling off a short distance, then a torch flared, illuminating the space around him.

They appeared to be in a large natural cavern, the ceiling above them so high it was shrouded in darkness. De Severy stood a short distance away, standing before an ancient wooden door set into the rock. He gestured for Gaspar to join him as he produced the old key he'd brought with him from his room.

"Hold the torch, Gaspar," he said as he handed it to him.

He inserted the key into the lock on the door and gave it a twist. It turned effortlessly, and de Severy pulled the door open. The sound of rushing water reached Gaspar's ears just as the smell of salt water assailed him. He followed de Severy through the door, finding they were in a much smaller cavern which became progressively smaller until it looked to be only a narrow cave leading off into the dark. A torrent of water raced by the narrow ledge on which they stood, off into the depths. The ledge led off toward the cave, disappearing inside.

De Severy lit another torch set in a sconce on the wall and turned to Gaspar. "This is where your task begins, Gaspar. The cave ahead leads up and out of the fortress beyond the city walls. It's narrow and treacherous, but I myself have made the climb, so I know that a man of your abilities will have no problem with the passage.

"It's a dangerous climb. One which will take you many hours, but this is the only way out that will shield you from those who would steal what you carry.

"At the end you'll be clear of the city walls on the far side of the harbor. This will place you outside the circle of the Saracens on the shore of a small, almost hidden bay.

"I, myself, placed a small boat just inside the mouth of the cave where it ends. You're to use the boat to row beyond the shallows and the rocks, which guard the bay. You'll find a Templar ship awaiting you beyond the bay. The captain of the ship knows only that someone is coming. He doesn't know who you are. I've given him instructions to take you to Sidon.

At that, de Severy removed a small pouch connected to a thin chain from around his neck and placed the rolled up parchment inside. He then reached up and slid the chain over Gaspar's head and tucked the pouch under his tunic.

"What you have around your neck is a map to the resting place of a great treasure. Everything else you know about the Order, our mission in the Holy Land, our service to the pope and to kings, all of it is nothing next to this. It was bestowed upon one of the founders of our order when he first came to the Holy Land. He was made its protector. Eventually, it was taken back to France and has been guarded by one of our Order since.

"You're the next in line. You must guard it with your life and trust no one but yourself. There are those who guess at its existence and who seek to possess it. When you reach the end of the cave, open the map and memorize the location of the hiding place. Then destroy the map.

"When you get to Sidon, you must make your way to France and to your destiny."

Gaspar's hand went to the pouch under his shirt.

"What could possibly be so important?"

De Severy was silent for a moment before he said, "That I won't tell you, brother. You must trust what I say is true. I fear that if you knew what you'll be guarding perhaps even you would falter under the weight of it. No, don't ask such a question. Take it and complete your task, knowing in this you will have served our Lord and our Order.

"Take it now, brother, and may God be your protector and your guide."

De Severy turned and passed through the old door, closing it behind him. The sound of the turning key in the lock and of the ancient bolts sliding closed sent a chill up his spine. He obviously wasn't going back that way.

He took the flaming torch down from the sconce, as well as an unlit one resting against the wall. Holding it in front of him, he inched his way into the passageway. With the pouch pressed against his chest, he began making his way to the surface.

He squirmed, twisted, and crawled on his hands and knees, several times on his belly for so long, the flame on the end of the second torch burned out. He'd continued on for hours in total darkness until he began to see a dim light ahead. A few minutes later, he was crouching in the mouth of the cave, looking out onto a quiet and tranquil cove below him.

The mouth of the cave was hidden behind a pile of boulders as was a small wooden dhow which looked barely large enough to contain him.

He carefully eased out of the cave, listening for any sound or signs of life. Once completely out of the cave, he stood stretching his tired, cramping muscles. De Severy had been right. He could hear nothing of the battle around Acre nor did it appear anyone was in the area.

He sat on a rock just outside the cave and pulled the pouch from under his shirt and over his head. Opening it, he extracted the parchment. He unrolled the brittle and worn paper until it lay open before him.

It was a map of the coast of France, Brittany to be exact. Next to a red Templar cross were the words "Monastery of St. Michael," and next to that, "Under our banner sleeps your charge."

Gaspar's fingers caressed the red cross marking the resting place of whatever it was which awaited him. Again he wondered what could be so important. But only for a moment. Pulling a dagger from under his shirt, he sliced and ripped the map until it was nothing more than scraps.

He dragged the little boat out from behind the rocks hiding it and climbed down a short incline to a sandy beach. Gentle waves lapped at the shoreline, but presented no problem for him as he placed the boat in the water. Wading out a short distance, he climbed into it. Taking the paddle, he began heading toward the narrow, almost invisible entrance to the cove. He paused briefly, as he dropped the fragments of the map into the water, watching them sink below the surface.

The cove was shallow, full of rocks, and the entrance was guarded by a series of large boulders which made it impossible for anything larger than a row boat to enter.

The sun beat down from high in the sky, and Gaspar was quickly sweating under the sweltering sun. As he approached the entrance of the cove, he could see a glimpse of open ocean beyond and much larger swells breaking on the boulders. He wondered how far he would have to venture into the open waters before he found the Templar ship.

Gaspar began to paddle harder as he passed through the boulders, the boat slewing wildly in the conflicting currents. He thought for a moment it would be smashed to pieces. He was sure he'd be sent to the bottom, when suddenly the boat shot through the last of the rocks, breaking free into the open sea.

Here the swells were larger, but de Severy had chosen well as the boat rode up and down the sides of the waves smoothly. Gaspar found, besides staying dry, he was able to move the boat with relative ease.

De Severy hadn't said how far out the Templar ship would be so he continued to paddle, the land behind him slipping steadily away.

After some time, Gaspar turned and looked behind him. In the distance around a point of land he could see smoke billowing into the air. A huge pillar of smoke and fire, visible even at this distance, rose from the city as high as he could see into the blistering sky. He knew then he looked upon Acre's fall.

This far out in the ocean, he could hear no sounds, but he imagined what was happening. It was apparent Kahlil had made his final assault and Acre had been set to the torch. Gaspar bowed his head, whispering a silent prayer for his brothers and all the innocents who had, no doubt, met a brutal end at the hands of the victorious Saracens.

His reverie was broken by the sound of a voice.

"Gaspar! Gaspar! Over here, man!"

Gaspar looked in the direction of the voice. Over the swells he caught a glimpse of mast and sail. Then it was gone as he dipped into a trough between the waves. He began stroking furiously in the direction of the boat, hearing his name called out again. He caught sight of the boat again as he reached the crest of a swell and saw he was getting closer. He continued paddling, gaining momentum until he could see several men standing along the gunwale of the ship urging him on. One man stood in the forepeak waving him in, calling his name. "Keep rowing, Gaspar. We'll throw you a line."

His muscles, already fatigued, cramping from his climb through the cave, ached as he fought the waves. Suddenly, he stopped rowing, peering intently at the boat.

De Severy had said no one knew he was coming. He'd said the ship's captain knew only someone from the fortress would be meeting the boat far enough out to sea to avoid the Saracen ships. No one was supposed to know his name.

He sat in the boat, every instinctive warning bell he possessed going off in his head. He strained to see who stood in the boat calling his name. He still couldn't make out the person's face, but he clearly was a Templar as he wore the white surcoat with the red cross on his chest.

His gaze traveled over the rest of the boat. He could see at least ten other men, two of them ready to throw the ropes they held, lining the railing.

Something wasn't right. Gaspar knew it. But what choice did he have now but to row to the ship? He was at least a mile off shore, and there was nothing waiting for him anymore in the direction of Acre except a bloodthirsty Saracen horde. Even if he turned toward shore, chances were the boat would catch him.

No, he would have to take his chances. Perhaps de Severy had decided whoever manned the boat needed to know his name and had somehow gotten word to him.

He began rowing again, and after a few minutes he was able to catch a rope that sailed through the air from the boat.

He was pulled alongside and, with the help of a rope ladder, lowered over the side, he soon found himself on the deck of the ship. When his feet hit the deck, he collapsed, his muscles finally giving way. Someone pushed a flask of water into his hand, and he drank until he was full.

"I thought for a moment you'd given up, Gaspar. It looked like you were going to row back to shore," a quiet voice said.

He looked up to find himself staring into the face of the Grand Master of the Order, Theobald Gaudin.

"De Severy was right to pick you. I know of no other who could have managed that climb through the cave, then the trip out to sea. Of course, I guessed it would be you."

Gaspar looked around him at the faces of the other men on the ship. He didn't recognize any of these men. They weren't Templars, of that he was sure. As he looked from face to face around the deck of the boat, he noticed a large stain on the deck near the mast. He had little doubt it was blood and obviously fresh.

He looked back at Gaudin, who was smiling down at him.

"There's been a slight change in plans, Gaspar," he said. "De Severy was afraid you might need help in your task. He sent me to assist you. I'm to travel with you to your destination."

"De Severy said nothing of this. He also said this would be a Templar ship manned by Templars. Who are these miscreants?" Gaspar asked.

"Well, you're right, they're not Templars. I had to press a few Genovese sailors, who were more than happy to escape Acre, into service as all of our brothers were required for the defense of the fortress. Now tell me where it's hidden. Where are we going once we reach Sidon? You've done your job, Gaspar. Let me help you now."

"You're lying," whispered Gaspar. "You should be in the ruins of Acre with the rest of our brothers."

Gaudin was silent for a moment, no trace of the smile left on his face. He knelt next to Gaspar, close enough so the sailors gathered around couldn't hear their conversation.

"Yes, I suppose you're right. It was foolish of me to believe you'd fall for my story. And it was foolish of de Severy to believe he could send you out of Acre without my knowing.

"I've been watching him for weeks, knowing full well eventually he'd make his move. I followed him to his hidden stairway and found the doorway to the cave. One of my spies in the fortress found out about his plans to have the boat waiting offshore. When I saw you leave dinner last night, I knew he was sending you away.

"It was simply a matter of exiting the harbor, and finding the waiting ship. No small feat, mind you, with the ships of friend and foe alike clogging the way. My status among the Templar's garnered me free movement with them. A chest full of Temple gold took care of a Saracen Admiral.

"The captain of this ship knew me as Grand Master of the Order and thought I was the one he was waiting for. He suspected nothing until I slid a blade deep into his gut. Unfortunately, the other brothers on board came to his aid and had to be dispatched as well.

"Now you have a choice, Gaspar. Give me the map you carry peacefully, or my Genovese friends will take it from you after which they'll slit your throat and feed you to the sharks."

Gaspar was furious with rage, but contained it as he tried to fashion a plan of escape. He had no doubt the fate described by Gaudin was what was in store for him regardless of whether he gave him the location described on the map or not. Obviously The Templar Grand Master was a traitor and a murderer. Gaspar knew he couldn't be trusted.

But what were his options? Gaudin knew about the map and obviously was willing to kill his brothers, never mind betray them, to possess it, which meant that he wanted it for evil purposes. De Severy had warned him traitors would seek what he protected.

He wouldn't divulge his secret.

Calm fell over him, a feeling of peace and tranquility that he embraced. It was a state of mind which had always come over him right before battle. It wasn't that he had no fear, but it was a state of mind where the fear was banished to a part of his mind where it wouldn't intrude on what lay before him. It had served him well throughout his many encounters with potential death, and he embraced it now as he knew he faced death again, perhaps for the last time.

He looked from Gaudin to the Genovese thugs arrayed around him. He could see most were armed with short knives or clubs. The Templar leader's broad sword hung from his belt. The Grand Master was wearing his full armor. Gaspar was armed with the dagger that rested under his shirt.

What he was tasked with protecting wouldn't fall into Gaudin's hands. He was going to fail to reach the location on the map. He wouldn't fail in his mission to keep whatever was hidden there out of the hands of evil.

In a flash, Gaspar struck out with his left hand, catching the still kneeling Gaudin in the throat, sending him sprawling backwards gasping for breath. With his right, he drew the blade and launched himself at the closest of the sailors. With great swiping arcs of his blade, he caught two of the killers unaware, slashing their throats.

The screams of the injured caused panic in the others for a moment, giving Gaspar time to lower his shoulder, ramming another thug into the railing, the gratifying sound of cracking ribs reaching his ears.

The panic in the rest of the sailors was over. Gaspar turned just in time to raise his arm in defense as a club came crashing down. He stopped the club with his left arm, but felt the bones give way a moment before excruciating pain exploded up his arm into his brain. The club-wielding assailant was rewarded with Gaspar's knife finding a space between his ribs before slicing deep into his chest.

Gaspar felt someone jump onto his back, an arm encircling his neck, trying to choke him. He spun around and thrust himself backwards into the railing hearing the breath go out of his assailant and the arm weaken slightly. Just then, he felt the slashing of a blade across the arm holding the knife.

The tendons were severed, the knife falling from his hand. He slammed backwards again in desperation, trying to free himself from the man hanging on his back.

The arm around his neck gave way as the body behind him went over the railing into the sea.

Just as he felt his burden slip away, he turned to find himself face to face with Gaudin, the broadsword in his hand poised to strike.

In rapt fascination, Gaspar watched as the blade drew back, then suddenly arched forward in a stabbing motion. The blade entered his body just below the rib cage, and he felt it exit his back.

There was no pain at first. He looked up to find Gaudin's eyes boring into his, the traitor's face a mask of hatred, malice, and triumph.

The pain blossomed when Gaudin slowly withdrew the sword, the blackness coming with it almost overcoming him. He fought back against it even as he watched his blood spill across the deck of the ship.

Gaudin's face intruded into his vision, his lips moving in a pantomime of soundless words. Slowly, as he concentrated on his face, he could make out what he was saying.

"Give me the map! Your life is over, Gaspar. Give it to me!"

Gaspar raised his shattered left arm and lifted the empty pouch from his neck. Gaudin reached out, snatching it from his hand. The Grand Master tore open the pouch and let loose a string of curses upon finding it empty.

"Where is it? What have you done with it?"

Gaspar leaned back until he rested against the gunwale. He gestured to Gaudin. "Come close. I'll tell you the location," Gaspar whispered.

Gaudin leaned in close, lowering his head to Gaspar's. "Tell me where it's hidden, Gaspar."

Summoning every ounce of ebbing strength he could muster, Gaspar threw his arms around the traitor, holding him fast. "Time to die, Gaudin," he whispered.

With a mighty heave he catapulted both himself and Gaudin over the gunwale into the ocean.

The Grand Master's heavy armor quickly pulled him down under the waves. Gaspar let go and, through open eyes, watched as Gaudin, mouth open in a silent scream, sank into the depths until he was gone.

Gaspar was enveloped by the cold green waters. As he slipped deeper below the waves, his eyes now closed, he felt the pain of his injuries begin to slip away. The cold shock of the water faded into a warmth which enveloped his consciousness. He felt himself falling, drifting this way and that, as if being rocked to sleep.

He opened his eyes and saw his mother's face looking down at him, her fingers, so long and soft, lovingly stroking his cheek. She was singing to him that little peasant song he loved so much, something about running in fields of clover. He lifted his hand and felt her hair, the golden cascades of it falling down to tickle his face. He smiled back at her, closed his eyes, and went to sleep.

CHAPTER 19

Zurich, Switzerland, May 2010

The plane touched down in Zurich in the early morning hours just after dawn. Alex had returned to reading the book after his nightmare, if that was what it was. He'd been strangely shaken by the dream and was relieved when he was able to escape the confines of the jet.

Alex had asked Lucas if he knew of a hotel in Zurich. The lawyer had arranged not only the hotel, but a car to pick him up at the airport.

As he exited customs, he spied a tall man dressed in black holding a card that read "Mr. Alex Donovan." The man offered to take Alex's only bag, a small leather carry-on, then escorted him to the curb and a black Mercedes Benz. Ensconced in the back of the car, Alex took in the sights as they made the twenty minute trip to the Hotel zum Storchen.

Once they arrived at the hotel, a grand looking granite building on the banks of the River Limmat, Alex paid the driver and entered the lobby.

For 650 years the Hotel Zum Storchen had been hosting guests in high style, and the understated elegance wasn't lost on Alex.

He checked in, booking the room for three days. After depositing his bag in the room and taking a quick shower, he decided to have breakfast before setting out for the bank. He put both books and the charm in the room safe and went back downstairs.

After an absolutely decadent breakfast of pastries, cheeses, and coffee, he gave the concierge the address of the bank. He was pleasantly surprised to find it only a short walk away on Zunn Bahnhof.

He set off and found himself walking down cobbled sidewalks, alongside narrow streets. The buildings along his way were all rather imposing, solid looking stone structures, which gave off an air of strength. Most had shops on the lower floors, a mishmash of jewelers, boutiques, and high end food purveyors. A few restaurants were mixed in as well. Everything was clean and tidy, and the people he passed seemed well off and happy.

He was surprised when he found himself in front of the bank's address. The building wasn't much different from those around it and looked more like a home than a bank. Other than a small brass plaque next to the highly varnished wooden door which was engraved with the bank's name, a person would never guess it was, in fact, a bank.

Alex tried the door and found that it was locked. He spied a black button above the bronze plaque and pressed. A clipped and proper voice spoke in German, "*Bergen en Cie, Kann ich Ihnen helfen?*"

Alex couldn't speak or understand German, but responded, "My name is Alex Donovan. I have an account here."

After a brief pause the same voice responded, this time in English, "Please come in, Mr. Donovan."

Alex could hear the sound of several locks being released and, when he tried the door a second time, it swung open silently.

He entered, finding himself in a spacious and well appointed foyer. Dark wood paneling, plush carpeting, and the quiet sounds of classical music created an atmosphere of quiet nobility. Standing at the far end of the foyer was a distinguished looking woman behind an obviously old but immaculate lawyer's desk. She moved from behind the desk and approached Alex on soundless footfalls.

"Welcome to Bergen and Cie, Mr. Donovan," she said, holding out her hand in greeting. "Would you like to have a seat? Direktor Bergen will be with you in a moment. In the meantime, may I get you something to drink, coffee perhaps?"

Alex took the outstretched hand. "No thanks, I've had a few cups already this morning."

The woman directed him to a leather chair and, after he took his seat, she returned to her desk where she sat down. As she sat, he noticed her reach under the edge of the desk, apparently pushing a button out of his view. A moment later Alex heard a door open and turned to see a man walking down the long hallway behind the receptionist, toward him.

The man came into the foyer wearing a smile which seemed put-on and professional.

"Mr. Donovan. Welcome to Bergen and Cie. I'm Direktor Hans Bergen. What can I do for you today?"

Alex had stood at the man's approach and again took the proffered hand.

"Yes, well. It seems I have a bank account with your bank. I have an account number and a key, but I don't know anything else about the account. I've come to see what's in it," Alex responded.

The banker's smile didn't change a bit, and he responded, "I take it you've never been to our bank before?"

"No. This is the first time."

"And how, may I ask, did you come to be in possession of the account number and key, and how do you know this account is held with us?"

Alex sensed even though the man's expression hadn't changed that he had become a bit more guarded.

"My grandfather recently passed away. He left this information with his attorney. My grandfather's name was Randolph Donovan."

At the mention of his grandfather's name, the banker's expression and attitude immediately changed. "Ah! Randolph Donovan; you're his grandson. Please, please. Come with me. We have a conference room where we can talk."

Turning to the receptionist, he said, "Helma, please bring some coffee and pastries to the conference room."

The banker then led Alex down the long hallway and entered a large room containing a massive table which ran almost the entire length. Along the walls of the room were half a dozen portraits, one of which was of Hans Bergen.

Noticing his gaze the banker said, "Those are all my ancestors, all managing direktors of the bank before me. I'm the sixth generation Bergen at the helm, so to speak," he said.

He directed Alex to a seat at the table, and then sat across from him. The receptionist entered as they sat and placed a gleaming silver service tray before them and a plate of delicious looking pastries. Bergen said nothing more until the woman had left and closed the door.

After Alex declined coffee and pastries, Bergen sat back in his chair and fixed Alex with an intense stare. Alex was getting a bit put off by the staring man, when a door hidden in the wooden paneling swung open silently. A tall man in a rather severe black suit entered, carrying a plain manila file folder which he placed in front of the banker. He then turned and left the room through the hidden door, which closed silently behind him.

Bergen finally looked away from Alex and opened the file folder in front of him.

"May I have the account number and key, Mr. Donovan?"

Alex retrieved a slip of hotel stationery he had written the number on and the key from his pocket. He slid the paper and key across the table and watched as the banker compared the account number to something in the file. He then took out a small magnifying monocle from his jacket and examined the key for a moment.

Apparently satisfied that they did indeed match, he said, "The account number is one that we have here in our bank. It is, actually, our oldest account. And the key is embossed with our logo."

Alex thought about that for a moment, looking up to see the portraits on the walls. Assuming Herr Bergen was in his fifties, Alex tried to do some quick math to determine how old the account could be. It didn't make any sense because there was potentially two hundred years worth of Herr Bergens on the walls.

As if sensing Alex's confusion, the banker said, "The account has been with us long before your grandfather. It is, as I said, the oldest account we have here. It's been with us over two hundred and forty years."

"I don't understand. How did my grandfather come to possess it?" Alex asked.

"I don't know, nor is it our business to concern ourselves with those kinds of questions," Bergen answered. "All that matters is possession of the account number. I do remember the first time your grandfather came here. I was a young man at the time. I think it was in the early sixties. The last time he was here was in the late nineties I believe."

"Can you tell me what the balance is in the account?" Alex asked.

Bergen paused for a moment, then answered, "I think perhaps you're confused as to what type of account this is. While we do have accounts which are like traditional bank deposit accounts, this is not one of them. It is, actually, a vault account. We only have a few of them. This one is our largest as well as the oldest. Perhaps you'd like to see what's in it?"

Bergen was right about one thing, Alex was confused. He'd expected some sort of bank account. Instead, it seemed to be some sort of safe deposit box.

"Yes. I'd like to see what's in it."

The banker stood and said, "Well then, let me escort you to the vault."

They exited the room, this time through the hidden doorway in the wall. Alex went through the door to find himself in a completely different environment. Everything appeared to be made of highly polished steel, and at the far end of the short hallway stood two large, serious looking uniformed men. Both had automatic weapons held in front of them, their eyes fixed on Alex as if measuring his every step. They stood in front of what looked to be elevator doors.

Bergen went up to the door and pressed a button in the wall. A panel slid up to reveal a device Alex recognized as a scanner. Placing his face to the scanner, Bergen waited as the device scanned his face. After a moment, Alex heard a soft chime, and the doors to the elevator slid open.

Alex followed Bergen into the steel-walled compartment past the guards and turned to face the doors, which closed silently. Immediately, Alex could feel the elevator descending. "Was that some sort of facial recognition device?" Alex asked.

"That and more," Bergen answered. "Not only does it use the most advanced facial recognition technology in the world, but it also scans my eyes, and reads my brain waves. It can tell if I'm in a heightened state of anxiety and, if it concluded that I was distressed, say someone was holding a gun to my head, it would refuse entry; quite amazing and expensive.

"Our vaults are all located four stories below the main floor of our building," Bergen continued. "They were bored out of solid granite and are inaccessible from the outside. They were expensive to build as well as maintain. Your vault was paid in advance in perpetuity."

Alex glanced at Bergen. "You mean it was paid for when it was built and it's paid up forever? How is that possible?"

Bergen gave a slight grin. "As I said, this account is unique. The original owner of the account, who that was, I don't know nor did any of my ancestors, actually gave the original founder of our bank, my great, great, great, great grandfather the money to build the bank. He also gave him a large part of the original capital with which he started the bank. In exchange, this vault was to be maintained in perpetuity for him and his heirs, one of whom is apparently you, Mr. Donovan."

The elevator came to a stop, and the doors slid open. A long wide corridor stretched off into the distance. A soft hum permeated the air, and light radiated down from the ceiling.

"This is our vault complex," Bergen said as he stepped from the elevator and headed off down the corridor. "We have twenty-five vaults and several hundred smaller safe deposit boxes here. The space is completely climate controlled. Humidity and temperature are strictly maintained with a variety of redundant power sources and systems. Many of our clients have upgraded their vaults in interesting ways, limited only by their imaginations and money, of course. Your vault remains as it was when your grandfather had it. He undertook some modernization of it, but it remains much as it was when it was built. If you choose to do so, we can work with you to bring your vault into a more technologically updated state."

Alex followed the banker as they walked down the corridor. He could see that the individual vaults each had a metal cage-like entrance which housed a utilitarian looking set of chairs and a metal table. Beyond the metal cage was an impressive looking doorway, much like a bank vault door, set into the rock.

"There's a separate elevator somewhat larger than the one we came down on. It's capable of carrying a small transport vehicle to our secure loading area. Sometimes our clients have rather large things they like to keep here," Bergen said.

"When you said vault, I expected a small compartment," Alex said. "Not Fort Knox."

Bergen chuckled softly. "I would submit to you, Mr. Donovan, that you'd have an easier time breaking into Fort Knox. Ah, here we are."

Alex found himself at the end of the tunnel and in front of the last vault. This one was much larger than the others. As he watched, Bergen drew a key from his jacket pocket and inserted it into the lock on the cage door. He turned the key and pushed the door open. It swung open on silent hinges. Bergen stood aside and gestured for Alex to enter. He allowed Alex to pass through the gate, then handed him the key.

"The way this works, Mr. Donovan, is I give you the key to the gate," Bergen said. "It's the only one. In this way you can be assured of complete privacy. Use the key you brought with you to open the lock on the inner vault door. You may close it behind you as it can be opened from inside. Once you're finished, use the phone on the table, and I'll return to escort you back upstairs. If you wish to take any items from the vault, I can provide you with any number of carrying devices or, if the item is large, you may use our utility vehicle to carry items upstairs in our freight elevator. If required, I can also arrange armed guards and transport once you leave the bank premises if you desire.

"Please take your time and call me for any assistance you might require. Do you have any questions?"

Alex looked around him for a moment before answering, "I have a million questions, Herr Bergen, but somehow I don't think you can answer them."

Bergen smiled a knowing smile. "Trust me, Mr. Donovan, when I say this is not the first time I've taken this walk with clients who had no idea what waited behind the doors of their vaults. Some were happy with what they found. Some were not."

With that, Bergen turned and headed off down the corridor, back toward the elevator, his expensive shoes tip-tapping away out of sight.

Alex closed the gate and turned to face the vault door. It was old and, unlike many of the other vaults that had seemed more modern, this one looked ancient. He reached into the folder and found the metal key. It, too, looked old.

He walked up to the door and inserted the key, turning it gently. The lock gave way smoothly and, taking a deep breath, Alex pulled open the door.

CHAPTER 20

Zurich, Switzerland, May 2010

Alex stepped into a large space hollowed out of solid rock. It was lit by a row of overhead fixtures. He pulled the door closed behind him, surprised briefly by the echoing snap of the lock engaging. The light, an older style of fluorescent lighting, while not dim, was such that it took a moment to acclimate his eyes.

The vault looked to be about thirty feet wide and close to one hundred feet deep. It was packed from floor to ceiling with boxes, crates, and chests of varying sizes. A narrow aisle down the center of the room allowed Alex to walk between the stacked containers as he examined them.

All the containers had writing on them in a language similar to that in his grandfather's old book, as well as a series of numbers.

He stopped in front of several old chests bound with metal straps. He grasped the lid of one and lifted. The scent of cedar, incense, and age filled the air, and he wondered how long it had been since the box had been opened.

The chest was full of small bundles, the smallest no bigger than his hand, the largest no bigger than two feet square, all wrapped in purple velvet cloth. He removed one of the items, slowly unwrapping the covering, until he was staring at a stunning miniature painting of a woman holding a small child.

He'd seen pictures of icons and somehow knew what he held was an old one. It was so full of reverence that he felt himself mesmerized by the tiny painting.

He carefully set the icon aside and retrieved a second bundle. Unwrapping the covering revealed a slightly larger icon, this one a painting of Christ on the cross.

One after another he exposed stunning works of art until he had ten of the icons staring back at him. He estimated the chest contained at least thirty of the paintings.

He opened a second chest to find it similarly filled with the velvet-wrapped treasures. He repeated this with four of the chests, which were lined up next to each other with the same results. Stepping back, he counted twenty-two of the chests. If each contained the same number of icons, there were easily close to seven hundred of them, maybe more.

He moved deeper into the vault, passing more crates and boxes until a stack of oblong crates caught his eye. Ten of the approximately six foot long boxes were stacked together. He picked one and released the double clasps holding the lid in place.

Lifting it, he found the same velvet cloth draped over the contents. Pushing aside the plush fabric, he stared at an ancient sword. He carefully reached in and lifted it from the box. Surprised by the weight, he grasped it in both hands.

The handle was wrapped in leather, worn and stained, obviously well used. The blade looked to be about four feet long and shown brightly in the light. Alex ran a finger down one side of the blade. While razor sharp, it was pitted and dented, and he realized, while beautiful in a simple utilitarian way, the sword was no ceremonial museum piece. This weapon had been used, violently.

He set the giant sword aside and lifted another layer of fabric to find a second sword. This one was shorter than the first, but looked equally deadly. The blade was curved, ending at a beautiful jewel-encrusted handle. It was much lighter than the first sword. Alex could wield this one with one hand.

The blade was razor-sharp as well but, like the other one, it also had obviously been used. In fact, this blade had a large slice in it approximately halfway up the length of it, as if something had almost cut it in two.

He set the second sword aside, delving deeper into the case to find weapon after weapon layered one atop the other. The box contained twelve swords of different sizes and shapes.

Looking around, Alex began to notice a pattern to the arranging of the crates. He could see that certain boxes were grouped together, and the numbers on the boxes in each group ran consecutively. Obviously the vault was more organized than it first appeared.

He was about to open another box in the next stack when he noticed a wooden table in a small cleared area in the center of the vault. A wooden chair was pushed under one side. In the center of the table was a large-leather bound book. Next to that, was an empty crystal goblet, an old corkscrew, and a dark colored wine bottle. Alex approached the table, his eyes drawn to the bottle. He reached out and, lifting the dark heavy bottle, realized it had the exact same label as the one he'd found in his grandfather's wine cellar just day's ago.

A chill crept up his spine as he pulled out the chair and sat, dragging the book toward him. He opened it, turned a few pages, and knew he was looking at a ledger. Each page contained several columns under which were dates and numbers that looked to correspond to the numbers on the crates. Some of the numbers were below one column on the left, others below another column on the right. Alex could tell the ledger was an inventory of the crates and the notations next to them were a record of things brought into the vault and other things taken out.

The language of the writing rendered the entries and notations unreadable, but he could read the dates. He turned back to the first page and located the first entry. June 12, 1780. The date corresponded roughly with the opening of the bank.

Alex turned the pages, noting the dates of the visits to the vault. The frequency varied, sometimes multiple visits in a year, especially toward the front of the ledger, sometimes large gaps in years.

Someone had kept a meticulous record of the contents and visits to the vault. An idea, a question really, formed in his mind. He turned back to the first page and examined the handwriting. It was a beautiful, flowing script done in an old fashioned style. Quickly leafing through the pages, Alex found all the entries written in the same handwriting.

As the years flowed by, the phantom hand documenting the passage of time, the writing remained the same. 1790, 1810, 1819, 1826, 1834; on the years passed. Turning the pages faster, knowing already what he would find, he passed an entry for 1882.

1885, 1901, 1908, 1912; and still the same flowing script. Alex leaned back in the chair, realizing he'd been holding his breath as he'd turned the pages. One hundred and forty years had passed between the first entry and the last one Alex had read, all made in the same unique handwriting.

He was no handwriting expert, but Alex had no doubt the same person had been visiting the vault for all those years.

He leaned forward again, this time slowly turning the pages until he'd reached an entry dated October 10th, 1960. Below the date was only one numbered entry and notation, this one under the right side of the ledger. Apparently one item had been removed.

He turned the page and, while surprised by what he found, he definitely wasn't shocked. The next entry was dated February 14, 1961. Under the heading were several notations, some in the left column, some in the right. The only difference was this time the handwriting was his grandfather's.

There was no mistaking it. The language, still unreadable to Alex, was the same as all the other entries. Only the handwriting differed. He turned several more pages to find entries in his grandfather's writing spanning the years from 1961 through September 2nd 1999.

Herr Bergen had said he'd last seen Randolph sometime in the nineties. That had to be the last visit his grandfather made.

He was about to close the ledger when he nonchalantly turned the page. This time what he found not only shocked him, it scared him.

He stared at the entry on the page before him, May 29th 2010; yesterday. But it was what was written below the date that had given him such a jolt. In perfectly readable English were the words:

"Greetings to my dear friend, Alexander."

The words were written in that same flowing script as the original entry in 1780.

Alex tried to gather himself, tried to calm his nerves. What kind of joke was being played on him? Herr Bergen had said nothing about having a visitor to the vault yesterday.

Alex looked at his watch and realized he'd been inside the vault over an hour. He stood suddenly, wanting out. The vault contained what looked to be hundreds, if not thousands, of crates. He would return for further exploration, but for now he wanted an explanation for the bizarre entry in the old ledger.

He headed back toward the vault door, stopping at the first crate he'd opened, and removed the painting of the woman and child.

Using his key, he let himself out of the vault, closing and locking the door behind him. He set the items from the vault on the table and picked up the phone. After two short rings the voice of Herr Bergen came on the line. "Yes, Mr. Donovan. How can I help you?"

"I'd like a briefcase, please, for a small item."

"By all means, I'll be right down."

After a wait of no more than five minutes, Alex heard the sound of the Direktor's feet making their way down the corridor.

He arrived at the gate carrying a black leather briefcase. Alex unlocked the cage door, letting him in.

"I hope this will be satisfactory, Mr. Donovan," Bergen said, handing the case to Alex.

"It will do just fine."

Alex placed the icon in the leather case, then turned to Bergen.

"Why didn't you tell me someone had accessed the vault yesterday, Herr Bergen?"

A momentary look of confusion and panic crossed the banker's face before he gathered himself. "Whatever do you mean, Mr. Donovan? No one was here yesterday. As I told you, the vault hasn't been accessed since your grandfather's last visit in the late nineteen-nineties."

"Well, that's odd, since someone left me a little note in there with yesterday's date on it."

"You must be mistaken, Mr. Donovan. I can assure you no one was in your vault yesterday. Perhaps you'd like to review our surveillance tapes. We have twenty-four hour camera coverage of all the vaults and the elevator access."

Alex stared into the banker's eyes. How far did he want to push this? He assumed Hans Bergen knew something, but apparently wasn't going to divulge what that was.

Alex turned away and picked up the case. "I think I'm done here for the day, Herr Bergen."

The trip up from the vault was made in stony silence until they reached the conference room.

"Is there anything else I can do for you, Mr. Donovan?" Bergen asked.

"Not today. I'd like to return tomorrow to spend more time in the vault."

"Certainly. The bank opens at 9:00 a.m."

Bergen showed Alex to the door and let him out into the street. Alex headed back in the direction of his hotel. The trip to the vault had raised more questions than it had answered and had given Alex an eerie sense of foreboding. He had no idea what his next step should be. Suddenly realizing how hungry he was, he decided to head back to his hotel for lunch on the veranda. He had a lot of thinking to do.

CHAPTER 21

Zurich, Switzerland, May 2010

Bergen watched via a closed circuit TV camera as Alex walked away from the bank toward his hotel. He dabbed at his forehead, mopping up beads of nervous sweat, cursing his lack of composure.

Donovan's question about who had accessed the vault had caught him completely off guard. Not because the American was wrong; in fact, he was right, but because Bergen had no idea that the visitor had left traces, apparently purposeful traces, of his visit.

The call had come two days ago on the cell phone, which until that moment, had never rung. As he had for the last fifteen years, on January 2nd, he'd received the phone via a courier service, with the same instructions. He was to carry the phone with him always, 24 hours a day. He was not to use the phone for any reason other than to answer it if it rang. And every January 2nd he was to destroy the phone, using the bank's incinerator, upon receiving a new one.

For fifteen years he'd followed the instructions to the letter just as every Bergen who had served as managing director before him had. Obviously, the mode of communication had changed over the decades, but it had always been this way. The Chairmen, as the Bergen's knew them, had demanded it.

Since 1780 when Hiram Bergen, the founder of the bank, had first been handed the strange, but fortuitous, capital to launch the bank, it had been this way. While the Bergens had been the face of the bank and handled all of the day to day management, the Chairmen had loomed in the background.

No one had ever seen them nor met with them face to face. The visits to the bank had always been done at night. All bank employees, including the Bergens, were told to leave the building. Over the years, as technology and security advanced, it had become more difficult, but all security systems were turned off and the bank left unsecured when the Chairman visited. There was never a record of the visits, and to this day none of the Bergens had any idea who their benefactors were.

In early 1961, Bergen's father had received a phone call telling him Randolph Donovan would be accessing the vault. Over the years, until last night, the Chairman hadn't contacted the Bergens again, and Randolph Dononvan had been the only person to access the vault.

So when the phone's ringing had startled him at his desk, he had answered with more than a bit of trepidation.

"Hello, Hans Bergen," he said.

"Good afternoon, Herr Bergen," came a quiet voice. "How are you today?"

Bergen tried to place the strange accent. "I'm well, thank you. What may I do for you?"

"Do you know who I am?"

Bergen noticed that the voice seemed to be oscillating and changing pitch, and he wondered if the person on the other end of the line was using some sort of scrambling device.

"You're the Chairman, I presume."

"You presume correctly, Herr Bergen. I need your assistance. You're going to receive a visitor very soon, a Mr. Alexander Donovan. He's the grandson of Randolph Donovan. Randolph passed away a few weeks ago, and his grandson has assumed his duties. He'll be accorded all the same access and assistance he requires just as his grandfather was. Do you understand?"

"Absolutely. I'll assist him personally," Bergen replied.

"You're not to give him any indication you had prior knowledge of his visit. Is that clear?" asked the Chairman.

"Absolutely clear."

"Further," the voice continued, "I require access to the vault tonight. I haven't been inside the vault for many years, but I've made myself familiar with all of your security systems. At exactly 12:00 a.m., you'll ensure that all bank personnel, including yourself, have vacated the premises. You'll also turn off all security systems and surveillance cameras both inside and outside the building. At 3:00 a.m., you'll reactivate the security systems, and all personnel will be allowed back into the building. Do you have any questions, Herr Bergen?"

"No, sir," Bergen replied.

"Very good. Thank you for your assistance, Herr Bergen."

Before Bergen had a chance to reply, the line went dead.

He had done as the Chairman requested. Under the guise of performing some tests of the security system, Bergen had ordered all of the security personnel out of the building at midnight. Notably perplexed, they had complied and, after turning off every security system and all of the bank's surveillance equipment, he'd spent a nervous three hours while Bergen and Cie, one of Zurich's oldest and richest private banks, sat virtually defenseless and open to the world.

In the end, there had been no trace or evidence of the visitor until Alex Donovan's pointed question.

Bergen had always known the bank's bizarre past would touch him in some way. Now, as he tidied up his desk and slowly regained his composure, he hoped the arrival of Alex Donovan and the reemergence of the enigmatic Chairman didn't signal trouble. He'd had a quiet run as direktor of the bank. He prayed it stayed that way.

CHAPTER 22

Zurich, Switzerland, May 2010

Alex sat on the terrace of the hotel contemplating the leather brief-case in the seat beside him. A barely touched plate of tiny sandwiches and a glass of German Riesling sat on the table in front of him.

He couldn't get the sight of the enigmatic note out of his mind. If his eyes were to be believed, the handwriting belonged to someone well over 200 years old.

The question lurking in a not very deep corner of his mind kept coming ever closer to the surface. He knew he was on the trail of his grandfather's immortal friend, Gaspar. Apparently, based on the note in the vault, Gaspar, who else could have written that note, knew as well.

Too excited to eat his lunch, he paid his bill and located the concierge. After a brief discussion, the concierge gave Alex a list of three art galleries, all located within walking distance of the hotel. Alex picked the one closest to the hotel and, after a five minute walk, he located the gallery on the lower level of a riverfront four-story building.

Entering, he found himself surrounded by several paintings, all displayed in glass cases strategically lit by soft lights. A security guard sat to one side of the room, and after pointedly examining Alex, he returned to watching a bank of security monitors.

A short, pear-shaped man with one of the most obvious toupees Alex had ever seen waddled out of a doorway near the back of the gallery, approaching Alex.

"Good afternoon, Sir. How may I help you?" the man said in German.

"I'm sorry, I don't speak German, only English."

"Ah, not a problem, sir. My name is Roberto Lang. Welcome to my gallery. What can I do for you?"

"My name is Alex Donovan. I'm in Zurich on business, and your gallery was recommended to me by the concierge at the Hotel Zum Storchen as a gallery specializing in old paintings."

"Yes, we specialize in older art works. Let me show you some of our current offerings and you can tell me what you're interested in."

"Actually, I'm not in the market to purchase a painting. I was actually wondering if you might be able to take a look at a painting that recently came into my possession. I know nothing about art and was hoping you might be able to tell me a little about it."

A momentary look of disappointment crossed the dealer's face as he realized he didn't have a paying customer. He gestured for Alex to follow him as he headed toward the back of the gallery.

"By all means, Mr. Donovan. Do you have this painting with you?"

"Yes, I have it here in my briefcase."

"Well, let's go into my office and take a look at what you have."

They entered a small office in the back of the gallery, and Alex sat on one side of a desk piled high with art books, auction catalogs, and, strangely, an almost three foot tall stack of comic books.

The dealer noticed Alex's observation and laughed. "I love old masters and make a good living buying and selling them, but I have a soft spot for old comic books and have quite a large collection of them. Now let's see what you have."

Alex reached into the satchel and pulled out the tiny velvet-wrapped painting. He noticed the dealer's frown when he saw the size of the bundle. He handed the painting across the table, and the dealer took it, gingerly peeling back the covering.

Alex heard the almost instantaneous gasp the dealer made when the painting was revealed. Lang reached into his desk and retrieved a pair of white linen gloves. Next, he pulled out a rather large monocle with a strap on it that he slid over his right eye. He leaned over the painting closely, examining it, mumbling incoherently and seemingly unaware that Alex even existed.

After about five minutes of painstakingly examining every inch of the tiny work of art, he stood and walked to a bookcase overflowing with books and magazines along one wall of the office. He began a frantic search through the piles, obviously looking for one in particular, all the while, Alex could hear muffled curses as books and magazines were tossed unceremoniously aside. Finally, with an exclamation, he grabbed a large book and returned to the desk.

He immediately began leafing through what Alex could now see was some sort of catalogue or reference book. Again, incoherent mumbling was all Alex could hear and, just as he was about to inquire as to what the dealer was looking for, the little man slammed his hand on the table and said, "Yes! I knew it!"

Looking up at Alex as if he'd just remembered he was in the room, Lang said, "Where in God's name did you get this, Mr. Donovan?"

Unsure how to answer, Alex said, "My grandfather recently passed away and left it to me."

"Here in Zurich?"

"Yes. It was here in Zurich. At a bank that he used."

"You have no idea what this is, do you?"

"Well, I thought it was some sort of icon but like I said, I know nothing about art."

Lang took the book in front of him and, turning it so it was facing Alex, he said, "Look at this, then read the paragraph below the picture. It's in English."

Alex leaned forward and found himself staring at a picture of a painting that looked similar to the one on the desk. This one was clearly of the same woman, but in this painting she was holding a much younger child; a baby, in fact. Even Alex could see the similarities, though. He began to read the brief description beneath the painting:

One of what is believed to have originally been a set of twelve miniature icons painted by Rembrandt was auctioned last month at Christie's annual Old Masters sale in London. The painting is the only one known to have survived from the set of twelve icons painted when the artist was a young student in the early 1620's. They were the only icons he ever painted and were commissioned by an unknown patron. To this day, none of the other paintings has ever been seen. Sale price was ten million pounds. The seller was believed to be English. The buyer was an anonymous phone bidder. April 23, 1989.

Alex looked up from the book to find the dealer staring at him intently with a crazy grin on his face.

"That little painting you plopped down on my desk, young man, is worth at least ten million pounds, probably a lot more. I don't think you should be walking around Zurich with it in your case," he said.

"How can you be sure it's one of the twelve? How do you know it's not some sort of forgery?" Alex asked.

Again, Lang laughed. "I know, because I was at that sale in 1989, and I bid on the icon that sold that day. I was hired by a Japanese collector who had used my services several times before to be his buyer and agent. I had researched and studied it extensively. He wanted the icon desperately, but we were out of the bidding at five million pounds. It was an amazing sale. The phone bidder never stopped. He just kept bidding relentlessly until everyone else had dropped out. Usually when you get to those types of prices, bidders will pause, and you'll get a sense they're trying to decide how high to go. That buyer never hesitated once. I knew at five million pounds he'd buy it. That was why I advised my client to get out."

"And you're sure this is one of the twelve?" Alex asked.

"Absolutely. His signature is there; Rembrandt, that is. The colors and style are exactly the same, and it fits with the theme of the twelve icons. Each was a painting of Mary, the mother of Christ, with the Christ child at twelve different points in his life, from year one to year twelve. I would say yours is the sixth or seventh in the series."

Alex was stunned. He thought of the hundreds of paintings sitting in the vault. He'd noticed other icons similar to the one he had in front of them. Now that he knew what he was looking at, there was no doubt the rest of the missing Rembrandt Icons sat in the containers in the vault at Bergen and Cie.

The dealer was talking again. "Of course, you would want to have it professionally examined by an expert who could document all of the points of authenticity, dating, paints used, etc. I could recommend someone here in Zurich, although there are a couple of experts in Italy and London I can think of as well. You'd need that for insurance purposes, but I can assure you it's what I say it is. I'd also be more than willing to represent you if you should wish to sell it. Did your grandfather leave you any other paintings like this?"

Alex quickly answered, "No. This was the only one."

The dealer eyed him closely. "I'd recommend you get this back into the bank or some sort of secure facility. What you have is an amazing piece of history, never mind an almost priceless work of art. If word of this find gets out, the art world will be in a frenzy. If you decided to sell the painting, that wouldn't be a bad thing; the more publicity, the better. Again, if you need someone to represent you, I can assist you."

"I think I'll take your advice and get this back to the bank tomorrow," Alex said.

There was something about the dealer that gave Alex pause. He understood the man's interest in the painting, but something else seemed just below the surface of his excitement.

Alex stood from his chair. "Thank you for your assistance, Mr. Lang. I'll think about your offer and, if I do decide to make the painting available, you'll be the first person I call."

"I'm at your service, Mr. Donovan," Lang said as he stood offering an outstretched hand.

Alex took the hand, almost recoiling at the wet and clammy palm. As nonchalantly as he could, Alex exited the gallery and made his way, this time with a more circumspect stride and a suddenly suspicious eye on those around him, back to the hotel. He went straight up to his room and locked the door behind him.

After showing Alex to the door, the dealer quickly returned to his office, closing and locking the door. Excitement coursed through his veins and, with nervous fingers, he entered a number into his cell phone that he'd committed to memory many years before. The monthly check had seen to that.

The call was connected and after only one ring was answered, "Yes?"

"This is Roberto Lang,"

"I know who this is."

"Ah, yes. Well, I wanted to let you know one of the paintings on your list just showed up in my gallery."

Silence filled the air for a moment before the voice quietly asked, "Which one?"

"One of the Rembrandt Icons."

Lang thought he heard a slight gasp of surprise. The voice, now not so sure of itself, asked, "Are you sure?"

"Of course I'm sure. This is why you've paid me all these years, isn't it? Because I know these paintings you seek?"

"Do you have it in your possession?"

"No. The man who brought it in left with it."

The voice erupted in anger, "Damn it, Lang! Who was it?"

"The man's name was Alex Donovan."

"Ah, of course."

Lang waited for almost a minute before the voice on the other end of the line quietly asked, "Do you know where he's staying?"

"I think he's staying at the Zum Storchen. He found me by asking the concierge there about art dealers. It was quite lucky he chose to come see me first."

"In this matter, Lang, luck has little to do with things. You've done well. You deserve a bonus. I'll send a man shortly with an envelope full of my gratitude. Let me know if anything else develops in this matter."

The line went dead.

Lang set his phone aside and rubbed his hands together. A bonus. While he would have loved the commission that would have come from selling the Rembrandt, his benefactor had been more than generous for many years. The news Lang had delivered had obviously been exactly what he'd been looking for. He hoped the bonus would reflect that.

An idea began to form in his mind. Perhaps there was a way to maximize this information he now possessed.

He picked up his phone again and dialed a local number. After three or four rings a voice in a thick Italian accent answered, "What?"

"Alfeo? It's Roberto Lang."

"Do you have my money?"

"Actually, no, but--"

"Then why the hell are you calling me? I told you no more bets until you pay me what you owe. Do I have to come over there and take some of your ugly paintings?"

"No, no. I have some information I thought might be worth something to you. In fact, it's worth much, much more than what I owe you."

"I'll be the judge of that. What is this information?"

"Oh, I think you're going to like this."

Lang laid out his plan to the Italian and, after coming to an agreement, hung up the phone. He leaned back contentedly in his chair. Yes, this was working out to be a most auspicious day. He opened the top right drawer of his desk and retrieved a brochure. It was a realtor's flyer for a villa just south of Nice. Perhaps it was time to make a call to that real estate agent.

Alex lay on the bed in his hotel room. It had been too late to go to the vault, so he had opened the room safe and, removing the Icon from the satchel, placed it inside. As he did so, he saw the translation of Gaspar's story and removed it.

Confusion engulfed him. What was the next step? What was he supposed to do now?

Perhaps the book would provide some sort of clue, some direction on how to proceed. He had left the story at the point of Gaspar's death at the hands of the traitor, Gaudin. He began to read once more.

CHAPTER 23

Acre, The Holy Land, 1292

G aspar opened his eyes. Blackness and cold enveloped him in a cloak of steel so binding, so suffocating, that almost instantly his mind began to crack at the edges. He could feel the madness snaking deeper and deeper into his brain eating away at whatever sanity he still possessed.

Where was he? What pit was this he'd fallen into? In a flash of violent memory, he saw the blade sliding into his gut, the steel tearing and searing his insides as if it was a scalpel wielded by some demonic surgeon. All of it came back then in a rushing tide, pushing back against the creeping insanity, focusing his mind on who and what he was.

In a moment, the memories were washed away by a tidal wave of anguish and remorse. His very soul was being torn apart by guilt and anger at having failed God and his Order. In that instant of overwhelming sadness, he realized this was his hell.

The madness surged and, just before he welcomed it, in the hope it brought with it oblivion, his consciousness exploded in a shower of golden light.

The light was so brilliant it seemed to be inside him, radiating through him, warming his frozen soul. The heat of it lifted his madness and drove it screaming from his mind, as if cleansing it with fire. He sensed he was rising; no, being lifted higher and higher, his whole being freed from the suffocating cloak of darkness.

He realized that he could now see. He saw a wall of black water turning blue, now green, then amazingly a hand clutching his, dragging him upward through a torrent of foam and confusion, the world around him growing brighter and clearer as he picked up speed. The momentum of his rise became so fast that, as he realized he was breaking the surface of the sea, his mind exploded in a flash of light.

Gaspar awoke to the sound of someone in the throes of a violent attack of vomiting. The episode seemed to go on forever until, as his consciousness cleared and reason began to reclaim his mind; he realized the sounds he heard were coming from him and that his body was being racked by intense spasms of sickness.

Great gouts of liquid were being expelled from his lungs as he struggled for air, fighting and clawing through the violence for some semblance of humanity.

And then it stopped. With eyes shut tightly, he reveled in the ability to draw breath, savoring the taste of salty air cascading into his lungs. His fingers dug into warm sand, clenching and unclenching, feeling the ground as if for the first time.

He could feel the warmth of the sun on one side of his face and the scratching but wonderful caress of sand on the other. The sounds of birds and the sea reached his ears. He lifted his head with what seemed a titanic effort of will and opened his eyes.

He took in the sight of the ocean, waves gently surging over the shore. Gulls swooped, darting into the surf, some alighting nearby, turning curious, and no doubt hungry, eyes his way. The sun was high in the sky, beating down with welcome warmth. A breeze blew in off the water, cooling his skin.

He pushed himself up until he sat facing the ocean, his mind still foggy and incomplete. He sat there just staring out to sea, not really thinking of anything other than what was within his vision.

He didn't know how long it was or why he became aware of it, but at some point he knew he wasn't alone. Even then he didn't move. He just stared out to sea. It was the sound of a song that drew him back to the land of the sane.

It was like nothing he'd ever heard before, and it filled him with such joy he began to laugh and cry at the same time. The notes were rich and full, soaring over him out to the water, reverberating back, it seemed, off the waves and wind to caress him again.

The song went on. He felt as if the notes and the sounds were coaxing something inside him to rise and fill him. He felt a sense of well being and place begin to return and, as if his mind was being rebuilt, he began to remember things from a little boy's world; dreams, dalliances, places, and people who spoke to him telling him stories of his own life as if painting his mind with remembrances.

Then he saw scenes from a still young, but older boy's life, some full of sadness, some of joy. A vision of a funeral for a man and a boy not much older than he, and he knew somehow, perhaps by the pain, they were his father and brother.

The vision continued with snippets from his life, until he saw himself on a ship and then in the end, he saw his own death.

In an almost painful moment, the singing stopped and so did his dream. He turned, looking to his side to see a man, an old man, sitting a short distance away, staring at him. He was balding, but with long flowing hair. His face was kind and gentle, framed by a beard flowing down his chest to his waist. He was dressed in a long white robe over which he wore a simple brown tunic. Gaspar noticed that his feet were bare and buried in the soft white sand of the beach.

"One takes for granted the feel of warm sand on one's feet, Gaspar. It is a pleasure so simple, but one I enjoy whenever the opportunity presents itself."

The old man's voice was so melodic it bordered on hypnotic. Gaspar stared back at the man for a moment before blurting out, "Is this heaven? Have I been saved from my watery grave and lifted into God's house?"

The man smiled and said, "No, Gaspar. Look to the east. This is Acre's harbor."

Gaspar turned, looking in the direction the man pointed, and saw, he was indeed sitting on the beach of Acre's harbor. But it wasn't the Acre he remembered. It was quiet, desolate, and only rubble and piles of stones remained of the once great fortress. It looked to be abandoned, and for some time at that.

"It has been almost a year since you left the city, Gaspar. It is gone now. Nothing remains of what you knew."

Gaspar turned back to the old man. "I don't understand. I was dead, wasn't I? Am I now alive again?"

The old man was silent for a moment before responding, "You were dead, brother. You lost your life out there in the ocean, but I brought you back. I raised you from your watery grave and brought you here to this beach. Even now, you are not fully alive as you once were. Whether or not you return fully to the land of the living is up to you and is why you find yourself here once more."

"I don't understand," Gaspar said. "If I'm not fully alive, what am I?"

"It is not so much what you are as where you are, my friend. This place where we sit is like a window. You are looking through the window at the world you once knew. You can see the world, but you are not yet a part of it. There is a door you can open to return. If, after we are through here, you choose to do so, you will open that door and be back in the world you knew. It will be your choice."

Gaspar stared at the man. "Who are you? What are you?"

"My name is Boniface," the old man answered. "As to what I am; what do you think I am?"

"Are you God?" Gaspar whispered.

The old man laughed. Not a laugh of derision, but a genuine laugh of mirth as if Gaspar had told a fine joke.

"No, Gaspar. I am not God, but I have been in the presence of the one you call God. You see, I am what you would call an angel, an archangel to be exact."

"You're an archangel?" Gaspar asked.

Boniface chuckled. "Perhaps I should have donned a set of wings? Or perhaps you expected someone more dramatic in appearance? Yes, I am an archangel."

Gaspar pondered this for a moment before speaking, "I'm confused. If I died, why did I not go to heaven? In fact, where was I for the last year? Why did you bring me back to this partial life?"

Boniface smiled and said, "It is one of the more common misconceptions of your faith that every soul goes immediately to some designated place, heaven, hell, or purgatory. Some souls possess a strength that allows them to resist the pull of whatever realm they are destined to.

"Some of the souls are evil, some are good. Some have things or people that bind them to this world so strongly they chose to stay among the living for a time.

"You see, even in death there is a choice. Eventually every soul must move on. Most who stay eventually make their journey on their own. Others must be judged and then taken by force.

"You are one of the good souls who made a choice not to go on from this world to your afterlife destination. You chose not to go because of your anger, the sense of failure you felt upon your death."

Gaspar interrupted, a question forming in his mind. "Where was I destined to go upon my death?"

Boniface quietly answered, "Your destination was purgatory."

Gaspar stared out to sea watching, but not really seeing a flock of birds diving at the water's surface.

He'd lived virtually his entire life in the service of his Lord and the Order. The fact he'd been destined to purgatory, and not heaven troubled him greatly.

"It troubles you that you were destined for purgatory," Boniface said, reading his mind. "It should. It is a place of atonement, and that atonement is difficult. It is different for each soul who goes there. The time spent there is unique to each soul.

"You were a devout and God fearing man, Gaspar. Your commitment and service was unquestioning but..." And here Boniface paused, his eyes looking into Gaspar's and holding them in an intense gaze. "You dealt death when you knew it was wrong. There were times, many in fact, when you followed the orders of your superiors even when you knew them to be wrong. You killed, when in your heart you knew that to do so was in violation of God's law.

"You confessed those sins and God heard those confessions. He knew them to be sincere and from your heart. It was those confessions that saved you from the damnation of Hell, but confessions do not absolve you of your duty.

"Your confession earned you the right to purgatory. Your piety, commitment, and anger prevented you from beginning that journey. I am here to give you another chance, another choice."

Gaspar was stunned at Boniface's words. The archangel had laid bare his sins, and he knew what he said was true. For years he'd slaughtered other humans, knowing deep in his soul that many of those deaths couldn't be justified. He'd followed blindly, all the while believing it was his duty to do so.

He'd known all of this, and now he felt the weight of his sins come crashing down upon him. Boniface had said he had another chance for atonement, another choice.

"What must I do, Boniface? I failed to complete the task I was given. How can I atone for my sins and my failure?" Gaspar asked.

"You have two choices," Boniface answered. "You can come with me now to purgatory and begin your time there. I can not tell you how long it will take or how difficult it will be. Or, there is a second path that only a few are offered. It is offered to you because of your commitment, your desire to serve and your skills. If you choose this path you will be able to fulfill your commitment and complete the task you were given. A task every bit as important as you were told it was.

"It is offered because you are a warrior, and it is a warrior's life I offer you."

"At what point are you going to cease this incessant rambling and tell this poor soul what we ask of him?"

Gaspar whirled around at the sound of a new voice behind him. Sitting cross-legged just a few feet away was what appeared to be a Saracen prince.

He was dressed from head to foot as if he were prepared to attend some royal event, clad in vibrantly colored silks, tasseled and bejeweled robes, and upon his head sat an ornate turban. He looked to be no older than twenty, with only a wisp of a beard and mustache.

Gaspar's hand instinctively went to his side feeling for his nonexistent sword, for lying across the Saracen's crossed legs was a nasty looking scimitar.

"Ha!" The stranger laughed. "Even now the warrior within him rises to the surface. As much as it pains me to say it, I do believe you have chosen wisely, Boniface. Now, can you please tell this mortal what we require of him? The infernal solitude of this place vexes me."

Gaspar turned back to Boniface, a questioning look on his face.

"You are late, as usual, Arusmus," Boniface said.

"Yes, well, it was a most delectable, sweet soul that delayed my arrival. I do so apologize," the stranger said mockingly.

"Excuse me!" interrupted a confused Gaspar. "Just who are you?"

"This is Arusmus. He is my opposite," Boniface said.

"Your opposite?" Gaspar asked.

"Oh, please! Can we move this along? What Boniface means to say, in his convoluted way, is that I am an angel as well, a fallen angel."

Gaspar stared at the cross-legged Arusmus. He turned back to Boniface, who simply nodded.

"You're a demon?" Gaspar blurted.

"Demon is such a crude human term and not very nice. But yes, a demon if you prefer, an important one at that," Arusmus said, laughing.

"Arusmus and I must agree that you are worthy, capable of the life you are being offered. We have agreed you are," Boniface said. "Now perhaps is the time to explain what we are offering you."

"Amen!" Arusmus whispered sarcastically, giving Gaspar a wink.

"Since the beginning of mankind, there has been a need for men like you, Gaspar," Boniface began. "From the very beginning, when the first human soul failed to follow its destiny and travel on, there was a battle between the forces of heaven and hell over these souls.

"Some of these souls were evil and caused great havoc among the living, while some just languished, never fulfilling their ultimate destiny.

"You see, Gaspar, in the realm of the living, neither side, Heaven nor Hell, is supposed to actively interfere in the matters of men or the souls who chose to stay here. But it was apparent something had to be done or else the world would eventually become uninhabitable due to the ever increasing number of wayward souls interfering in the lives of men."

"Wait a moment," Gaspar interrupted. "You said neither side is supposed to actively interfere in the affairs of man. What then of praying to God for help in times of need? What of miracles? How can you say good and evil, you or Arusmus, can't influence the acts of men?"

"Let me put it this way," Arusmus said. "If you were tempted to murder, I could not lift your hand and plunge the sword into your victim. I may whisper to you encouragement to commit such a deed, and I may rejoice when you have killed, but I can not make you sin.

"Likewise, Boniface can not keep you from killing. He may whisper his platitudes of peace and love, hoping you will resist your urges, but he can not stay your hand.

"It is a balance, an equilibrium that allows humans to live their lives and choose their paths without the interference of angels."

"It is about choice," Boniface continued. "You have the choice to sin or not to sin. Only you can decide your fate."

Gaspar was silent for a moment as he processed what he'd heard, then looking from Boniface to Arusmus, he asked, "What do you need me for? What could I possibly do for beings such as you?"

Both angels were silent for a time before Boniface broke the silence. "We want you to be a hunter of souls."

A hunter of souls; the very idea of it sent Gaspar's mind reeling. How did one do such a thing?

Gaspar could feel the eyes of both angels boring into him. He had a sudden unpleasant feeling as if both of them could read his mind.

At that thought, he heard Arusmus chuckle. He turned to find the demon smiling at him. "Oh, yes, Gaspar. Every thought running through your mind is open to us. I can tell what you are going to say before the words pass over your lips. It comes in quite handy when dealing with mortals."

Boniface interrupted, "Let me explain how this works. If a soul fails to move on from this realm, it falls to Arusmus and me to determine what action to take. If a soul is destined for heaven, then I instruct the hunter to deliver it there.

"Likewise, if the soul is bound for hell, Arusmus summons the hunter. If a soul is bound for purgatory, both Arusmus and I must summon the hunter."

Gaspar interrupted, "Why do both of you have a say in the souls destined for purgatory?"

"Because, Gaspar," Boniface said, "not every soul is able to atone for its sins. Not every soul continues on to heaven from purgatory."

The fact that his salvation wasn't guaranteed by a trip to purgatory wasn't something Gaspar wanted to dwell on.

"You said you were offering me a warrior's life. What did you mean by that?" Gaspar asked.

Arusmus spoke up. "As you can imagine, not every soul destined for hell wishes to go there. Many get quite angry, violent even, when the moment of truth arrives. Violence will come your way occasionally. You will need your skills at dealing death to survive."

"What Arusmus fails to add is the matter of crossing from the realm of mortals to the realms beyond," Boniface said. "In those realms it is not against our rules for one side or the other to intervene in each other's matters or the matters of someone like you. Occasionally Arusmus' brethren take an interest in a soul not destined for their realm."

At this Gaspar looked at the demon who gave a nonchalant shrug and said, "Not every one of my brothers is as dignified as I."

"These souls and demons could kill me?" Gaspar asked.

"Do not forget angels, Gaspar. Right, Boniface?" Arusmus said quietly, looking at the archangel.

"Yes, Gaspar. You could lose your life, the life that would be restored to you," Boniface said.

Putting aside that thought and the myriad of questions flooding his mind, Gaspar asked, "How long would I have to do this?"

"Until you atone; how long that would take is up to you," Boniface said. "This is all about choice. You can not be forced to make this choice. You can not be forced to atone."

Gaspar was about to give voice to a thought when Arusmus, obviously probing his mind, said, "Yes, your soul could end up with me."

Gaspar stared into the demon's eyes, seeing in an instant not a Saracen prince, but a being permeated with pure evil. He could feel it radiating from him, and without speaking, he heard Arusmus whisper into his mind, "I am not your friend, Templar. I would love nothing more than to torment your soul forever in ways you can not begin to imagine."

The demon's lips hadn't moved but Gaspar had heard him clearly.

The sound of Boniface's voice drove Arusmus from Gaspar's mind, "Arusmus speaks his truth, Gaspar. If you so choose, you could lose your soul. I do not want that, and I do not believe that is your destiny. I chose you because of your strength. Arusmus agreed because he wants to see you fail. Nothing makes the fallen ones happier than to steal the souls of the strong."

Gaspar felt anything but strong at the moment. "How can I possibly make this choice? It's impossible to decide!"

Boniface stood and walked over to Gaspar. Looking down, he offered his hand, saying, "Stand, Gaspar. It is time we showed you things."

CHAPTER 24

Acre, The Holy Land, 1292

Gaspar took Boniface's outstretched hand and stood. Once he was standing, the angel reached out and placed his hand gently on Gaspar's forehead and closed his eyes.

Gaspar felt as if he was propelled into a black space as a feeling of weightlessness overcame him. He lost all sense of direction and place and just before panic set in, he opened his eyes to find himself standing on the top of a tall building. He looked around to find Boniface sitting at a small table a short distance away drinking from a small chalice. Arusmus was leaning over the parapet of the roof, looking down on a vast city below them.

They were on a rooftop terrace that gave them a view across the entire skyline of the place.

"Ah, Rome!" Arusmus said, lifting his face to the sky and breathing in deeply. He seemed to be inhaling the very essence of the city. "Now, this is much better than that lonely and deserted beach, eh, Gaspar?"

"This is Rome?" Gaspar asked.

"Indeed," Arusmus answered. "The Lord's city, as they call it. You would not believe the number of souls I have harvested from this city so full of such pious and God-fearing mortals."

Gaspar didn't miss the sarcasm in his voice. They were joined by Boniface, who looked out over the city with them. It appeared to be late afternoon as the sun was low in the sky. Still, the sounds of a vibrant, chaotic metropolis reached their ears high on the rooftop.

"Why are we here?" Gaspar asked.

"We are here to show you what happens when souls do not move on from this realm," Boniface answered. "We are going to show you what is required of you. Somewhere out there in the warrens of this place is an evil soul who has refused to leave this world. He is destined for hell, but has no desire to move on. Today he will be taken there whether he wants to go or not."

In spite of his confusion and doubts, Gaspar could feel excitement building in the pit of his stomach.

"Nothing like the thrill of the chase, is there?" said a grinning Arusmus. With that, the demon vaulted over the side of the parapet and began floating downward toward the street below. Looking back and laughing, the falling Arusmus said, "Come on, Gaspar! Jump! We have a soul to find."

Gaspar noticed the beginning of a smile crossing Boniface's visage as he leapt the parapet and now, floating in mid-air, said to Gaspar, "Come, this is something you will not be able to do when you receive your life back. You will not be hurt."

Gaspar, still staring open-mouthed, clutched the wall with both hands. He'd never been a fearful man, but he'd never been exhorted to hurl himself into mid-air, off a tall building, by an archangel and a demon.

"Just use your mind. Jump out. Tell yourself to slowly fall to the ground. Let your mind control you and the space around you," Boniface said.

Taking a deep breath and actually closing his eyes, as if that would help to cushion the fall, he was sure was coming, he threw his legs over the edge and propelled himself into the air.

There was nothing. No plunging feeling, no pain. He opened his eyes to find he was floating above the ground next to Boniface. He looked below to find Arusmus already on the ground walking away through the crowds lining the street below.

"Come, Gaspar. Just tell yourself you want to go down to the street," said Boniface as he began to float downward to the ground.

As the thought entered his mind to float downward, he began moving slowly in that direction. He looked around as he made his way to solid ground, reveling in the feeling of weightlessness until, before he knew it, his feet were touching the cobblestoned sidewalk.

"Not bad, Gaspar," he heard Arusmus whisper into his mind. "I thought you might be too fearful to do it. Now come along. Our quarry is just a short walk away."

Gaspar looked down the street and could see the receding back of the demon as he made his way in and out of the crowds.

Gaspar realized Arusmus and Boniface were still dressed as they had been, something that made them stand out among the crowd of Romans. That he was clothed in a simple white robe did nothing to help him blend in.

"The mortals here can not see us," Boniface said as he headed off in the same direction as Arusmus. "We are completely invisible to them. There are others, though, who can see us." At that he pointed across the street in the direction of the opposite sidewalk.

Gaspar looked in the direction Boniface pointed and was startled to see two beings watching them intently. Both were strange creatures that looked as if they had been fused together from cats and humans. Their heads were like those of small house cats while the bodies could have been those of powerful human warriors. They were heavily muscled and, while they walked on two legs like men, they moved with all the grace and stealth of a feline.

"What are they?" Gaspar asked.

"Two of Arusmus' brothers," Boniface answered. "It is rare they would see one such as I, but I think it is you who draws their interest. They can sense your mortality, but are confused by your current state. You will see many other beings, some evil, some good, if you look closely."

Indeed, as Gaspar looked around, he began to pick out different beings among the mortals. As he hurried to keep up with Boniface, he saw the strangest creatures all unnoticed by the throngs of humans.

Sitting on the back of a cart horse was a beautiful woman whose body was surrounded in an aura of golden light. Her face, when she looked at him, almost made him weep with joy. She was so radiant that Gaspar stopped in his tracks transfixed, unable to move. She then turned away, and he found himself staring open-mouthed at a second face where the back of her head should have been. This second face was the twin of the other.

"She is a guardian angel," Boniface said while reaching out and pulling Gaspar along. "They are not always so visible. I would guess something is about to happen to the mortal whom she is assigned to."

The voice of Arusmus once again intruded into his mind. "Would you two hurry up please? I have found him."

"Come along, Gaspar. You must see this for yourself," Boniface urged.

They came upon Arusmus sitting at a wooden table outside the door of a nearly empty tavern. He had a glass in his hand, filling it from an urn in front of him.

"Have a seat," he said while gesturing toward two empty chairs. "Our wayward soul is right across the street. It should not be long now."

Gaspar sat down, as did Boniface, and looked in the direction Arusmus indicated with a nod. Directly across from them was another tavern, this one quite busy and full of people. The tables in front of the tavern were full of mortals eating and drinking, the mood festive. All of the patrons seemed to be in good spirits except for one.

Gaspar noticed a man sitting alone at a table, a plate of uneaten food and a carafe he didn't touch, in front of him. The man sat staring at the other patrons with an obvious look of loathing and malice as if angry at the frivolity taking place around him.

As Gaspar watched, he sensed something about the man he couldn't place. Just as he began to turn his attention elsewhere the man seemed to shimmer, losing shape and form ever so slightly. Gaspar blinked, thinking his eyes were playing tricks on him, and found that the man now looked normal again.

"Very good, Gaspar," Boniface said. "That is the soul for which we search. What you saw was his mortal form weakening and becoming unstable. The longer he stays here, the harder it will become for him to maintain the façade of mortality. In the meantime it allows him to mingle with mortals, unknown for what he is."

"So the humans around him can see him and have no idea of what he is?" Gaspar asked.

"That is correct," Boniface said. "If his form weakens and he allows it to fade, they can see that. He can allow it to fade completely if he chooses, but each time he does so, it becomes harder to reform himself. So he will try to maintain his mortal form as long as he can. This soul is a strong one. He has been here for some time and has wreaked havoc among the living."

"Who is he?" Gaspar asked.

"His name is Remuluc," this from Arusmus, who refilled his glass, swallowing the liquid in one motion. "He was a teacher of languages. Well respected and sought after by the wealthy of the city. They paid him well for the right to have their children instructed in Latin, Greek, French, and Arabic, to name a few. What they did not pay him for was to prey upon those same children. He had a perverse love for young children. Before he was discovered and beheaded by a mob of angry parents, he molested and killed over twenty children. The nastiest sort of mortal. Now he belongs to me."

A movement on the periphery of Gaspar's vision caught his eye. He turned to see a dark form moving along the sidewalk in the now lengthening shadows of sunset. He peered more intently, unable to quite make out the form that seemed to be able to move like a shadow itself.

"And now we begin," whispered Boniface. "Watch carefully."

Gaspar looked back at Remuluc, who was now standing. He was looking around the street as if he sensed something not quite right. For a moment his eyes lingered over the space inhabited by Gaspar and his companions, but then moved on.

"He didn't see us?" asked Gaspar.

"He may have sensed something not quite right about this space, but we are invisible to him. His pursuer is not," Boniface said.

Then a tumult erupted across the street. Remuluc, apparently sensing something even Gaspar couldn't see, sent a half dozen patrons flying head over heels as he catapulted himself through the tables and down the street at a speed that shocked Gaspar.

Close on his heels, he could now see a man in dark clothing clutching what looked like a short, thin sword in his hand, giving pursuit. The man had exploded from the shadows, and Gaspar knew this was the hunter.

"Come on, you two!" exclaimed Arusmus, heading off in pursuit. "This should be quite a show."

Gaspar followed Boniface as they effortlessly kept pace with the fleeing soul and his dogged pursuer through the throngs of yelling and screaming mortals. The chase went on through streets and alleys, at times into shops and houses, leaving a wake of startled and sometimes injured humans.

At one point the fleeing soul grabbed the bridle of a horse. As Gaspar watched, the soul's mortal form flickered and undulated, and he knew somehow it was trying to merge with that of the horse. The beast was so terrified, it took off, dragging a cart full of vegetables down the street. The soul now being dragged through the mud and filth eventually lost hold of the bridle and was trampled underfoot and wheel.

Once again fully formed, it leapt up, speeding off, the hunter in close pursuit.

Finally, Gaspar found himself in a dark trash-strewn alley that ended at the back of a brick building with only one way out, back the way they had entered. He caught up to Arusmus and Boniface, who were standing watching the spectacle unfolding before them.

At the end of the alley the soul of the murdering Remuluc stood with his back to the wall, cursing and screaming in a multitude of ever-changing languages at the dark clad stranger who stood blocking the way out.

Neither the wayward soul nor the hunter gave any indication they perceived the presence of the three spectators.

"It's time to go home, Remuluc," said the hunter in a deep, resonating voice. "Your days here have long since passed. Time to pay the piper."

"Who are you?" came the voice of the damned soul. "What makes you think you can compel me to do anything? Perhaps I should just crush you like a bug and send you to hell."

"By all means, give it a try," said the hunter, slowly sliding the sword under his coat, holding up his now empty hands in front of him.

The child killer Remuluc leapt forward with an unholy scream, attacking the hunter with the fury of twenty men. The attack was parried with a speed Gaspar would have never believed had he not witnessed it himself. Back and forth it went, with Remuluc attacking, trying to lay his hands on the elusive hunter, who danced and weaved around him, seemingly impervious and untouchable. Screams of rage echoed in Gaspar's ears as the frustrated soul was stymied at every turn.

Slowly, Remuluc's energy became spent, and Gaspar realized the hunter was wearing the soul down, robbing it of strength and venom.

Suddenly, in a move Gaspar almost missed, the hunter drew his sword and lunged forward, grabbing the head of the soul in one hand. With the other hand he plunged the sword into the side of Remuluc's neck until the blade was firmly embedded. The soul instantly stopped moving and screaming. It sagged against the hunter as if it had lost the ability to stand on its own.

"Now, that wasn't so bad, was it?" the stranger said. "If you had just gone along peacefully, none of this would have been necessary."

Remuluc's mouth slowly opened and closed like a fish out of water, but no sound emerged. His eyes blinked furiously, but he seemed incapable of any other movement.

Gaspar was watching the hunter whose back was to him when he saw him tense. He went deathly still and appeared to be listening intently. Slowly, while still holding the unmoving soul, he turned to face the three observers. He cocked his head slightly and said, "I can't see you, Boniface, but I know you're there, and who do you have with you? Is it that scum, Arusmus? I sense another as well, although for the life of me I can't place the nature of who's with you. If I had to bet, I'd say a mortal. Yet I can't see him."

Gaspar looked to Boniface to find him with an almost paternal smile across his face. Boniface waved his hand slightly at which point Gaspar sensed a feeling as if a wisp of a weight was lifted from him, and he found himself looking directly into the eyes of the hunter.

The man stared into his eyes for a moment before turning his gaze to Boniface.

"Well, well, Boniface and Arusmus in the same space, at the same time. It must be an auspicious occasion to warrant this little gathering. And what did you bring with you?" he asked. "Not a mortal."

He turned from Gaspar to Boniface, a look of bewilderment suddenly crossing his face. Nothing was said between them, but Gaspar could have sworn he'd seen something like relief passing over the man's face.

The voice of Arusmus intruded on the moment. "May I introduce William of Yorkshire. William, this is Gaspar de Rouse, most recently of the lovely port city of Acre and the watery depths of the ocean surrounding it. A Templar Knight as well, I do so hate that batch of cretins; no offense, Gaspar. We thought we should show Gaspar a true master in action. As always, you did not disappoint."

William stared hard into Gaspar's eyes, and Gaspar realized he was reading his thoughts.

"I learned their little trick a long time ago. I also learned how to close my mind to them. Something of utmost importance for one such as I. Tell me, Gaspar, are they trying to recruit you?"

Before Gaspar could answer, Boniface spoke, "How long have you been doing the Lord's work, William?"

"It's been three hundred and forty-five years, two months and ten days. But you know that, Boniface," William answered. "And it hasn't always been just the Lord's work I've been doing."

Then quietly and in a profoundly earnest voice, he asked, "Is there something you want to tell me?"

"Perhaps we should complete the task at hand, the delivery of this poor soul to his destination, before we go any further in that regard," Boniface said.

William gave him a hard look, then turned to Gaspar. "Get used to the never-ending dance, friend. Sometimes getting straight answers from these two seems the work of ten men."

William lifted the still blinking Remuluc in his arms and embraced him chest to chest.

"I assume you're all tagging along. Let's get this over with."

And with that he lowered his head to Remuluc's until their foreheads were touching and, closing his eyes, both the wayward soul and his captor vanished from sight.

"Come along, Gaspar," said Boniface as he placed his hand on Gaspar's forehead. "There is much more to see."

The darkness once more enveloped him as he was transported out of the world of the living to some unknown destination.

CHAPTER 25

In the realm of the boatman, 1292

The sound of water, unmistakable in a thundering way, greeted his consciousness, cutting through the dark like crashing waves of stone. He could see these gray monsters speeding toward him, giant crests curling along their edges like sneering hungry lips, even though the blackest dark enveloped his mind.

He felt a hand drift gently across his face, bringing a sense of burgeoning light even through his hard-clenched lids. Slowly, as if afraid opening his eyes would chase away the embryonic light, Gaspar stole a glimpse and saw a light not unlike the dawn.

With that first glimpse, the tiny ripples on the surface of what looked to be a large lake or broad river gave chase to the phantom waves, leaving only the lapping of water on pebbly shore.

Boniface stood absolutely still, and beside him the demon, Arusmus, did the same. Both stared off across the water as if waiting or listening for something to happen. Gaspar glanced around him to find William, still holding the limp Remuluc under his arm like a rolled up carpet, standing behind him. He, too, stared into the dark horizon.

A different sound reached his ears then, the sound of water being cut and the sliding of a thing through the ripples coming his way. He imagined some creature gently swimming through the calm waters, its body gliding through the surface in an almost silent approach.

Then the sound of a gentle splash and he knew an oar had struck the glassy surface. A boat was coming their way, from where he couldn't tell.

William's voice interrupted his straining thoughts. "The boatman comes. The landing is over this way, Gaspar. Follow me."

He headed off along the shore, and after confirming that Boniface followed as well, Gaspar went after the hunter along the sandy shoreline.

After a short walk he began to make out a light, perhaps a lantern of some sort. As they gained on its location he could make out a wooden quay stretching some distance from the beach into the water.

When they reached the dock, William turned onto it and began walking toward the far end. Gaspar followed until they reached the terminus, which was lit by an iron lamp hanging from a pole.

"We'll wait here for a moment. It won't be long now. See the boatman's light?" William asked.

Gaspar peered into what seemed the perpetual dawn and could just make out a slowly approaching light. He could hear the now unmistakable sound of a boat cutting through the water toward them.

"Where are we, William?" he asked.

"This is the realm of the boatman," he said. "This is the first stopping point in the journey from the mortal world into the worlds of Boniface and Arusmus. It's a realm of perpetual twilight where neither good nor evil prevails. You notice our angelic friends have become somewhat quiet? Well, it's because neither holds sway here, nor do they lay claim to this place."

He turned to find both Arusmus and Boniface simply staring off over the water. It was as if both angels were there in the flesh, but their minds, perhaps their souls, were somewhere else.

"They can't harm each other here," William continued, "in fact, I've wondered for many years whether they even inhabit their forms in this place. I've never been able to get either side to explain it fully. It's actually the only place where I ever feel at peace anymore. No angels, demons, or their assorted pets and playthings hounding me or trying to steal my thoughts. You'd do well to remember that as you ponder the choice I'm sure they've offered you."

Gaspar was about to speak to William's comment when a quiet sound reached his ears. He looked toward the approaching light and could clearly see the shape of a boat approaching. A figure stood in the stern, slowly pushing a paddle back and forth through the water.

The sound he heard was singing, a low, quiet sound that instantly struck him as a woeful lament. The notes of the song were hauntingly desolate and so full of unhidden anguish that tears began to fall down his cheeks at their sound.

"You get used to his songs. The first few times I heard them, I did what you're doing now. I finally came to understand why he sings the songs he does, and it helped insulate my soul against them," William said, seeing Gaspar's tears.

"Why does he sing these songs?" Gaspar asked.

"He sings this song for Remuluc. He sings a song of loss over a soul destined for hell. If the soul we carried was bound for heaven, his songs would be so joyful you'd shed tears of happiness. If we were traveling to purgatory, his songs would be songs of strength and fortitude, hoping to give the soul courage for what lies ahead. I think it's his way of trying to ease the burden of the job he does. Or maybe he's just insane, I don't know. I've tried to talk with the old man, if that's what he is, but he's never said a word in all these years."

Gaspar stared transfixed as the boat, now only yards away, slowly glided toward him, the song now fading in volume, the notes drifting off like spectral tears into the hazy twilight of the horizon.

His gaze fell upon the man, the being, whatever he was, in the stern of the boat. If such a thing as an aged God lived and breathed, this thing wielding a paddle that Gaspar wondered if he could even lift, was surely it.

The man's face looked to be of an age beyond measure, but his body was as lithe and youthful as a man of twenty. He was clad only in a simple loin cloth, nothing more. The muscles, like cords of heavy rope, stood out under his skin and moved as if snakes inhabited his body. The hair on his head was long, but bare on the crown and was of a white that reminded Gaspar of the snows that fall on the mountains of the Pyrenees.

But it was the eyes that held Gaspar, for they looked not at him or anyone else on the dock but beyond them into places only he could comprehend. Gaspar could see a thousand years in those eyes, and it chilled him to the bone.

"I would wager it's many thousands if it's one," whispered William.

The boat bumped against the quay, and Gaspar took the measure of it. It wasn't a large boat; probably only large enough to hold the party standing on the dock. It was wide of beam, though, and looked as if it had been built from a solid piece of wood. It had no seams down the sides, but the grain of some dark heavy tree could be seen running down the length of it.

The boatman threw a rope to William, who pulled the bark tight against the dock and bade Gaspar aboard with a wave of his hand. Gaspar carefully climbed into the boat near the front, watching as the still silent and seemingly comatose Boniface and Arusmus took seats just behind him.

William unceremoniously tossed the limp Remuluc onto the floor of the boat at Gaspar's feet before jumping in and settling beside him.

Almost immediately the boatman began pushing the boat away from the dock toward the horizon.

"Where are we going now?" Gaspar asked.

"We're going to the fallen side," William answered. "The boatman will take us to the spot where we'll disembark. Then we must make our way to the place where I'll turn over this wretched soul to Arusmus' brethren. It's a trip that never ceases to exact its toll upon me, for even knowing what I know about the souls I transport to this place, I shudder at what awaits them. Even now I don't wish it upon anyone."

Gaspar turned to William and asked, "Why did you choose this life, and did you choose wisely? Was it worth it?"

William was silent for a moment before he answered, "Who can say? I've seen purgatory; the place I was destined for. I've stood outside the walls and heard the laments and the wails of agony flowing from the place like some sort of river of pain. But I've also heard the joy mixed in with those cries. I've heard the sounds of joyous release when souls attain their goal and their penance is over. It's like nothing you've ever heard. The upwelling of happiness; no, perhaps it's re-birth gives me hope.

"What I've endured, I believe, is less painful than what those souls have gone through, but in other ways no less difficult. You see, I don't know if what I've done, what I've accomplished, is enough. Have I atoned for my sins? Will I be relieved of this duty and be transported to the heaven I crave? Or has this life of immortality, living among sin and depravity, still dealing death on too numerous an occasion, left me bereft of salvation? Will Arusmus have my soul?

"I still don't know. And that haunts my every breath. At some point those two will have to tell me, for I don't believe I can continue this life much longer.

"Don't underestimate the weight of immortality when one lives among mortals, Gaspar. I was always a solitary man as a mortal so I gave no thought to loneliness. I've felt the sting of demon's claws ripping at my flesh and have endured the endless brutality of wayward souls upon my body. I'd prefer to feel the fangs of a dozen of Arusmus' brethren upon my skin than to live another day alone. Immortality is the ultimate state of loneliness."

Gaspar was struck by the depth of sadness and longing William's words contained. This man who appeared as hard as stone, who gave every impression of being able to stand toe to toe with the worst of hell, seemed like a lonely and wayward child, but only for a moment, for as quickly as he'd let down his guard, Gaspar sensed it rising again as William turned to the two angels behind him. Waving a hand in front of them, he said, "Are you two with us or are you still like babes in the womb?"

Boniface was the first to show some signs of life as his eyes began blinking rapidly, looking this way and that.

"Ah, past the limits of that place finally," he said.

Arusmus as well seemed to reanimate and, looking around, said, "If I could strangle God for His creation of that place, I would give up my soul to do it!"

"I think your soul is already spoken for, demon," William said. "I do wonder, though, if I should have availed myself of the opportunity to have introduced your neck to my knife while you sat there like some spellbound invalid."

Arusmus said nothing, but if hate could be seen, Gaspar would swear he saw it flowing from his eyes into William.

"So, Gaspar, has William explained where we are going?" Boniface asked. "Has he told you of what awaits us on the shore where Arusmus and his fellow angels reign?"

"He's told me where we're going," Gaspar said, "but he hasn't told me what to expect once we arrive."

"Perhaps Arusmus should be the one to enlighten you," Boniface offered.

The demon still stared maliciously at William, who returned his gaze unwavering.

"I think it best to just wait and let Gaspar see for himself what awaits the child killer at his feet. I would not want to spoil the surprise," Arusmus whispered.

And then, as if announcing that their voyage was about to end, the boatman began to sing again.

CHAPTER 26

In the realm of the boatman, 1292

The song of lament began again, the notes powerful and deep, prompting Gaspar to turn and watch the boatman as he paddled and sang.

"We'll be there shortly," William said.

"So soon?" Gaspar asked.

"In these realms, great distances are traveled in the blink of an eye, Gaspar," William said. "If you were to live a hundred years in the mortal world, I doubt you'd even begin to cross this river. The worlds these two invite you to inhabit stretch on forever, and our mortal minds can't begin to comprehend their vastness. I quit trying many years ago in interest of maintaining my sanity."

William nodded in the direction the boat was traveling, and Gaspar could now see a light similar to the one on the dock they had so recently left.

In a quiet voice Boniface spoke, "When we land, Gaspar, you are to go with William and Arusmus. It is a short distance to where Remuluc will be handed over. Arusmus has agreed to escort you and to guarantee your safety. You must see what awaits this soul and what happens at the end of his journey. William will be your guide. Do exactly as he says."

"You'll not be coming with us, Boniface?" Gaspar said in a troubled voice.

"I can not leave the dock on the fallen side. This place belongs to those like Arusmus. Even I would not fare well there," Boniface answered.

A chuckling Arusmus interrupted, "Yes, I would imagine there are legions of my brethren who would rise up for a chance at Boniface. Do not worry, Gaspar; with me along, no one will bother you. At least not today. Even William will breathe a little easier, right, dear William?"

William said nothing in response to the demon's prodding.

Gaspar was startled by the bumping of the boat against the dock and followed William, again carrying Remuluc, and Arusmus from the boat. Nervously, he turned to Boniface, who simply nodded as if to say "Go."

The little group walked down the quay until it ended on a sandy shore, not unlike the one they had left at the beginning of their trip.

Arusmus headed off in the direction of what appeared to be an ancient stone building a short walk down the beach. Gaspar watched as William paused at the end of the dock, his head swiveling from side to side as if looking for some hidden danger.

"Come on, William," Arusmus called over his shoulder. "Have a little trust for a change. I said you both are under my care today. I give you my word."

The sound the demon uttered, a kind of chortle that rattled Gaspar's soul, did nothing to calm the nerves of the obviously suspicious William.

"Normally, once off the dock, we're in their lands and all bets are off. Even though I'm bringing them a soul, they would love nothing more than to ambush me and tear me apart. Most of the time they stand down, but these demons have no morals. I've had to kill more than my share just to get back to the dock on many an occasion. Stay close and do what I say," William cautioned.

Stepping off the dock, William headed after Arusmus, who had almost reached the stone building. The moment Gaspar, set foot in the sand he was assaulted by an almost overwhelming sense of dread. The revulsion that swept over him was so great, he thought he'd collapse from the very weight of it. He stumbled and, for a moment, thought his heart, suddenly pounding in panic, might explode in his chest.

William reached out a steadying hand. "Easy, my friend. Just take deep breaths for a moment and steady yourself. They're testing you. They want to see what you're made of. You mustn't panic or flee. Nothing excites these scum more than a mortal in spiritual distress."

"What am I feeling, William?" Gaspar asked.

"You're feeling the evil of this place," he said. "The untold numbers of souls torn asunder and devoured here have left their trace. The demons here can use that leftover power as a weapon."

Suddenly Gaspar's mind was invaded by the voice of Arusmus, "Come now, Gaspar, I am disappointed in you. Are you so weak that simply stepping into my realm brings you to your knees in abject terror? I thought you much stronger than that."

"Get out of his head, Arusmus," came William's voice, inside his head as well. "You know very well the effect this place has on one who's never been here before. Cease your cheap tricks and stay true to your word or I'll drop this soul in the river, and you can spend the next thousand years trying to fish him from the belly of whatever beasts call it home."

Instantly, the feeling of dread and fear lifted, and Gaspar's heart began to beat normally. The soul-grating sound of Arusmus' demonic chuckles faded from his head as William gestured to follow.

They made their way to the building where Arusmus stood waiting, a sardonic grin plastered on his face. Gaspar could now see what had appeared to be a building was actually a stone wall stretching off into the distance as far as he could see. Arusmus stood before a large gate, his hands raised slightly from his sides as if holding back an unseen force. Two heavy wooden doors stood open behind him through which he could see nothing but an impenetrable darkness.

Gaspar was startled by a commotion to his side and turned to find William struggling to control the lost soul still tucked under his arm. Remuluc, even though he still seemed to be under whatever spell William had placed on him, was now struggling and thrashing, his mouth thrown wide open in what he knew was a silent scream of terror. Gaspar thought the killer's eyes were going to burst from his head as they stared wildly at the open gate.

"He knows now what awaits him, Gaspar," Arusmus said in a quiet voice. "He senses the end. What he does not know is it is only the beginning. A soul as strong as his will serve us well for a thousand years, and the torments awaiting him leave me weak with anticipation."

Arusmus stared into Gaspar's eyes. "Watch carefully, Templar. Imagine that this could be your end."

Arusmus raised his left hand slightly, and a wind of such strength that it knocked Gaspar backwards to the ground erupted from the gates. He looked up to see William standing in place, still holding the now violently thrashing Remuluc, braced against the wind.

A moment later, a smell so foul he began to wretch reached Gaspar's nose, and from the gate sprang a dozen creatures seemingly conjured from a nightmare. They were loathsome beasts covered in oily black scales, growling and howling like wild animals. They walked on two legs and had two arms as well, but that was where any resemblance to humans ceased. Their heads were those of birds of prey, but with the mouths of some sort of lamprey-like beast, full of glistening yellow fangs. They moved in a hellish cadence of demonic communion as if their minds were linked as one.

They clustered around Arusmus, but their eyes were focused on Remuluc. It was only the fallen angel's command that held them in check.

"It is time, William," Arusmus said. "Let us show Gaspar what happens at the end of this road."

William's eyes never left Arusmus as he reached into his coat and removed his sword. The beasts began to shriek and wail in voices so loud Gaspar had to clamp his hands over his ears to keep his mind from cracking.

William placed Remuluc at his feet. Never taking his eyes off Arusmus, he slid the blade deep into Remuluc's neck. He paused for a moment, one foot planted on his back, and then, in one fluid movement, he twisted the blade slightly and pulled it from his neck while diving backward, rolling to a stop beside Gaspar, then, jumping to his feet, he held the sword out in front of him.

The beasts were on Remuluc in an instant, the soul disappearing beneath a twisting and convulsing pile of demons. Gaspar was reminded of watching wild dogs tearing at the bodies of the dead and wounded on the battlefields of his past life. The sounds of unholy screams tore at his mind until he had to look away.

He found Arusmus still staring at him, not a trace of his sardonic smile to be found.

The demon's voice ghosted into his mind, "I do so hope you will take up our offer, Gaspar, because, unlike Boniface, I believe it will be the death of your soul. What you see here today will be nothing compared to what I will do to you when you are brought writhing and whimpering before me."

Arusmus lifted his hand, and the pack of rabid demons pulled back from their prey. Gaspar reluctantly looked to see that what had been a human form was now reduced to nothing but scraps of bloody bone and sinew spread across the sand. But the sounds of Remuluc's tortured voice continued its wailing and, looking closer, he could see a huddled and battered form, a ghostly apparition almost unseen, now lying on the sand.

Arusmus walked over to the apparition and, reaching down gently, almost paternally, he lifted the vaporous thing and held it to his chest. Turning his eyes to Gaspar, he opened his mouth wider and wider until it was a huge gaping abyss. Then, with both hands, he jammed the wailing soul into the opening and swallowed. He then raised his arms above him, lifted his head to the sky, and let loose a cry of demonic joy that shook the ground.

Then he was gone, Arusmus, the demons, and the soul of Remuluc, as if they had never been.

"Come on, Gaspar," William said, reaching down and pulling him to his feet. "Arusmus is gone now, and so I assume is his protection."

Gaspar hurried after William, who wasted no time making his way down the beach. They reached the dock without interruption and walked to the end where the boat sat waiting. Gaspar stepped into the boat, followed by William.

The boatman silently pushed off, heading back into the river. Boniface said nothing for some time, and Gaspar, still reliving what he'd just seen, had no interest in talking. William, too, was silent.

Gaspar tried to push the horrific images of Remuluc's end from his mind. He'd been a warrior and, as such, he'd witnessed scenes of devastating horror, some doled out by his own hand. Never had he felt so completely desolate. He felt as if his very soul would break apart. He wanted nothing more than to cry to the heavens in anger.

How could this be? How could his God allow such a thing to happen, even to one such as Remuluc? To know that this fate was what waited for so many laid waste to his mind. He felt a hand on his shoulder and heard Boniface's voice from behind.

"That is exactly how your God feels every time he loses one of his creations. He feels every one. Even those like Remuluc who became possessed of such evil. He was born free of evil, and that is how your God remembers him. That is how you should remember him."

Gaspar said nothing for the remainder of the trip across the river. Silence weighed heavy on the boat, with only the sound of the water and the rhythmic paddling of the boatman intruding on his thoughts.

When they reached the dock, they all disembarked, walking toward the beach. Gaspar turned back to find the boatman staring into his eyes.

He thought he saw the old man's head nod slightly in his direction before he turned and pushed the boat off into the twilight.

A song reached his ears as he watched the boat disappear into the haze. Gaspar didn't know how he knew it, but the song was a song of hope, the notes lifting his spirit ever so slightly.

"Come, Gaspar," whispered Boniface. "I want to show you more."

CHAPTER 27

Paris, May 2010

Dominicus sat behind the wheel of a gray Peugeot sedan, a nondescript vehicle that never drew unwanted attention. He was parked in a quiet Paris suburb of nineteenth and twentieth century mansions. Well-made, three foot tall, wrought iron fences decorated the small front yards of each house.

His attention was on one house in particular, three residences down the street from where he sat. His attention was actually on the man tending to the small, but stylish garden in front of the house. Oblivious of his surroundings he pruned a well-trained, rose bush climbing the iron fence.

Dominicus pondered the phone call from Zurich he'd received earlier. The art dealer's report had surprised him. Not so much that the painting had shown up, but who had been carrying it.

The more he thought about it, the more he realized he should have anticipated that Randolph Donovan would ensnare his grandson, Alex, in the Arimathean's world.

He thought about all he knew about the younger Donovan. During their surveillance of Randolph, the Order had compiled dossiers on each of

Randolph's children and later his grand children. None of them had been noteworthy except one, Alexander Donovan.

Dominicus picked up an I-Pad from the seat next to him and with a few swipes of his finger, eventually clicked on a folder. A picture of a man filled the screen. The face looking back at him, while handsome, radiated an aura that Dominicus had seen many times before. His mouth and jaw line imparted ruggedness, but it was his eyes that told the story. They were the eyes of someone who had seen unfathomable violence and lived to tell about it.

He scrolled down the screen with his finger, stealing a glimpse back up the street at the man still sculpting away at the rose bush. A scan of Donovan's military identification card appeared, followed by a series of official looking documents. Alex Donovan's entire military record had been accessed by one of the Order's members in the Pentagon. Dominicus had read through it several times and couldn't help but be impressed.

Donovan had been decorated several times, in secret, for bravery and injuries sustained during combat operations. The last injury and the events around it were what caught Dominicus' attention.

He had read the after-action report from Donovan's last mission four times now. The operation was a search and destroy mission in the mountains of Afghanistan. A particularly nasty terrorist, responsible for the deaths of four Navy service men, who had been drinking in a German bar when it exploded, had been hiding out for some time. He was untouchable, and according to intel reports, planning new strikes.

When the C.I.A. received a tip that the killer in question was hiding out in a small village in a remote valley in the Hindu Kush, Alex Donovan's Seal team had been dispatched.

Alex and three other members of his team had been transported via helicopter into the remote valley, and for three days kept the village under surveillance from concealment in the hills above.

On the fourth day, a goatherder, a boy no more than ten, had stumbled upon one of Alex's team hiding in a small cave. The Seal had captured the boy and alerted Alex who rushed into the cave just as the other Seal put a knife to the boy's throat. Alex stopped him from killing the boy and after a brief, but heated discussion, he sent the boy away. Hurriedly, he set about evacuating their positions knowing their presence might be revealed.

Sparing the boy was the only mistake Dominicus could find that Alex ever made as a warrior. Before they could evacuate, Alex's team was surrounded by over one hundred Afghan tribesmen, loyal to the terrorist.

For over six hours, the Seals fought a running battle through some of the most treacherous territory in the world. Slowly one by one, despite inflicting heavy losses on their pursuers, the Seals began to fall. Out of ammunition and fighting to the death with knives and then hand to hand, they all died except Alex.

Near the end, as the sun dipped behind the mountain tops, while wounded in three different places, Alex made his stand. In a shallow ravine exposed to fire from above, he took shelter behind a group of large rocks. With his last few rounds of ammunition, he traded fire with the Afghans, dispatching six by the time darkness set in, but not before a ricochet from an AK-47 hit him in the left knee.

Perhaps afraid to attack in the dark and unaware of the severity of his wounds, the Afghans decided to wait for light to resume their attack. Delirious from the pain and loss of blood, Donovan drifted in and out of consciousness, until some time during the night, something strange happened. It was something that caught Dominicus' attention instantly.

Donovan had related that at some point during the night he awoke to find a tall man standing over him. The man was dressed like an Afghan tribesman and at first Donovan thought the man meant to kill him. Instead, the man picked up Donovan, and miraculously avoiding the Afghans who waited in the dark, transported him through the mountains for several hours until dawn began to break in the east.

The man never said a word, he just carried him through the night until they reached a small village. There, the people, showing an almost reverential deference to the Good Samaritan, took Alex in and provided him with water and food.

Before the man left, he dressed Donovan's wounds and then disappeared without ever saying a word to Alex. Blaming it on his delirium, Alex was unable to give a description of the man who had saved him.

Three days later, after a member of the village had hiked to an Afghan Army post, another Navy Seal Team arrived by helicopter and evacuated Alex.

Donovan couldn't explain his savior's actions. Dominicus thought he could and it gave him pause.

Donovan's appearance had set him on edge. The young man spent the last ten years living a sedate and non-eventful life since retiring from the Navy, after his career-ending injury. Somehow Dominicus knew that didn't matter. Donovan could be a formidable opponent. It was time to get to Zurich.

Setting aside the I-Pad, and making sure the object of his surveillance was still at work, Dominicus retrieved a small leather case from the glove compartment. Opening it, he extracted a syringe filled with a clear liquid. Taking out a needle from the same case, he fitted it into the syringe and looked around for any sign of pedestrians before exiting the car.

He walked down the sidewalk until he was standing across the fence from the gardener. It was only then that the man sensed Dominicus' presence. The shock of recognition gave way to confusion.

"Dominicus. What are you doing here?" the man asked.

"Hello, Jonathon. Your roses are beautiful."

Dominicus' right hand flashed out, over the fence, grabbing Jonathon by the arm, pulling him close, as if in an embrace. To any observer, they would appear to be hugging like old friends.

Dominicus' left arm went around Jonathon's neck and the syringe hidden in his hand came to rest against the man's jugular vein. Staring into Jonathon's eyes, Domincus saw them go wide with fear as he plunged the needle in deep.

"You have doubts Jonathan. We cannot abide that," Dominicus whispered in the man's ear.

It was all over in ten seconds. Dominicus, not bothering to say another word, turned and headed back down the street to his car.

Jonathon on the other hand, could only hold onto the fence as he realized he was dying. The cold, heavy feeling spreading through him eventually reached his heart which stopped beating instantly. He collapsed amongst his beloved roses as Dominicus slowly drove by in the Peugeot.

Dominicus headed north out of Paris, studiously adhering to the speed limit. He hadn't given a second thought to his former compatriot, Jonathon. What consumed him now was Alex Donovan.

His thoughts were interrupted by the quiet chirping of his cell phone.

"Yes." Dominicus said.

He listened for almost a minute.

"Very good. I'll deal with it myself. I should be at the airfield in five minutes. The plane is standing by and I'll be in Zurich within the hour," he said into the phone, before disconnecting the call.

A frown creased his forehead. This was an unneeded diversion. The phone call had been from a person tasked with monitoring the phone tap on Roberto Lang's phone.

Apparently, after talking with Dominicus, the bastard made a call to someone else. Dominicus listened to a recording of the phone call.

He pulled off the motorway and, after driving down a small country road for a few miles, pulled into a small airfield. A lone metal hangar stood beside an immaculate, paved runway. Sitting on the tarmac was a Gulfstream G4 jet.

Dominicus pulled up to the hangar and a man immediately exited the building and approached him. Grabbing a small leather bag out of the back seat, Dominicus handed the man the car keys and headed to the plane.

The whine of the jet engines picked up a notch as he ascended the stairway and before he was ensconced in a leather chair in the main cabin, the jet was already taxing down the runway. He had called an hour before and told the pilot to ready the plane for take-off the minute he arrived.

The Gulfstream was owned by a corporation in the Cayman Islands which actually was just a front for the Order. The pilot had made many of these flights over the years for Dominicus.

As the plane roared into the sky, and the pilot directed it toward Zurich, Dominicus laid his head back and closed his eyes; within moments, he was sleeping. The last vision that flashed through his mind before he drifted off was of Alex Donovan being carried through the mountains by the unknown stranger. He thought he knew the man's name.

CHAPTER 28

Zurich, Switzerland, May 2010

Alex sat on the bed in his hotel room contemplating the pictures before him. As he had read the story of Gaspar, as related by the painter Bartholomew, the paintings in the old manuscript had followed the story. On one page was a painting of an old man standing in the rear of a boat paddling it across a turbulent body of water. On another page was a beautiful painting of four men sitting in the same boat, the man standing behind them obviously singing in full voice.

On and on it went, the narrative of Gaspar's adventures illustrated in fabulous artwork.

As Alex had read of Gaspar's journey to the gates of hell, the paintings had left him breathless and at times had evoked a palpable feeling of dread.

He was transfixed, and even the persistent pangs of hunger failed to drive him from the book. Unable to resist, he decided to read on for a while longer, then he would get some dinner from the hotel's restaurant.

A beautiful drawing of an ancient castle perched on the edges of a sheer cliff above a crashing ocean marked the spot in the book where he had stopped reading.

He began again.

The coast of England, 1292

Gaspar awoke to the sound of gulls and the crashing of waves on the shore. This time there was no darkness as a bright rectangle of dawn flooded the room from a window high up in the wall.

He slid off the bed, shivering at the cold. Pulling on his robe and stepping into the sandals which sat at the foot of the cot, he walked out of the small room into a long hallway. He saw a stairway at one end and headed toward it, going down the stairs into a large foyer. Before him was a large wooden door that stood slightly open. He went to it and, going through, found himself on a cliff overlooking an ocean disappearing into the horizon. A gray sky, leaden with dark storm clouds racing by, greeted him.

He stood for a moment trying to gain his bearings, remembering the events of the previous night. He'd spent almost the entire night tormented by nightmares of his sojourn to the gates of hell. The safety of the dawn had finally chased away the recurring dreams where he'd taken the place of the damned soul Remuluc. His dreams had been full of the sounds and sensations of demons slowly peeling away his mortal flesh, revealing the indefensible soul beneath. The fallen angel Arusmus had repeatedly devoured his soul in what had seemed an unending torment.

Now with the fresh sea air filling his lungs, cleansing his mind, he thought of where he was and how he'd arrived. He remembered only traversing the blackness from the realm of the boatman, ending up in a dark, forbidding castle William said was his home. He'd followed his host to a tiny room where he'd collapsed in complete exhaustion.

Great drops of rain began to fall as thunder cascaded down in waves around him. He lifted his head to the sky, letting the drops caress his face until he was soaked to the skin by the wind-driven torrent. Gentle rivulets of rainwater ran down his face and, opening his mouth, he savored the salt on his tongue. They tasted like the tears he'd shed in the dark of the night.

"While I love a good bath as much as the next man, perhaps you'd be better off coming in out of the rain, Gaspar."

Gaspar opened his eyes to find William striding up a dirt path leading to the cliff. As he passed him, entering the house, he said, "Besides, it's January on the coast of England. One could catch his death out in this weather."

Gaspar followed the Englishman into the house. William closed the heavy door and bade him follow. "Come on, I think our angelic friend Boniface is the only wise one here, as he's ensconced in front of my fire."

Gaspar followed William down a large, vaulted foyer into a great hall with a ceiling soaring above the flagstone flooring. At the far end, Gaspar could see a huge fireplace with a roaring fire in the hearth and could instantly feel the warmth radiating from it, filling the room. He looked around the room as he headed for the fire and saw great banners, flags, and tapestries hanging from the massive wooden beams of the rafters. Along the walls hung the skins and mounted heads of animals, many of which Gaspar had never seen before.

The floor under his feet was covered in rugs of all colors and sizes, every one of them a stunning work of art.

Sitting in an ornately carved chair by the fire was Boniface. He turned, greeting Gaspar with a smile. "Did you sleep well, Gaspar?"

"I actually have never slept so poorly in all my life," Gaspar responded as he stepped to the fire, feeling the warmth drying him. "I spent the night being devoured by Arusmus and his demonic hordes."

"Yes, well, I guess that is to be expected after seeing such an infernal display. How many times have you witnessed the passing over of souls to Arusmus and his brethren, William?" Boniface asked.

William stood before the fire, next to Gaspar, holding his hands toward it, warming them. He didn't respond for some time. When he did, it was in a quiet voice. "No one ever showed me that before I made my choice. No one ever asked if I could bear the weight of handing over a thousand souls to the likes of Arusmus. To this day I can remember each and every one of them. Every time I watch it, I feel like a bit of my soul gets devoured as well.

"I know they go there in scores every day, every hour, but it's I who hands over those few who cross my path. I'm the one who takes them there and feeds them to those beasts."

"You may be the one who takes them there but they made the choice to go," Boniface responded. "You are simply the vessel which transports them. If not you, another, and when you're gone, another. There'll always be one like you. Lost souls like Remuluc will always be. Likewise, you carry across the river in the other direction those who have attained what you seek, and you know the joy that comes from that journey. Does that not help to assuage your guilt?"

"In many ways it makes it worse," William said. "I've seen what we're meant for, the opposite of what awaits in the realm of the fallen. Every time I take a soul to the gates of heaven, it becomes harder to leave one at the gates of hell."

Gaspar was silent during their exchange, knowing full well both were speaking for his benefit, Boniface trying to assuage his fears, and William warning him of what he faced. If he was forced to choose at this moment, he would ask to be taken to the boatman for the ride to purgatory.

Boniface knew this.

"I think it is time we go in search of one of those souls destined for our Lord's realm. I want Gaspar to see what it means to help a wayward soul complete the journey to heaven. He has seen what lurks beyond hell's gate. Now you must see what waits beyond heaven's."

Boniface stood from his chair and moved to Gaspar's side.

"You certainly know how to play this game well, Boniface, I'll give you that" William said. "Fine, I'm ready when you are."

CHAPTER 29

Ireland, 1292

The three of them stood on a hill looking down on a tiny hamlet in the waning light of the day. Smoke rose from the chimneys of many of the houses, and Gaspar rubbed his hands together, trying to work some warmth into them.

He had no idea where they were. The journey from William's castle had been quick, and he found himself getting used to the feeling of stepping into blackness and arriving in far off lands.

"This is the land of the Irish, Gaspar," came Boniface's voice. "The soul we seek refuses to leave this place. Grief and sadness ties her here. It is time for William to convince her to complete her journey."

William had already begun making his way down the hillside ahead of them. Gaspar and Boniface followed a short distance behind.

They reached the first of the little hovels on the outskirts of the village and began making their way down a muddy main street winding through the houses. Gaspar watched as William searched, stopping now and then, raising his face to the sky. With eyes closed, he looked every bit the wild creature straining for a whiff of his prey. After a moment like this, he would move on peering into windows and down alleyways.

Suddenly he froze. Boniface and Gaspar stopped behind him. This time his head was bowed, and Gaspar could see his lips moving silently. This went on for some time before the sounds of a soothing song began to escape from William's mouth. Slowly, as the tune increased in volume, he lifted his head, and with eyes still closed, he began to sing in full voice. It sounded like the song Boniface had been singing on the beach when Gaspar had risen from his watery grave.

Gaspar looked at Boniface to see that he, too, had his eyes closed, a look of beatific peace on his face. His lips mimicked the movements of William's, but no sound emerged.

Gaspar found himself slowly falling under the spell of the music until he was slowly rocking from side to side, eyes closed, reveling in the beautiful notes. They stood there, the three of them, in the middle of the muddy street, for what seemed like hours until suddenly William's song stopped mid-note. Gaspar opened his eyes to find a young woman clad in the simple dress of a peasant, standing in the street before them, staring silently at them, a look of wonder on her face.

"Who are you?" she asked in a quivering voice.

William took a step toward her, his hands outstretched. "We're your friends, Ailis. We're here to help you."

A look of confusion crossed her face. "You can help me? Are you angels?"

William glanced at Boniface, then back to the girl. "I'm not an angel, Ailis. But I've been sent by angels and by your God."

"Are you here to help me get back to my son?" she asked.

Gaspar could see William take a deep, almost forlorn breath before he spoke. "I'm not here to reunite you with your child. Not here and now. But I will help you get to a place where you'll ultimately be with him and your husband again. Do you understand me, Ailis?"

The girl gave an almost defiant shake of her head, and in a flash she darted away down the muddy lane. William's shoulders fell; then he took off in pursuit of her. Gaspar began to run after them when Boniface reached out, stopping him. "I know where she's going, Gaspar. Come with me."

They walked down a series of narrow alleyways between the houses until they came to a small, ramshackle home with a dimly lit window. Outside the window, peering in, was the wayward soul. Ailis. Her hands gripped the sill as if she would never release it.

Gaspar saw William standing a short distance away in the shadows, quietly watching. The sounds of quiet sobs came to his ears, and he realized Ailis was crying.

Through the window past her, Gaspar could see the huddled shape of a man, his shoulders hunched and quaking. He realized the man was crying great tears of loss. In his arms he cradled a small sleeping child.

Boniface's voice whispered into his mind, "She cries for him and he cries for her. She died some time ago, giving birth to her only child. It is that grief, the love of a mother, which binds her here. Now William must convince her that heaven awaits her, and it is there she'll be reunited with her loved ones."

Gaspar watched as William slowly moved to the woman's side. Placing a hand gently on her shoulder, he began singing again, almost whispering a soothing and beautiful tune. Before long, Ailis was leaning against William. Amazed, Gaspar heard her begin to sing the song with him. Together, they stood side by side outside the window until their voices seemed merged into one.

Her cries had ceased, and Gaspar could see her gaining strength and vitality until he began to see the faintest outline of light around her, an aura of slowly pulsing radiance.

"They sing a song which tells of the love of God for His children. It gives her strength to know there is one who feels her pain and understands it," Boniface whispered into his mind. "William sings it to tell her she has nothing to fear by leaving this place, and someday both her husband and her child can join her in heaven."

Gaspar left silent his question of whether, in fact, this might be a lie. Was it not possible these loved ones might not join her in heaven, but might, in fact, end up somewhere else? It seemed almost a trick; a trick played with the best of intentions, but a trick none the less.

"Hope is not a trick, Gaspar, and love is not an open wound into which we pour the salt of falsehoods. We leave that to the fallen. What William tells her is the truth, and she begins to see the beauty in his words. She will go with him now, and she will have that hope and love forever."

Gaspar watched as William gently moved Ailis away from the window and turned her to face him.

"Are you ready to go home, Ailis?" he asked.

A gentle nod was his answer. Slowly, he embraced the young woman and lowered his forehead to hers. He reached up, gently closed her eyes, and, together, they disappeared into the night.

Gaspar walked quietly to the window and peered in. He watched as the young husband carried his child to a small bed. After laying the child down and covering him with blankets, he placed a gentle kiss upon his forehead. The man blew out the candle lighting the room, and moving to the window through which Gaspar peered, he looked out into the dark, star-filled sky and, closing his eyes, he began to pray.

Gaspar listened as the man whispered a prayer of love and thanksgiving for the gift of the child now asleep behind him. When he'd finished his prayer, he reached out and closed the window on the night.

"Come, Gaspar," Boniface whispered. "William and Ailis await us."

CHAPTER 30

In the realm of the boatman, 1292

G aspar and Boniface joined William and Ailis at the end of the quay as they waited the arrival of the boatman. Already Gaspar could see the boatman's lantern and he could hear a joyous song floating across the water. At once his spirits were lifted as the song washed over him in what seemed like waves of love and light.

The boatman slowly came into sight, and Gaspar marveled at the change in the old man and his formerly dark and forbidding bark.

The boat seemed to be lit from within by amber light spilling out over the water with a warm and soothing glow. The wood, dark and forbidding before, now seemed welcoming and safe.

The boatman appeared imbued with energy and life where before he had seemed suppressed by the weight of his task. His features hadn't changed, but Gaspar could swear he looked as if he might break out in some sort of frantic jig of happiness.

The boat came to a rest beside the dock, and William helped Ailis into the boat. After everyone had taken seats, the boatman pushed off, and they began to make their way across the water. The song of the boatman, while still joyful, now carried a hint of something else Gaspar couldn't place. The tune had slowed, the tone taking on a reverent quality. He sang now as if afraid of disturbing something with the song's tenor.

"He sings now because he knows all of heaven listens and awaits the arrival of Ailis," whispered Boniface. "He knows the songs of heaven, but he is not an Angel. When he sings the song, it is touched with what is left of his mortality."

Gaspar turned to Boniface and said, "The boatman was a mortal once?"

"A mortal, yes; not a human mortal, but a mortal none the less," he said.

Gaspar's questions were interrupted in mid-thought by Boniface's raised hand. "Just listen, Gaspar. Just listen and watch. Let these moments flow through you and caress you."

Gaspar turned back to watch Ailis at the front of the boat. He watched as she swayed from side to side in sync with the song of the boatman, her form still radiant and pulsating with light.

Off in the distance, Gaspar could see a glow on the horizon growing in size and intensity. He found himself leaning forward, straining to reach out to the light.

He looked at William to see he was sitting silent with his face raised to the sky, eyes closed.

Suddenly, a wave of light slipped across the water toward them. As it came closer, Gaspar could see that it was actually a myriad of individual lights weaving around each other, creating a pathway down which the boatman steered.

Slowly, the light enveloped the boat, and Gaspar sensed Boniface standing behind him. He turned to find the being that was Boniface morphed into a shaft of light, golden and effervescent.

"This is who I am, Gaspar. This is the real being you know as Boniface, and these are my fellow heavenly beings."

The words were whispered into his mind, and as he watched, the light that was Boniface rose up from the boat, merging with the light surrounding them.

Suddenly the song of the boatman ended, and Gaspar looked back to the front of the boat to find they had come to rest against the side of a long narrow walkway. The walkway was made of wood and stretched off into the distance as far as he could see. William had already risen, taken Ailis' arm, and helped her out of the boat onto the walkway.

They began walking away when William turned and spoke into Gaspar's mind, "Come, my friend. Come with me to the gates of heaven."

Gaspar rose and followed, stepping onto the narrow boardwalk. He struggled to keep William and Ailis within sight as they walked into the distance toward a bright, blinding light.

The sounds of a gently tolling bell reached his ears, the sound so fine and delicate it seemed to be nothing more than a chime blown by a gentle breeze. But he could sense a building strength in the gentle ringing; a slowly building crescendo drawing him farther and farther along the narrow path.

Suddenly, the bell stopped, and silence crashed down on him, freezing him in his tracks. He looked above him to find he was within a walled space, the ramparts soaring above him as far as he could see. Along the walls, sitting in alcoves recessed into the stone was a host of beings staring down at him, unspeaking, not breathing, so still that for a moment Gaspar thought they might be statues.

But they weren't statues. He could see their eyes, bright shining orbs, locked on him, following his every step. They looked like giant bats, but covered in golden feathers with faces that made him smile.

And then it all exploded in a mind-numbing symphony of voices so full of love and joy that Gaspar fell to his knees under the weight of it.

As he watched, the beings along the walls took flight, and in full voice they swarmed downward, engulfing him, swirling around him, lifting him into the air higher and higher, until he was above the palisades, carried ever higher into the sky.

A feeling of euphoria engulfed him. With eyes closed, he began to sing the song invading his soul; the song sung by what he knew were angels. He sang louder and louder, sensing the words, not knowing their meaning or even the language, but singing none the less.

"Gaspar. Gaspar! Open your eyes, man!" William's voice shocked him out of his reverie, and he opened his eyes to find he was standing on a great open plain.

"You must be careful not to lose yourself in their songs, my friend. We're not of this place, and if you were to give in to the songs, you might never make it back."

"Why would I ever want to leave this place," Gaspar asked. "Is this not heaven? Is this not what you and I have dreamed of?"

William laughed. "Actually, this isn't heaven. That's heaven. Or should I say, through there is heaven."

Gaspar looked in the direction William pointed and saw a simple shack off in the distance, far away over a desolate, dusty plain; a solitary worn down building Gaspar had seen a hundred times in the fishing villages along the coast of the Holy Land; a building that looked as if it would topple over in a not overly stiff breeze.

William and Ailis headed off in the direction of the shack with Gaspar in tow. As they approached it, Gaspar noticed a small man sitting at a low wooden table on the porch contemplating their approach. He sucked on the long slender stem of a pipe, the bowl of which seemed to be made of an iridescent green stone. A haze of ivory-colored smoke which emanated from the pipe hovered beneath the low overhang of the porch, seemingly impenetrable and unmoving.

Upon reaching the shack, Gaspar could see what he thought was a man sitting on the porch was, in fact, an old woman. She was a tiny thing, no taller than Gaspar's waist. Her hair was surprisingly long and thick, the color of a raven's feathers. Her face was as smooth as a baby's, but radiated untold age in a manner he couldn't quite fathom. Her eyes fixed on Gaspar's for only a moment before moving to Ailis and settling on her in a penetrating and intense gaze.

No one said a word for some time before William finally broke the silence. "I come before you, Mother, with one of your own. Once lost, she is now found and wishes to join the flock."

The old woman swung her eyes from Ailis to William, and a huge toothless smile spread across her face.

"Ah, my favorite shepherd come calling with a wayward lamb. Besides the poor lost soul beside you, what other weak and helpless thing have you brought with you?"

With that her eyes settled on Gaspar, who instantly felt as if his every thought, action, and deed from the day he was born until now was flowing out of him into the gently inhaling mouth of the woman slowly sucking on the strange pipe. He could feel his very soul merging with the smoke being drawn into the woman who, now with eyes closed, was mumbling some incoherent words that steadily grew faster and more garbled.

Just when he thought his whole being would be drawn into the pipe, the woman exhaled a long, slow breath of a thick and viscous cloud which rose back to the ceiling and, with it, Gaspar's soul was released from whatever force the old woman had conjured to ensnare it.

"He is certainly capable, this one, William. I wonder, though, if he can deal with the loneliness. I wonder at the strength of his heart. It may need to be hardened for what lies ahead."

"That I don't know, Mother," William replied. "What little I know of him seems well suited. But that's not why I'm here."

"Yes, yes. I know that, boy. I just offer up my observations as one who's seen hundreds of your kind come and go. This one intrigues me. He has the makings of a legend."

With that, she turned away from Gaspar and reached behind her. With one small, bird-like hand, she lifted a huge book that was bigger than she was. She placed it on the table before her. Opening the book, she ran her hands over the pages, eyes closed for a moment, before she spoke.

"So, Ailis. I have before me your life. In this book is everything that ever was or could have been in your life and in the lives of those you touched. This is what is left of your mortal soul. Tell me, child, what do you want here?"

Ailis looked from the woman to William, who gently nodded.

"I wish to pass through the gates behind you, Mother," Ailis whispered. "I wish to live with my God forever."

The woman inhaled deeply on the pipe, causing the bowl to glow brighter for a moment before she exhaled.

"Once beyond these gates, my child, you will never be able to return. You are not like the various angels and other beings who come and go, traveling the infinite worlds around us. No, this is your world, and a wondrous world it is, but it is all you will know for eternity. Do you understand this?"

"It is all I want," Ailis said.

With her smile once again renewed, the old woman stood and came around the table. She reached out her hand to Ailis and whispered, "Then take my hand, child. Walk with me."

Ailis hesitated for a moment and turned to William, who seemed on the verge of tears.

"Thank you, my friend," Ailis whispered. "Thank you for saving me. I will always remember you."

Ailis reached out and touched William's cheek, then turned and took the woman's hand.

The woman guided her toward the narrow, wooden front door of the shack. She opened it and standing aside she bade Ailis enter. The young girl didn't hesitate for a moment and crossed over the threshold.

As she did, the world around Gaspar suddenly melted away and was replaced by a scene of stunning brilliance and beauty. Where there once was a dilapidated old shack, now there stood a grove of giant trees, their leaves a golden shade of green, the canopies of foliage stretching across the sky as though they held up the now stunningly clear blue of a radiant star-filled dusk.

A clear flowing stream of water, shining like the sun ran through the glade, translucent bubbles rising from it into the air, dissipating like rain in reverse.

All around Ailis, who was now transforming into the same bright light Boniface had morphed into, were more of the pulsing and flowing beings of light that had met the boat earlier.

The songs had begun again and, as Gaspar watched Ailis, she began singing the songs in an unearthly voice that reached out and lovingly caressed his soul. He turned to William to find tears falling across his cheeks, the wisp of a smile changing their course.

He turned back to find Ailis had completely transformed into a surging shaft of light growing in size and scope for only a moment, then collapsing upon itself into a shaft of speeding brilliance that streamed off through the trees into the blinding horizon beyond.

The sound of the woman's voice in his head reached him, and in the blink of an eye, the shack reformed and the old lady sat at her table as if nothing had happened.

"You will come this way again, Gaspar. It may be with a host of souls like our Ailis, but in the end I would wager my favorite pipe I will someday have your book opened before me. Pray it tells a story that gains you the passage you seek," she said.

With that she rose from her chair, walked through the door, and closed it behind her, leaving Gaspar and William alone on the plain.

CHAPTER 31

In the realm of the boatman, 1292

Gaspar and William walked together across the plain for some time before Gaspar spoke.

"Have you ever been beyond the doorway Ailis went through?"

"No," William answered. "It's not allowed to us. Through that door is a world we as mortals couldn't survive. It's the same with the doorway to hell. Only the souls of mortals can cross into those realms."

"So does that mean we must die again, William?" Gaspar asked. "How is it if we succeed in our quest to become like Ailis we would cross over that threshold?"

"I once asked Boniface that exact question. As usual, he gave me some sort of cryptic answer about another path from this mortality to the realm of souls. Perhaps you'll have better luck prying loose his secrets," William offered.

The two men crested a small rise and looked down to find they were nearing the shore and the wooden walkway stretching off across the water. In the distance, they could see the boatman waiting in his boat.

They were heading down the hill when Gaspar stopped. He sensed something, but couldn't quite place what it was. William had continued down the slope, moving away from him. Suddenly Gaspar realized the ground beneath his feet was shaking ever so slightly. William had now stopped as well, sensing something amiss.

Instantly, Gaspar knew what the shaking ground meant and, whirling around, found himself facing a massive charging horse.

"Run, Gaspar!" William yelled. "Get to the walkway!"

Gaspar stood staring at the approaching charger. On the horse's back, carrying a huge broadsword, was a rider clad only in a simple loin cloth. The being was huge and looked as if it had been carved from a solid block of granite. He looked to be twice Gaspar's height, and he held the sword, as long as Gaspar was tall, in both hands above his head, ready to strike. His eyes shown with an unholy anger, his mouth open in a silent scream of rage.

There was little doubt the charging beast would run them down long before they reached the safety of the boardwalk.

In an automatic reflex born from years of battle, Gaspar charged forward toward the approaching behemoth, taking a momentary bit of pleasure when he saw the rider's face display a look of surprise.

Just before the beast was upon him, he launched himself through the air in a rolling sideways dive, catching the horse's legs just below the knees.

Explosions of light erupted in Gaspar's head, every bit of breath violently forced from his body under the impact. Just before blackness overtook him, he smiled at the sight of the giant horse cart wheeling forward, head over heels, expelling the huge rider skyward, both horse and rider tumbling to the ground in a rolling heap.

* * *

William stood transfixed at what he'd just witnessed, but only for a moment. Drawing his sword, he charged toward the shaken giant, who was trying to right himself from the ground. William could see Gaspar in a motionless pile. A momentary probe of his mind told him the knight, while badly hurt, was still alive.

The giant was now standing and appeared to be regaining his senses as he searched for his broadsword, which had gone flying in the collision.

William gave him no chance to find it, launching a frantic attack with every ounce of strength he could muster. Dancing and whirling around the giant, he slashed and stabbed, attempting to inflict some sort of damage on the huge creature.

The damage was minimal, the blade slicing, but seeming to cause little distress. But it was the momentary respite which saved both his life and Gaspar's, for in a flash of brilliant light, an orb of iridescent lightning exploded from the shoreline into the giant, knocking him to the ground and rendering him motionless.

William stepped back and watched as the glowing light slowly ebbed and transformed into the calm, serene form of Boniface.

"What the hell is that, Boniface?" William asked, gesturing at the behemoth.

"That, William, is an angel; an angel who should not be here and who apparently has ill designs on our friend Gaspar. Now, go help him while I tend to this traitor."

William hurried to the crumpled body of Gaspar, kneeling beside him. Expertly, he probed his body with his hands, looking for injury. Then, lowering his forehead to Gaspar's, he closed his eyes, probing his mind, willing him to wake.

After a few minutes he could sense Gaspar's consciousness returning, then his eyes slowly opened.

"Did you kill that thing, William?"

"No, but our friend Boniface seems to have it under control. How do you feel?"

"Like I've been run over by a giant horse," Gaspar said.

Smiling, William said, "I have to say your little maneuver most likely saved our lives. Either you're uncommonly brave or amazingly daft."

Rising carefully to his feet with William's help, Gaspar said, "Believe it or not, that very move saved my life once during a battle with Saracen cavalry."

Gingerly, Gaspar and William approached the still immobile form on the ground to find Boniface now kneeling beside the giant.

"How are you, Gaspar?" Boniface asked, not taking his eyes off the being lying before him.

"I've been better. What is this thing?" Gaspar asked.

"This is an angel. His name is Sandolphon. The fact he is here and that he attempted to destroy you is of great concern."

"I don't understand," Gaspar said. "Why did he attack us?"

"That is what I was about to find out."

They could see that the immobile angel was staring at Boniface, who seemed to be holding him in place with his gaze. Suddenly, the angel began thrashing wildly on the ground, a choking unrecognizable voice erupting from his mouth. The indecipherable noise went on for some time before he once again laid still, his eyes staring wide open.

Slowly Boniface stood, turning to face Gaspar and William.

"It appears that my brother Sandolphon has crossed over the river and joined forces with someone on the fallen side. Unfortunately, I can not ascertain who corrupted him. But what he did tell me was that he was tasked with killing you specifically, Gaspar."

"What?" Gaspar exclaimed. "Who would want me dead and why?"

"I do not know that," Boniface answered.

"Well, can't you ask him?"

"Not anymore. He is dead."

Gaspar stared at the unmoving form on the ground before him. As he watched, it slowly began to waver, melting into a gently glowing wisp of light which faded, then blinked out, as if someone had blown out a candle.

"He willed himself into a state of death before I could learn anymore from him," Boniface whispered.

Gaspar turned to Boniface. "I don't understand. He killed himself?"

Boniface seemed engulfed in sadness. Amazed, they watched as tears fell down the archangel's face. His head was bowed, his shoulders gently shaking as he sobbed.

He lifted his head, his eyes meeting Gaspar's. "That is something all of us can do, even angels."

CHAPTER 32

Zurich, Switzerland, May 2010

Roberto Lang sat in his office nervously watching the clock. He had paced back and forth from his office to the front windows of his gallery a dozen times already, drawing annoyed looks from the otherwise bored security guard.

The unknown man on the phone had said he was sending someone with a bonus. Lang had hoped it would be here by now. He'd made a flight reservation to Nice three hours ago and had an appointment in two days to look at the villa of his dreams.

Finally, two hours after closing time, he decided his bonus wouldn't be arriving today. He said good night to the security guard and, heading out of the gallery, began making his way home. He'd wait there for news from Alfeo about the Rembrandt icon.

His loft apartment was a short walk away, and he arrived in less than ten minutes. His home was on the upper floors of an old mansion sitting alongside the river. Expensive and exclusive, it would bring a good price. He'd already called a local agent and instructed him to sell it quickly.

He stepped into the old elevator, his substantial girth filling the space. After a short, lurching ride to the top of the building, he arrived at his front door and unlocked it. As he stepped into his foyer, he noticed a plain white envelope on the floor. Reaching down, he grabbed the envelope, instantly feeling the substantial weight of it. No stranger to the feel of cash-stuffed envelopes, he tried to guess at the amount of money inside. Obviously, his bonus had come. In his excitement, he gave no thought to how it had ended up inside his apartment.

Hurrying to his living room, he sat at an old lawyer's desk overlooking the river. The envelope was blank other than one word on the front: *Roberto*.

Not wasting time to find a letter opener, he tore at the envelope until a thick wad of euros spilled out onto the desk. There was no doubt he now had enough for the down payment on his villa. This, combined with his coming pay day from the Rembrandt, would ensure a comfortable and sun-filled retirement.

He began counting the bills and had reached twenty-five thousand euros when a quiet voice behind him shocked him out of his blissful reverie.

"Fifty-thousand euros, Roberto."

It was the voice of the stranger who for so many years he'd heard over his phone. He broke out in a cold sweat, panicked, but galvanized to the chair in terror. The tenor of the man's voice cut through him like a knife.

"Have you ever heard of the seven deadly sins, Roberto? Of course you have. Greed is one of those. It usually comes in at third or forth on the list. Personally, I prefer the word avarice over greed. And I rank it a bit higher on the scale, as it were. Avarice, Roberto. I think that fits this situation perfectly."

In the moment before the hiss-like explosion of the silenced pistol and the impact of the double-tapped hollow points to the back of his head, Roberto Lang saw himself on a cliff top veranda sipping champagne, watching the sunset. It was the last thing he ever saw.

Dominicus Bureau watched as the art dealer slumped forward onto the desk. Calmly, he removed a white handkerchief from his jacket, unscrewed the silencer, and wrapped it in the cloth. He dropped it into his coat pocket and slid the pistol into its holster.

Reaching over the dead man, he picked up the scattered euros and slipped those into another pocket in his coat. Turning, he made his way to one wall of the living room. Eight paintings of various sizes were hung on the wall. Working quickly, he removed three paintings from their frames, all minor paintings, but together worth a not insignificant amount of money. Rolling them up, he slipped the art work into a shopping bag he retrieved from the kitchen.

When the art dealer was found, all signs would lead to a murder-robbery. Walking to the door, he quietly let himself out of the apartment. Fifteen minutes later he was sitting in a quiet café four blocks away drinking a wonderful cup of chocolate laced espresso.

This was going to be a busy night.

CHAPTER 33

The coast of England, 1292

The cliffs outside William's castle were more hospitable the next morning as a bright sun shone down from a cloudless sky.

Gaspar, William, and Boniface all sat on an outcropping of rocks overlooking the ocean far below. They had traveled back to this realm and, after drinking a potion William had made for him, Gaspar had slept peacefully through the night. He'd awakened to find no lingering after-affects from the battle with Sandolphon.

"So, Gaspar, tell me your thoughts after what you have seen these last two days," Boniface said.

Gaspar was quiet for a moment, then responded, "What I think is, the world as I knew it, what I believed it to be, is so far removed from reality that I can scarcely believe it. I must tell you I'm unsure as to what course to take. I've seen hell, and I've seen heaven. What of purgatory? Am I allowed to see that place before I make my decision?"

"Surely you are not going to indulge this mortal further, are you, Boniface?" came a familiar voice.

Arusmus sauntered over and sat across from Gaspar. The fallen angel was now dressed like an English lord. Gaspar noticed William turning away from him in disgust.

"He deserves to know the truth of what awaits him in that place," Boniface answered.

"Well, what say you, William?" Arusmus asked. "I don't remember you getting this grand tour when we bestowed this current life upon you."

William was silent, but Boniface answered, "William did not have the questions Gaspar has. He chose to take the life we offered, no questions asked. That was his choice. If Gaspar wants to see purgatory, then I will show it to him."

Arusmus shook his head slowly in disgust. His gaze fell on Gaspar, and in a sardonic voice he asked, "What troubles you, warrior? What scares you so?"

Gaspar turned to face Arusmus, his eyes searing into the angel's. In that moment, any fear of Arusmus he might have felt seemed to melt away. He remembered how he'd felt when he'd faced down Sandolphon, charging headlong into the giant's attack.

He stood and walked over to the seated angel. Towering over him, he looked down and spoke, "If you think it's you I fear, then you're sorely mistaken, demon. What I fear is making the wrong choice for my soul. I've seen what you have to offer. I caught a glimpse of what heaven offers, and if it takes a thousand years, I'll never stand at your gate with my soul at your tender mercies. If I stand at your gate, it'll be either to hand over those who deserve their fate or to separate your head from your wretched body. I'll make my choice when I'm damn ready, and there's nothing you can do or say to change that."

Gaspar turned, walking away until he stood at the edge of the cliff. He stared out to sea, letting the fury washing over him slowly fade.

Arusmus stood, fists clenched, and took a step toward Gaspar. He found his way blocked in a moment by a blade-wielding William, a thin smile creasing his otherwise stern features.

"What are you thinking about, Arusmus? Tread softly on my ground and with my friend," William said.

Boniface sat silent, still staring out to sea.

"Your friend, William? Is that what he is now? You have your work cut out for you if you think this cretin can take your place and set you free," Arusmus said.

"I'll take my chances with him," William answered. "I've seen what he's capable of. If he chooses this life, he'll at least be my equal. Of that you can be sure."

Boniface stood, slowly moving between Arusmus and William. "There will be no war here today. Come, Gaspar. Let us take this final journey before you make your choice. Come with me now to purgatory."

He reached out to Gaspar, who turned, allowing Boniface to embrace him once more.

The sound drifting across the water was unlike anything Gaspar had ever heard; one part gnashing of teeth, one part joyous exaltation. In a single moment he could hear pain and suffering, the wailing of beings in what seemed mortal peril, and in the next whispering breath, the sounds of ecstatic release.

It was frightening and reassuring at the same time.

Gaspar once again was seated in the boatman's bark, Boniface beside him. William sat in front of them as far from Arasmus, who sat behind Gaspar, as he could. The boatman's slow rhythmic paddle strokes pushed the boat ever closer to the source of the strange and convoluted voices.

"What you hear, Gaspar, are the voices of the souls in purgatory," Boniface said. "Some cry out in agony from the pain and suffering they endure while others proclaim their joy at reaching the end of their torment. What you hear is the cleansing of these souls, the final purification and burning away of the last vestiges of sin. In the end, when they have paid their penance, they see the true wonder of Heaven, and it is that which causes them to sing their final mortal song before joining God in heaven."

Gaspar was silent as he let the voices wash over him, the sounds rendering him speechless. He began to see the faint outline of a large structure in the distance, the glow of some sort of light pulsing and ebbing, silhouetting what looked to be a gigantic fortress.

As they drew nearer he could make out more clearly ramparts of stone, the height of which seemed never-ending. The pulsating light seemed to ebb and flow along with the lamentations and the joyous songs.

The boat pulled alongside a landing cut into the rock below the fortress. William was the first out of the boat, and Gaspar followed as he headed up a narrow footpath that looked as if the passage of eons of feet had worn it into the sheer face of the rock. Both Boniface and Arusmus followed.

The path switch-backed its way up the rock until, after a vigorous climb, they arrived on a broad flat promontory. Gaspar could now see that the walls of the fortress were actually part of the rock, the ramparts soaring up until they seemed to merge with the dark empty sky. Before him, set back into the stone, was a huge gate. On either side of the gate stood two giant statues that looked like lions, but with seven heads each. As Gaspar stared at the statues, he recoiled, startled when the eyes of both statues turned his way and blinked.

The evil chuckling of Arusmus was interrupted by Boniface's quiet voice. "Those are not statues, Gaspar. Those are the guardians of purgatory."

Boniface moved past Gaspar and William until he was standing near the feet of the gate keepers. He raised his face to the sky, then opened his mouth, and as Gaspar watched transfixed, a nebulous light, cloudlike, floated up to the guardian on the right. The being opened its seven mouths and swallowed the vaporous light, and after a moment both guardians moved as one to the gates.

In unison, they grasped rings attached to the doors and, giving what looked to be gargantuan efforts, slowly parted the gates to purgatory.

It was as if the doors leading to a menagerie containing a billion simultaneously singing voices were opened at once. Gaspar's hands flew to his ears in a vain attempt to shut out the noise. He felt the feather-light touch of Boniface's hand on his shoulder. When he turned to face him, Boniface gently blew into his face, and the noise subsided to a level that, while still loud, was at least bearable.

"The lamentations and exaltations of an infinite number of souls can take some time to get used to. Come with me now, Gaspar. Follow me into purgatory. Listen and learn, for when we're done here, it will be time for you to make your choice."

With that, Boniface walked past the guardians and through the gates with William following close.

Gaspar turned to find Arusmus standing silent and still, a frown on his face.

"Aren't you coming with us, Arusmus?" Gaspar asked.

The angel was silent for a moment before he turned to look at Gaspar. Astonished, Gaspar could see the tell-tale beginnings of tears in his eyes. The normally fearsome fallen angel stared forlorn at Gaspar before, in a quivering, almost childlike voice, he said, "I can not do it, Gaspar."

Turning, he walked away from the gates and down the path out of sight. Gaspar turned, hurrying after Boniface and William. When he caught up to them, just beyond the gates, Boniface turned to him and said, "Remember, Gaspar, Arusmus was like me once. He was, in fact, an archangel of the same stature and position. When he chose the path of revolution, he condemned his soul. This place is almost as unbearable to him as heaven would be.

"He can stand the cries of the suffering. Their lamentations are like the sweetest honey to his soul. It is the cries of redemption and salvation he can not stand. He hears the sounds of souls being released from this place on their way to heaven and what is left of his heavenly heart breaks anew. Someday you will learn even demons can lament their choices."

Boniface turned and, with the two warriors in tow, headed deeper into the fortress. As they walked, the light glowing above them grew brighter, and the sounds became more distinct.

Gaspar looked around him to see the walls which rose into the sky until they disappeared out of sight seemed to be coming closer together, their pathway narrowing slowly. The farther along the walkway they traveled, the closer the walls became until they were walking single file, Gaspar's shoulders almost touching the walls.

The light and sound in front of them grew more pronounced, more focused, and Gaspar began to make out the sounds of individual voices. His mind began spinning faster and faster as he tried to take in the infinite number of songs and cries invading his mind.

He closed his eyes in an effort to stave off the vertigo that seemed to engulf him. Reaching in front of him, he held out his hands, trying to find his way forward. A brief feeling of panic began to overtake him when, suddenly, he felt Boniface take his hand and whisper into his mind, "Here we are, Gaspar. Open your eyes and see. Open your ears and hear. Open your mind and understand."

Gaspar opened his eyes to find they were standing on the edge of a precipice; a cliff overlooking a vastness that took his breath away. Spread out before him was a golden sea of gently pulsating light. The light had a substance to it that, while not solid, seemed to have a depth and width to it.

As Gaspar focused on the light, he noticed brief flashes of brilliance exploding in different locations, and he realized these brief firefly-like bursts of light coincided with almost ecstatic songs of release.

"What you are hearing and seeing is the release of souls from purgatory to their journey on to heaven," Boniface said. "They've done their penance and atoned for whatever sin has kept them here. Now they are free."

"Are these all souls, Boniface, this mass of light? It seems to go on without end."

"You would never reach the end of this place, Gaspar. This is not only the repository for souls from your world, but from all the worlds in this universe and beyond. In your mind, there must be a beginning and an end. There is no such thing here. Come, take my hand. We are going to get a closer look."

Gaspar took the angel's hand and, as Boniface stepped off the precipice into the air, Gaspar followed without hesitation.

They floated downward ever closer to the lights. In wonder he watched his feet, then his legs disappear into the amorphous mass until they were fully engulfed. Now he could make out different and separate beings, spectral shapes that, while not fully human, seemed to contain the vestiges of mortal form.

As they made their way through the mass of teeming souls sinking deeper and deeper, Gaspar watched as they reached out to them, especially Boniface, and he marveled at the strange but pleasing feelings he felt when caressed by them. A tingling sensation, a feeling of warmth, washed over him, and he felt himself merging with the souls, becoming something other than human.

And then he found himself looking into the face of a man not much older than himself. The man, or soul, was smiling at him. Reaching out his hand, he took Gaspar's and held it. As Gaspar watched, the soul began to grow in brightness and strength. It seemed to be rejuvenated and filled by the simple act of touching him.

"The souls of purgatory take great comfort and solace in the contact with those who maintain their mortality," Boniface whispered. "That is why the prayers of the living are so important. It brings them solace and imbues them with the strength to carry on with their penance."

The soul released his hand and, with a look of peaceful gratitude upon its face, it faded away into the mass of souls now swarming the three travelers.

Gaspar turned to find William behind him, slowly spinning in a circle, his arms outstretched, a gentle whirlwind of souls fading in and out of substance as they reached for him. The warrior's eyes were closed, his head tilted back, a smile of such peace on his face that Gaspar, unable to resist, emulated him. Throwing his arms out wide he opened his mind, his heart, his very soul, and embraced a rush of souls that engulfed him.

A wondrous feeling of happiness and joy washed over him in a soul-quenching flood. He realized what he felt was the gratitude and joy of thousands of souls who drank from his spirit, filling themselves with his strength. He was reveling in the peaceful feeling when suddenly a flash of light exploded in his head, and searing white hot pain engulfed him. He was trapped in a wave of remorse and contrition, and he knew in an instant, a soul in the throes of its penance had invaded him and was trying to gather strength to combat the torment possessing it.

He was powerless to stop what consumed him and, helpless, he gave in to the sorrow and pain. His consciousness opened, and the face of an older woman invaded his mind. Slowly, the pain and the sorrow that seemed to be sucking the very life from him ebbed, and once again he began to feel the return of the wonderful feelings of peace. Her face, at first a mask of pain and guilt, had transformed into one full of gratitude. Gaspar realized as she slowly faded from his mind he'd given her the strength she needed to fulfill her penance.

"And so it goes, Gaspar, on and on for eternity; this process of redemption and contrition. This is purgatory. This was your destination."

Gaspar opened his eyes to find they stood again at the precipice above the teeming mass of souls.

"It is time to go now. It is time for you to make your choice. There are no more places left for us to go," Boniface said.

Gaspar awoke from some sort of sleep to find himself sitting on the sandy shore of Acre's harbor once more. Blinking in an attempt to clear his mind, he realized he could remember his trip to purgatory, but nothing after that.

"The time has come, Gaspar, to make a choice. We brought you back here as this is the place of choosing for you."

Gaspar turned to his right to find Boniface sitting next to him staring out to sea, his feet once more buried in the warm sand. Looking to his left, he found Arusmus also quietly staring at the blue green waters of the now calm bay.

"It is time, Templar. We can show you nothing more. The choice is yours to make. Will you go on your way to purgatory? Or will you choose the life of the soul hunter? Now is the time," Arusmus said.

Gaspar stood and walked slowly across the sand until he stood ankle deep in the cool water along the ocean's edge. The feeling of the water on his feet brought with it a cavalcade of memories, from his days as a child, walking along the shore to the deaths of his father and brother. He was swept along a tide of remembrances, crossing the battlefields of his time as a Templar knight through to the moment he hit the water, mortally wounded by Theobald Gaudin's broadsword.

He felt the cold and watery embrace of the water as he was pulled from the depths and back into this nowhere land between life and death.

And then he heard the slow rhythmic cadence of the boatman's paddle as he was transported once more to the gates of hell, the little shack that was the entrance to heaven, then through the giant doors blocking the pathway to purgatory.

All of it he saw as he struggled with his choice.

Later he would realize that it was the warrior within him, ingrained and imprinted on his soul that made up his mind.

He turned to find both angels now looking into his eyes. He walked slowly out of the water across the sand, each step a titanic effort until he stood looking down at the archangel Boniface and the prince of hell, Arusmus.

He fell to his knees before Boniface, and with head bowed, he said, "I choose the life you offer me. I choose to atone for my sins by serving my lord."

Boniface tenderly reached out a hand and lifted Gaspar's face until he was staring directly into his eyes and said, "You will serve the lord, Gaspar. You will also serve Arusmus' lord. Do not forget that."

Nodding his head Gaspar said, "Take me and make me into what you will."

With that, both Arusmus and Boniface stood. Boniface reached out to Gaspar, helping him to his feet and drawing him close, he embraced him, blowing gently into his eyes.

The last thing Gaspar saw before everything turned to black was Boniface's smile.

He awoke in William's castle to find William sitting quietly watching him.

"How did I get back here?"

"That's of little consequence, my friend. What is of import is you've made your choice and, by so doing, you've set me free. For that I'm eternally grateful. But before I can go on to face my destiny, we have work to do."

Standing, William said, "Now get out of bed. It's time to make you a hunter."

CHAPTER 34

Zurich, Switzerland, May 2010

Alex sat in the dining room of the Hotel Zum Storchen, clean linen, fine silver, and an uneaten dinner before him. He'd read late into the afternoon from his grandfather's book, reveling in the story of Gaspar. Not far from his mind was the realization that the words he read, written so long ago, told the story of a man who apparently was hiding in the shadows outside his door. Hunger had driven him from the book and into the dining room. Now, lost in what he had read, his appetite deserted him.

He retraced his trip to the art dealer. The dealer's story seemed surreal, and for a moment, he wondered at the odds of walking into a Zurich gallery and finding the connections he had.

He was deep in thought when some not so atrophied sense of danger caused him to look up and register the approach of a man from across the room.

The man was walking so purposefully in his direction that only a thousand-year-old granite statue would have failed to register the man's approach.

At Alex's recognition, the man's otherwise stone cold face sprouted a smile that threatened to crack his visage into a thousand pieces. Alex reflexively reached for the closest thing he could find resembling a weapon, grasping the fine silver bread knife on the table before him, a move not unnoticed by the approaching interloper.

"Alex Donovan! My good friend, how are you?" the stranger said as he reached the table.

Alex, every nerve lit white hot, stared at the stranger and took quick stock of the man who had so bluntly invaded his space. He was dressed all in black, from his highly polished shoes to the tightly drawn collar around his neck. He looked to be as tall as Alex and solidly built. His jet black hair was cut short and framed a square-jawed face that, while severe, still held the remnants of a long gone humorous spirit at the corners of the eyes and mouth. The man was old. How old, Alex couldn't tell. His outstretched hand was large and looked rough and calloused.

It was a hand Alex made no move to grasp. Every bit of his natural and trained sense of self-defense was at a high state of alert.

The stranger laughed and, without asking, pulled out a chair across from Alex. Sitting, he said, "Dominicus Bureau, good to meet you. What's for dinner?"

"I don't know you," Alex said.

"Truer words were never spoken, but seeing you wielding the hotel's finest, I hope you'll at least give me the courtesy of the opportunity to introduce myself and explain how I know you before you attack me with your bread knife and a slab of butter."

While his every instinct recoiled at the presence of the dark haired man across from him, Alex couldn't help but glance at his own hand tightly, clutching the bread knife, then the slab of butter in front of him, and in spite of himself, smiled a nervous smile.

Alex set down the knife. Leaning back, he gave the man named Dominicus his best stare of indifference and said, "You have one minute to explain yourself before I ask hotel security to escort you from the building."

"Fair enough, young friend. Shall I begin with the fact that I knew of your grandfather? Or perhaps, I should just cut straight to the matter at hand and say if it's the one called Gaspar you seek, perhaps I can be of some assistance."

At the mention of Gaspar, Alex froze. The slowly growing smile on the stranger's face gave tell to the fact Alex had given himself away.

"There aren't many men in this world who know that name, Alex. You search for him for some reason. I also search for him and hope perhaps we can be of use to each other."

"What in God's name are you rambling about? You're speaking a load of nonsense. I don't know any Gaspar. I'm here on business. End of story."

Like a stone curtain had slid down over his eyes, the stranger's smile faded. Alex could now see they were a stormy shade of gray, dark and flinty.

"Do you know what treasures he holds in that vault and others like it? The Rembrandt is nothing. A hundred Rembrandts couldn't begin to touch the things he's accumulated over his seven hundred years.

"But I don't search him out for those. I, like you, seek answers. I want only to talk with him to learn the truth about heaven and hell and the life after this. You see, Alex, I'm a priest. I'm in the Lord's work, and for forty-five years my quest, my mission in life, has been to find this man, and set the record straight once and for all. The world deserves to know the truth. That's all I want."

Before Alex even knew he was doing it, he'd reached across the table with his left hand and grabbed Dominicus' hand. Holding it as tight as he could, he turned it over and, with his right hand, grasped the bread knife. With all his might he stabbed the blade into the webbing, between the thumb and index finger, of the stranger's hand. He felt the blade cut through the flesh and sinew. The whole time his eyes were locked on Dominicus'.

He felt the blade pierce the hand and lodge into the tabletop. Audible gasps erupted from tables around him as people witnessed his attack.

Dominicus didn't even flinch. His hand now pinned to the table, he simply stared into Alex's eyes.

"I'm tired of nightmares invading my waking hours," Alex said. "I don't know anymore if those sitting at my table are real, imagined, or something else entirely. Tell me no more lies. Tell me only truth."

Dominicus slowly reached up with his right hand and, with a nonchalant movement, pulled the knife from his hand and laid it next to his plate. He turned to the diners next to them, a younger couple who looked aghast at his hand, and said, "Excuse my young friend, he suffers from an obscure form of Tourette's Syndrome that causes him to lash out violently at times."

He turned back to Alex who was again sitting back in his chair and said, "I can see why they chose you. A bit barbaric and rough, but I see it. Excuse me for a moment."

Dominicus took one of the dinner napkins and wrapped his hand tightly, staunching what was a not insubstantial amount of blood that soaked the napkin almost immediately.

"Having some bad daymares lately, my friend?" the priest asked.

"I've had some not so pleasant intrusions into my life lately. I imagined you might be one."

"Well, after dinner you can escort me to a discreet doctor I know who'll suture up this wound in my hand. In the meantime you, and I have a lot to talk about, my young friend. And this may not be the best place for that kind of talk."

Alex looked up to see two large men, obviously hotel security, moving across the dining room in their direction. Standing, he moved to intercept them.

"Gentlemen, thank you for your concern, but everything is fine here, just a small misunderstanding among friends."

The lead security guard looked inquiringly at Dominicus, who flashed a benign smile and raised his bandaged hand as if to say no harm, no foul.

Alex dug into his pocket, palming a wad of bills and slipped it discreetly into the security guard's hand and, with a brief, but emphatic squeeze, turned away dismissively.

"Shall we go, Dominicus?"

"By all means, Alexander. I know a great bar on the river bank, a short ride from here, where we can have a discreet dinner."

Dominicus stood and moved across the dining room as if nothing at all was amiss, Alex following in his wake.

No one moved to obstruct them as they made their way out the front doors of the hotel.

"I must say you handled that masterfully, young Donovan," Bureau said sarcastically when they had gained the large cobble-stoned car park in front of the hotel.

Alex eyed the front door where he could see the two security guards peering out at them.

"What's your game, Dominicus? And what kind of name is that anyway?"

A soft chuckle slipped from the priest's mouth before he responded.

"My mother had a crush on a Dominican priest when she was a teenager. She never forgot him. When she married my father and I was born, she named me Dominicus over the objections of my father, who preferred Ludwig. Frankly, I would have preferred Ludwig, but then I would have had to deal with the whole Beethoven thing."

A taxi pulled up to the curb, and the two men ducked into the back.

Dominicus gave the driver the address and the cab pulled away from the hotel.

"Where are we going?" Alex asked.

"To a quiet little pub along the river, just north of here that has a great wine list and even better food. As long as you don't give in to your inner psycho and start stabbing me again, we may be able to find a quiet spot there to talk about our mutual friend.

"By the way, you might want to think about putting the painting back in the vault. Your dealer friend is not very discreet."

"What are you talking about?"

"How do you think I got wind of your arrival, Alex?"

"The art dealer?"

"Exactly. We've known for a long time that Gaspar uses Bergen en Cie as a storehouse. One of many, I might add. We've spent a lot of money and time cultivating sources in the general area, and your art dealer was one. He got a small stipend every quarter to keep an eye out for strange and obscure art, specifically icons, and the comings and goings of strangers in that neighborhood. He called me not two minutes after you left. After calling me, he called someone else as well.

"The painting in your room is one, Gaspar, we didn't know for sure, but we suspected, had stashed away. When you popped up with it, I was informed. And here we are."

"Why are you talking about the art dealer in the past tense, Dominicus?" Alex asked.

Dominicus stared into Alex's eyes but said nothing.

The cab came to a stop in front of a wooden beamed structure that looked as if it had been plucked from the sixteenth century and plopped in the middle of one of Zurich's most fashionable neighborhoods.

Dominicus was out the door and into the bar before Alex was out of the cab, so he paid the cab driver and followed the priest into the pub.

He caught up to Dominicus at a table set in an alcove facing the door.

The bar was mostly empty, dark and imbued with a sense of mystery. The low ceilings, heavy beamed, almost brushed Alex's head.

Alex took a seat facing the door with his back to the wall. The priest smiled at his choice of seats. "I have eyes in the back of my head, young Donovan. You, though, are smart to be cautious with the things stalking you."

Alex said nothing as he saw a bar maid making her way to their table.

"Ah, yes, I think I'll have a bottle of wine, what with the throbbing pain in my hand. A bottle of the 1955 LaTour, please; two glasses," Dominicus said to the waitress.

"Expensive tastes for a priest."

"You're paying, my young friend, and with what you have at your disposal, that's like ordering a Coke."

"What's your game, Dominicus, seriously. My patience is wearing thin."

"Relax a moment. A little wine, then we lay our cards on the table, as you Americans are fond of saying."

Alex said nothing, but his attention was drawn to the doorway as two large men dressed in black leather jackets, black pants, and black boots, which looked as if they were made for breaking ribs, walked through the door and took up station at the bar.

"Mafia," said Dominicus.

"What?"

"They were outside your hotel this afternoon, about twenty minutes after you left Lang's."

"You knew they were there, and you allowed us to be followed?"

"Of course. Something you'll learn about me, Alex, is I'm not averse to confrontation. I've, over the years, found it the best tactic to make quick headway. Especially with gangsters; best to confront and deal with the issue early. Observe and learn, young friend."

With that, the priest stood and headed toward the bar and the two men.

"Hello, my friends! Can I buy you a drink?"

The two thugs said nothing.

"Now, now, gentleman. What will it be? My young friend over there in the corner is a rich American. He wants to buy you two wops a drink."

Still the Italians said nothing.

"Well, I must say, such rudeness would be expected from Sicilian whores. I guess I mistook you for men."

At that, one of the gangsters whirled around and reached for the priest. In a flash of speed that took Alex by surprise, Dominicus took the man's hand, bent it at an obscene angle, and threw the man halfway across the room.

Tables, chairs, and two rotund men, having a quiet cocktail, went flying in a shambles of broken wood and crumpled bodies.

The second thug started to stand, but before he'd risen halfway from his chair, the priest's forearm smashed into his throat. The crunch of broken bones and cartilage, all too familiar to Alex, from his days as a Seal, echoed around the room as the man went down in a heap.

Calmly, Dominicus turned, made his way back to the table, and sat across from Alex. The waitress stepped over the bodies strewn across the bar floor and deftly made her way to their table with a dusty bottle and two glasses. She expertly opened the bottle and, ignoring Alex, gave Dominicus a slight pour to taste, then, leaving the bottle, walked away as if nothing at all was out of sorts.

The priest expertly swirled the wine, then, sticking his nose into the glass, took a deep smell. Eyes closed, he savored the aroma. Then delicately, savoring the moment, he took a sip.

"The last time I had this wine was in a castle in Bavaria ten years ago. I was, as I am now, on the trail of your friend Gaspar. I had tracked him there after the sale, in Paris, of some old Arabic swords from the eleventh century. Missed him by hours, I think."

Dominicus poured a serving of the wine into Alex's glass, then sat back in his chair.

"So ask away, young Donovan. What about me do you want to know?"

Alex looked from the priest to the gangsters on the floor.

"Don't worry about them. The owner here is an old friend who is on the payroll. He has three strong sons whom I have no doubt will be here in a matter of minutes to dispose of our Italian interlopers."

"You say you're a priest. But you act as if you're working for someone. Who pulls your strings, Dominicus?"

"Do you have the book, Alex?"

"What?"

"The story of Gaspar. Do you have it?"

Alex said nothing.

"Ah. One thing you don't do well, my friend, is hide things. For many years now, we believed your grandfather possessed the book. How he got it, we weren't sure. But the fact Gaspar chose him to be his custodian led us to believe he had it."

"We? Custodian? I ask again; who is your master?"

"I'm a Catholic priest, Alex. Need I say more?"

Alex thought about the priest's statement for a moment before musing out loud, "The old priest in Rome who stole the book."

"Ah. Friar Ricardo Dore. He was a translator in the Vatican archives. He found the book while doing research on a celebrated Italian painter who ran afoul of the church in Venice in 1598. Seems this painter was a sought-after artist who took up with devil worshipers or some such nonsense. The Venetian diocese at the time incarcerated him and took possession of some sort of book full of paintings of a supposed heretical nature. He refused to recant his fables and denounce his sins. He was burned at the stake for his crimes. Medieval sensibilities were a tad less accepting than our modern ones.

"Friar Dore found the book, full of paintings, and telling the story of an immortal man, granted his immortality for the purpose of serving both heaven and hell. Dore wasn't supposed to find the book. It had been hidden away in an area of the archives that should have been off limits to him. He became enthralled by the book and, when he brought it to the attention of his superiors, it caused quite an uproar.

"To hide the fact Dore was right, that it was, in fact, a true story, he was told it was a dangerous fable and it was to be destroyed. A lie, of course, but Dore didn't know that. Friar Dore stole the book and disappeared. He was never seen again. Nor was the book; now you have it."

"I don't remember saying I have this book your looking for," Alex said.

"No, you didn't. But your eyes gave you away. Take a drink of this wondrous wine. You're paying for it."

"So you work for who? The Vatican?"

"I work for God."

"I think if you asked Gaspar who he worked for, he'd say the same thing."

Dominicus and Alex stared at each other for a moment, neither man speaking.

"I'm not sure I should trust you, Dominicus."

"Well, before this night is over, that's something you most likely will have to come to grips with."

"What do you mean?"

"Those weren't the only Mafia goons in this town tasked with keeping an eye on you. In fact, I would guess they will at some point, make a move for the Rembrandt."

"It's in my hotel room. I don't have it with me."

"They'll wait until you move it. Or, and I think this more likely, they'll just grab you and force you to give it to them, and, regardless of all your training and inner strength, you'll, in the end, give them what they want."

Alex's attention was drawn away from Dominicus by the arrival of an older man who gave a gesture of greeting to the priest, then moved toward the carnage in the bar room. He was trailed by three large men, obviously his sons, who quietly and efficiently hoisted the two gangsters on their shoulders and disappeared out the back of the room. The older man, obviously the proprietor, hustled the two patrons who had been caught in the melee to another table, placating them with a new bottle of wine.

Alex looked back to the priest. "Should I ask what they're going to do with your two Italian friends?"

"No, you shouldn't. It's of little concern to me or you. What's of more concern is how many and where the rest of their friends are."

"Should we get back to the hotel?"

"No, for now we're safe here. Besides, I fully intend on enjoying this wine with a great piece of meat."

As if on cue, the bar-maid appeared with two plates of steak frites. Dominicus attacked his portion with gusto, then, looking at Alex, said, "Fire away, young Donovan."

"Why does the Vatican want to find Gaspar now? You said you've been searching for him for over forty years. What do you really want?"

"The Vatican, the entity, doesn't know that I even exist. As I told you, there are only a small handful of people, including you and I, who know the story of Gaspar. One of those men is the pope. He, like all the popes before him, back to the book's first discovery, has known of Gaspar and has searched for him. I'm but the latest in a long line of men tasked with the mission of finding him. It's a secret passed on from one pope to the next."

"But why? It's pretty obvious he wants to stay hidden."

"Are you sure about that? Why did he seek out the painter and tell him his story? Why did he have him create the book?"

Alex thought about the priest's words for a moment.

"Something doesn't smell right about your story, Dominicus. There's something you aren't telling me."

The priest put down his fork and sat back in his chair.

"You really don't get why you're here, do you?"

"Actually, you're right about that. I woke up one day to find out I'm somehow linked to a man over seven hundred years old who chases wayward spirits for a living. Why am I here, Dominicus? You act as if you know."

The priest began to speak when they were interrupted by the owner of the bar who approached their table and began speaking in rapid German. As he did so, he slid a set of car keys into the priest's hand.

After a brief conversation Dominicus stood and, after downing his glass of wine in one gulp, said, "Dinner's over, Alex. I hope you still have some of those skills the U.S. Navy taught you. Let's go."

CHAPTER 35

Zurich, Switzerland, May 2010

Alex hurried out the front door of the bar after Dominicus. The priest, if that was what he was, was already sliding behind the wheel of a black Mercedes coupe. Alex stopped, looked down the street, and, before he could see it, he heard the roar of a high powered vehicle racing their way.

"Come on, Alex! Get in! Your Italian friends have decided not to wait."

The screech of tires woke Alex from his momentary pause, and he leapt across the hood of the car and swung open the passenger door just as the headlights of a car came glaring down the street. He jumped into the passenger seat and, before he had closed the door, the priest was powering away from the curb.

In a flash, Dominicus was expertly piloting the car through the maze of narrow streets at over seventy miles per hour.

Alex hastily buckled his seat belt, feeling a dull throbbing in his knee no doubt caused by his vault over the hood of the car and, looking over at the priest, said, "So, not only are you an expert at hand to hand combat, you're a formula one driver as well?"

The priest, not taking his eyes off the road, smiled and said, "There are quite a few things I'm expert at, my friend, that I think you'll come to appreciate."

The car chasing them had closed the gap and despite the priest's expert maneuvers, they couldn't distance themselves from their pursuers.

"Bastard is driving something with more guts than this thing has and he knows how to drive it," Dominicus mumbled.

As if to drive home the point, the car pursuing them rammed into the back of their car, sending them lurching forward. The priest slammed the accelerator to the floor, trying to put distance between them, but whatever was pursuing them had them out-gunned.

Again the gangsters rammed them. This time the Mercedes slid wildly as the priest fought to control it. Sliding broadside, the Mercedes hurtled toward the stone wall of a solid-looking building. At the last minute, the priest regained control, and the car shot down a narrow alley between two buildings.

Their pursuers shot past, and for a moment Alex thought they might have a chance at escape. The priest's barely audible oath and the screech of the car's brakes, coupled with the return of the headlights behind them, chased that fleeting thought away.

The Mercedes skidded to a stop just short of a stone wall; dead end.

"Hold on, young Donovan!" the priest yelled as he threw the car into reverse and floored the accelerator.

In an instant, Alex knew the priest meant to ram their pursuers. He braced himself on the dash and, looking over at the priest, saw a maniacal grin on his face.

"When this train wreck comes to an end, get out and fight for your life, my friend. Don't let them take you. Fight! From the first! Fight!"

The explosion a heartbeat later almost rendered him unconscious. As if a thousand gunshots had exploded in his ears, he experienced a feeling of weightlessness and silence. The breath was driven from him, and he gasped for air in the now deathly quiet.

His lungs caught, and he welcomed the ability to breathe. Raising his head, he looked over to find the priest slumped over the wheel, moaning slightly. Remembering his pursuers, he undid his seat belt and found he could open his door. He lurched out of the car into the dark. Only the sound of hissing steam reached his ears. Nothing moved in what he could now see was a black Range Rover.

He reached into the car, grabbing the priest by the shoulders, and pulled him into the alley. He propped him against the wall and took a close look at him. Blood flowed freely from his nose and mouth and, just when he thought the priest might be dead, his eyes opened wide and a smile spread across his face.

He looked from Alex to the Range Rover and said, "I knew it would work."

"Yeah, worked real well. I can barely move, and you look half dead," Alex responded.

"Nonsense. I've never felt better."

Alex started to respond when he was interrupted by the sounds of several voices at the mouth of the alley. Turning, he saw the silhouettes of men running toward them.

"Time to go, Dominicus," he said, helping the priest to his feet.

Putting an arm under his shoulder, he hustled the priest down the alley away from the Italians toward the stone wall, looking for a way out of their trap.

He found it in the form of a small metal gate built into the wall just before the end of the alley. The chain on the gate gave way easily under Alex's well placed kick, and he pushed the priest through the opening.

Stealing a quick glance down the alley, he could see several men approaching their Mercedes with guns drawn.

The priest was now moving on his own, and Alex hurried after him down a narrow walkway between two stone buildings. After stumbling their way down the walkway for a short distance, they found themselves standing in an open space alongside the river. It looked to be an empty lot surrounded on three sides by old stone buildings. While they were in a larger space, they were still trapped unless they planned on swimming.

Alex looked at the slowly moving water and, kicking off his shoes, made to strip off his pants, preparing to swim their way to safety.

"All well and good for you, my Seal friend. There's just one problem," came the priest's voice from behind.

Alex turned and said, "Whatever it is, you better deal with it because this river is our only way out of this trap."

"The river is the problem, my friend. You see, I can't swim."

"What?"

"I can't swim; never learned. Hate the water, in fact."

"You've got to be kidding me, Dominicus. Of all the things-"

"No use, Alex. If I go in there, I'll sink to the bottom like a rock, and I don't plan on ending my life in that manner. You, though, could make the far bank without much effort."

Alex looked at the priest and realized what he was saying.

"We had a code as Seals; no man left behind. They'll get here in a minute. Let's go. You hold onto me, and we'll swim for it."

What sounded like automatic weapon fire filled the night air, and Alex, no stranger to the sounds of a firefight in full voice, heard the sounds of yelling, screaming, and dying men.

Dominicus stood eerily still, listening to the mayhem that seemed to be coming slowly their way.

"What the hell is going on, Dominicus?" Alex asked.

The priest simply raised his hand as if to say *silence*.

Alex could clearly hear the panicked screams of men being slaughtered. The gunfire was slowly subsiding in a way Alex also recognized, and with a cold sweat breaking out all over his body, he realized someone or something was systematically wiping out their pursuers.

He was surprised a moment later by the hand of the priest on his arm.

"This is where we make our stand, young Donovan. It's no longer a matter of choice."

"What are you talking about?"

Before the priest could answer, Alex felt the air around him still and, as if the warmth had been sucked from the atmosphere, he felt a chill course through him that for a moment caused him to be physically ill. Just when he thought he'd pass out from the waves of nausea washing over him, he saw several figures emerge from the walkway and enter the clearing. They were unlike anything he'd ever seen, then, in a moment of blinding clarity, he realized he was in the middle of Gaspar's book.

CHAPTER 36

Zurich, Switzerland, May 2010

Demons, hideous creatures that walked on two legs but had bodies covered in black oily scales slinked into the clearing. They looked like monstrous eels with the bodies of humans. Moving in a synchronized motion, as if tethered to each other by some unseen chain, the creatures advanced in unison. They carried monstrous looking swords and axes that dripped with what Alex knew were the remnants of his mafia pursuers.

Dominicus' hand had become an iron grip on his upper arm, and in a quiet, exceedingly calm voice, the priest said, "Steel yourself, boy. I need the warrior who lies within you now."

And then, like a whispered lullaby, a voice sweet and melodic ghosted across the open ground. "Hello, Dominicus, old friend."

Alex swore he could see the old priest's shoulders shrink for a moment before he gathered himself. The priest drew a knife from under his shirt, a wicked looking double edged blade that looked to be about six inches long.

He handed it to Alex. "Take this. When they get close, go to work. I'll distract them."

And then, looking deep into Alex's eyes, he said, "You know, it's you they really want. It's why they risk everything, break every rule to come here like this. It's you they fear, so they come now when you're frail, still new in this flesh and untaught by the one you seek. If you find him, what he'll teach you puts all they work for in peril."

"Why me? How could I possibly be a threat to beings such as these?"

Dominicus smiled even as Alex noticed him flexing his hands and fingers, shaking his arms, and vigorously shrugging. The old priest was readying himself for battle.

"I'm not sure. But I aim to find out, which means we can't die in a Zurich alley tonight. It means we fight and we continue your search. I may be old, but I'm not ready to die."

With that, he pulled a silenced pistol from inside his jacket, turned and ran across the empty lot straight at the horde of nightmarish things now swarming into the open space.

Alex had dealt death, fought hand to hand to save his own life. What he saw unfolding before him was like nothing he'd ever witnessed. Mayhem and death, imbued with an unholy fury, exploded before him. One thing was sure; Dominicus wasn't your run-of-the-mill parish priest.

In a flash, Dominicus was among the beasts whirling and spinning, avoiding the slashing and stabbing weapons, firing until his gun was empty. First one, then two of the creatures went flying across the ground, crumpled into unmoving masses. Then Alex saw the priest had gained one of the wicked looking swords from the demons and was now slashing and fighting his way through the seething horde.

In the end, there were just too many, and as he parried and thrust, two of the beasts streaked by him, their eyes locked on Alex.

As if ten years were gone in a flash, Alex took up a knife-fighting stance with the blade held out in front of him. In a moment's rush they were on him.

Using their momentum against them, he whirled and lowering his shoulder caught one of the charging demons low in the chest, sending it flying over his back. Not hesitating, he slashed the blade in two giant arches catching the second demon in the abdomen, slicing up into its chest.

The scream of agony that erupted from the beast was ear-splitting. Not wasting a moment, he grabbed it by the neck from behind and repeatedly stabbed the blade into its lower back. Holding on for dear life as the demon thrashed and spun, he was amazed at the strength of the thing.

Finally, he could feel its life ebbing away and, letting go, he pushed it into the river. Turning, he found himself facing the other demon who, had gathered itself off the ground and now, obviously leery of his prey, slowly approached, looking for an opening.

Alex began to circle away from the river and, as he did so, the demon also began to circle until they seemed to be engaged in a slowly choreographed dance of waiting death.

Alex didn't have to wait long. The creature lunged at him with his sword. Alex parried the thrust with the blade of the knife and lunged into the demon. He found himself in a death embrace with a being of such immense strength, he realized the beast could crush him to death. In this close proximity, Alex could now see directly into the thing's eyes and was almost overcome by the evil and hate radiating from them.

It was into one of those eyes he thrust the old priest's blade again and again, until slowly the crushing embrace began to give way and the being crumpled at his feet.

Taking a step back, Alex suddenly fell to the ground, his knee giving way in a blinding flash of pain. Alex knew that he'd torn it apart somehow in the fight.

"Not bad, Alex. Not bad at all."

Alex looked up to see Dominicus standing above him. The priest was covered in blood and gore, and Alex could tell by the way some of the blood ran free-flowing much of it was the old man's.

Alex was about to take the priest's outstretched hand when the sound of clapping hands froze him to the ground.

"Bravo, gentlemen! Bravo!"

Alex peered past Domincius and found himself staring at a woman standing a few yards away from them. She was at the same time beautiful, and fearsome.

She was at least a head taller than Alex, with long thick black hair which almost touched the ground. Her skin was so white, it seemed translucent and seemed to glow in the dim light. He could see she was smiling, but the smile struck fear straight into his heart like an ice cold blade. She wore a long, black coat that brushed the ground, and he could see a pair of heavy boots on her feet.

Alex looked away for a moment back to Dominicus and found the priest's eyes closed, his head bowed, his lips slowly moving in what Alex instantly knew was a silent prayer.

"No use praying, Dominicus. God's not listening," the woman said.

Slowly the priest opened his eyes. He looked at Alex and said, "Here, take my hand."

After helping Alex to his feet, the old priest turned slowly to face the woman behind him.

"Hello, Cassandra. Or should I be using your fallen name today?"

"I do so much like Cassandra and this form. It brings back such wonderful memories of our times together. How have you been, Dominicus? I see you still love to fight."

The priest said nothing, but Alex could see the telltale flexing of his fingers and the tightening grip on the sword in his hand.

"Easy, my long lost lover. Are you in such a rush to die you'd deny me a few final words?"

Alex stared from the woman back to Dominicus. Lover? What in God's name was going on here?

And in the instant he thought the question, the bone-chilling laugh from the woman broke the silence.

"Oh, yes, Mr. Donovan. There was a time when Dominicus and I became intimate. He's old now, but what a specimen of manhood he once was. I remember that night well. It was--"

"Silence, you evil bitch!" thundered Dominicus. "One time I allowed myself to be tempted and gave in to the charms of what turned out to be a spawn from hell. One time I forsook my vows, and every day since, I've worked to rid myself of your stain. Now you come here again to torment me? I'll abide it no more!"

The fallen angel laughed bitterly, then said, "I'm so sorry to disappoint, Dominicus, but I didn't come here tonight to waste time tormenting your useless, old carcass. I came here to kill you and the thing standing behind you. I'm done with you, priest. You served your purpose, now its time to take your soul."

Slowly, the fallen angel raised her hands in front of her and began to advance, the smile never leaving her face.

"You may take my body, Cassandra, but you'll never have my soul. I've made my peace with God, and I willingly go to him now."

With that, Domnicus raised the sword and launched himself at the woman. Covering the ground between them in a rush, he swung the sword at the angel's head. Alex watched, horrified, as the woman calmly and effortlessly sidestepped the slashing blade, then caught the old priest by the throat with one hand. Lifting him off the ground, she calmly grabbed his arm holding the sword, and with a snap, broke the arm, eliciting a blood-curdling scream from the old priest.

Before Alex could act, she drew Dominicus close to her, kissed him full on the mouth, then, with little effort, threw him against the stone wall of one of the surrounding buildings. The priest's body hit with an unbelievable force, and the sounds of his breaking bones echoed in Alex's head. Dominicus slumped to the ground in an unmoving heap.

Slowly the woman turned to face Alex. All traces of the smile were now gone. What replaced it was an evil scowl. The woman began to shimmer, and her shape began to fade. As he watched spellbound, all remnants of human form disappeared in a cloud of light. What emerged from the light was a monstrous thing of beauty so dazzling that Alex had to raise his hand to shield his eyes.

What stood before him was what he'd read about in his grandfather's book; a fallen angel in its true demonic form.

"So, this is what's driven all of hell into such a torment? You?" said a voice he didn't hear with his ears, but came full voice into his head.

"I'm almost disappointed this is what I was dispatched to deal with. We shall see if your soul is stronger than your frail and useless human body. I'll enjoy taking it with me back to hell."

Alex's eyes had now adjusted to the bright light emanating from the angel. He took a deep breath and found himself strangely calm. A wave of remembrances washed over him as he experienced a sense of almost euphoric peace. The thing before him was about to devour him soul and all, but all he could see was the smiling face of his grandfather staring across the old desk at him. He looked down and saw his feet slowly swinging above the Persian rug. And then he heard Randolph's voice, "We're going to read Nabokov today. I think at eleven years old you're ready for him. Just don't tell your parents what we're reading. It's called *Lolita*."

He blinked away a tear and found himself back in the clearing, facing the fallen angel again.

"I don't know why you crave my soul, demon, but something tells me your wretched soul will reach its end before mine."

Alex raised the knife, braced himself on his good leg and, gritting his teeth in a sudden wave of anger, yelled at the thing in front of him, "Come and take me, you ugly bitch!"

It was as if a ten ton truck had hit him at full force. The wave of light that was the fallen angel engulfed him, and he found himself flat on his back, the thing above him pressing down on him with a force that began to squeeze the life from him. He could feel his bones cracking, his lungs exploding, and his heart pounding like a giant drum in his ears.

He realized at some point he was repeatedly and franticly stabbing the angel over and over to little or no effect. As the darkness began to engulf him, it dawned on him that the angel's hands were slowly crushing his skull. Bright explosions of light lit the back of his eyes and, in what he feared would be his final vision, he looked into the orange glare of the angel's eyes. What he saw in them surprised him, for what they contained was fear; the unmistakable burgeoning of fear blooming amid the angry flames of evil.

And then he was free. Not dead, but free of the life-crushing presence of the angel. He turned his head, the cool dirt a welcome distraction from the death trying to subdue him.

Watching his blood flow away across the trash-strewn lot, like so many lost and shattered dreams, Alex lay broken and near death. In a fog of delirium, he realized a pair of worn and scuffed boots stood in the midst of the bloody remnants of his life. A hand like a feather brushed his cheek and a voice whispered, "Not yet, young Donovan. Not yet."

Through a sheer force of will, Alex raised his head and wiped the blood and gore from his eyes. He saw the angel who, a moment ago, seemed ready to snuff out his life, stepping backwards in obvious fear.

A dark and shadowy form stood above him, facing the fallen angel. It was a man dressed in dark clothes, a long coat that almost reached the ground and a strange droopy hat on his head.

"You! What are you doing here?" whispered the angel.

"Did you think for a moment I would allow this blasphemy to occur?" the stranger responded.

Alex could sense the angel's fear when it said, "This thing at your feet isn't worthy. He can't be allowed to ascend to his dark destiny."

"That's not for you to say. And I wonder why you so vehemently oppose his ascension, if that's what he chooses? I wonder what you fear. Or perhaps it's your master's fear that sends you here."

"Is this thing worth this? Is he worth what I may do to you?" the angel responded.

Alex heard the man laugh, a laugh that for whatever reason gave him hope and strength.

"What you may do to me, Cassandra? After all we've been through? What you may do to me? Tread lightly and go on your way now. This is your last warning."

Alex watched as the two stood across from each other, saying nothing for a moment. Then, as if a colossal burden had been lifted from the angel's shoulders, she drew a short sword from under her coat.

"No, one of us dies here. This is where it ends."

In a voice that to Alex seemed full of sadness, the man said, "So be it."

Alex had seen death before, just never played out in such a medieval and dramatic fashion, as if it was some sort of choreographed opera taking place for his benefit only. The epic scene that unfolded before him left him spellbound.

The man drew a blade from under his coat, a huge broadsword he held in one hand with apparent ease. He took a step back from the angel and, with his free hand, gestured to the alley as if to say *take your leave*.

The response left Alex cringing and breathless. The angel flew as if she possessed the wings of a falcon through the air, sword whirling in a windmill of death Alex swore should have rendered the man into a thousand pieces of broken flesh.

Instead, the man calmly, and with no effort, stepped into the attack, Alex would have sworn through the whirling blade, and took up station behind the angel.

Still he didn't make a move to attack.

"Here, Cassandra, behind you," he said half mockingly, half imploringly, as if willing the angel away.

Swearing in a hundred voices and languages, the angel whirled and launched a furious attack, this time met by the blade of the stranger. With effortless ease, he parried every thrust, stab, and crushing blow. Alex was struck by the ease of his actions, as if he'd done this a thousand times, and nothing the angel could throw at him surprised him.

As Alex watched, he began to see a change in the angel. Her onslaught began to wane. The ferocious venom of her initial attacks seemed blunted and weak until, finally, the angel stood before the stranger, sword held in a quivering arm.

What happened next was like a scene from a hellish nightmare.

The stranger began to circle the angel; slowly, walking in an ever tightening circle around her, as she tried to keep him in front of her. He began to pick up speed, walking faster, faster; now running, the angel still keeping him in sight, until he was moving so fast that Alex could barely discern his form.

Then it happened. Alex, in his near death state, almost missed it. The stranger struck.

The blade flashed for only a moment, then, the angel stood still with the stranger's sword protruding from her chest, the haft buried tight against her body, the blade sticking obscenely out her back.

The angel fell to her knees, a soul-wrenching cry emanating from her throat.

The stranger had let loose of the sword, now a short dagger was in his hand. He moved behind the angel and stepped close. He removed the sword from her hand and tossed it into the dark, then grabbed the angel by the neck, holding her tight.

Wiping the still free-flowing blood from his eyes, Alex leaned forward, straining to hear. He listened as the stranger lowered his head to the angel's ear.

"I tried to save you. I even loved you for a moment once; just a moment. My heart no longer breaks, but you, you came close to breaking it once more. Please, Cassandra. Please, repent. I beg you."

Alex swore he could see tears flowing down the man's partially hidden face.

The quiet and now peaceful voice of the angel ghosted across the open ground, "Those days and those things, like love, have passed me by, Templar. If what you say is true, that you could have loved me, end this hellish existence now."

The man closed his eyes and, without hesitation, thrust the blade into the base of the angel's skull, holding it tight as she began to thrash and wail spasmodically.

Then, as Alex watched, she slowly quieted. Still in the arms of the stranger, her form began to flicker like an ebbing candle. He watched as she melted from a physical being into a halo of light burning bright for only a moment before flickering out and fading away, leaving the man holding his knife, his broadsword on the ground before him.

The man knelt there for a moment before turning and walking away, fading from Alex's vision.

A wave of nausea passed over him. His arms failed him, and he fell to the dirt of the empty lot, his face soaking up the coolness of the earth.

He saw Dominicus lying still and lifeless at the base of the wall. He wondered why he was so cold in the middle of a warm summer's night. He realized he could no longer move or feel his extremities.

And then he saw the stranger kneel next to Dominicus. The strange droopy hat he wore shielded his face as he knelt close to the old priest and, as Alex watched, he moved his hands over Dominicus' body as if searching out injury.

Then, quietly, his hands came to rest on the priest's chest, and the low rhythmic cadence of a song floated into Alex's ears. The sound was like a pleading call to someone or something. The notes caressed Alex and seemed to fortify him. He thought it surreal that the man could so devastatingly dispatch the creature from hell, then so passionately sing this song.

After a moment, the priest's body shuddered violently, and he sat up wide-eyed and gasping for air.

The stranger's hand reached out and cupped the old man's cheek and, as if comforted, Dominicus stilled.

"You! It's you!" cried the priest.

"Old, Dominicus. Will you ever learn the art of subtlety? These things you provoke will be the death of you."

"I always knew you existed."

"No you didn't. Not until now. Tell me, priest, do you believe that those who send you after me for these many years have pure hearts? Is what you seek worth all the blood you have spilled? Perhaps what you seek is not what you believe it to be."

"What do you mean?"

"You know what I mean, old man. Tread carefully down the road you walk. You live tonight only because I allow it. Think about your afterlife and if what you are doing is truly what your God would want. Forsake your misguided crusade, and perhaps I'll speak well of you at just the right moment, to just the right being, when it means the most. Now, sleep."

Alex watched as the stranger's hands caressed the old priest's face and, catching his head softly, lowered him back to the ground.

The man stood and moved out of Alex's view.

He lay there seeing nothing but the once again quiet priest, feeling only his shallow breaths, every one of which seemed might be the last.

And then he felt it, a slow warmth spreading over his body, starting at his feet, slowly rising upward. He realized what he felt were two hands, strong but tender, moving up his body.

The warm caress of breath on his ear startled him at first, then gave him comfort. The rhythmic breathing seemed to invade him and take over his own breathing, supplanting it and giving it strength. The hands reached his waist and continued up his back, the fingers probing, looking, he realized, for wounds, injury, and pain.

His breathing was now out of his hands. He had no control over it. He felt as if his own lungs were being compressed and driven by a force outside of himself and, with that force, came a strength which allowed him to open his eyes and turn his head.

The brim of the worn hat was all he saw before a hand grasped his chin and held it firm. The other hand gently massaged his shattered skull, imparting a tingling, warm sensation.

"You acquitted yourself well against those two demons, brother; a mortal against two of hell's warriors. That you still live is something worth noting."

He couldn't move or speak, and he would have sworn his heart hadn't taken a beat since the sound of that whispered voice.

"Your life ebbs away; it happens. If I had to count the times I've been at death's door, I'd drown in a rampaging river of memories. This is but the first for you. There will be more. The good news is this isn't your end, this is your beginning. But we'll have to do something about that knee of yours. It'll be the death of you otherwise."

He felt that hand again, strong but feather-light, move slowly over his crippled knee. Intense and pulsating warmth infused his leg, and in a flash of brilliant pain he lost consciousness, knowing he'd found the one he searched for; the man in his grandfather's book. He'd found Gaspar and he lived. It was not a dream.

CHAPTER 37

France, somewhere in the foothills of the Pyrenees,
August, 2010

A lex woke to the sound of a rooster crowing like a banshee well past the sunrise. It was as if the bastard bird hadn't seen a hen in weeks and was taking it out on him. The sun was flowing through a window, a window without glass. Heavy wooden shutters that looked as if they were a hundred years old did little to muffle the persistent crowing.

He lay on his side, listening to the bird and contemplating the thin shafts of light knifing through the shutter slats, and after a time, the dusty motes swirling within the light. He knew, somehow, he'd been asleep for a long time. Not hours, but days, maybe months.

In the end, it was the bird that drove him from the still comforting solace of the sheets. He slid from under the coverings reveling in the feeling of cool tile on his feet. It was already warm. Wherever he was, it was summer to be this warm so early.

A basin and a pitcher of water sat on a small nightstand beside the bed. He poured the water into the basin and splashed it on his face, then through his hair. It was cold. Not cool, but cold, as if from a mountain stream. A towel lay next to the basin and he dried his face and hands.

He was naked. Casting his gaze around the room he spied a stack of clothes on a low bench at the foot of the bed. He picked up a pair of worn, but soft pants and a brilliant white shirt. He slipped them on, taking only passing note of the fact that they fit him perfectly. Why wouldn't they? he wondered.

A pair of sandals, stained dark by someone's feet, were arranged next to the bench. He slipped his feet into them, the indentations of the toes and the heel lining up perfectly with his feet. They weren't his sandals, he knew that.

Spying a door next to the window he went to it, pulled it open and hesitated at the glare. His eyes adjusted quickly as he stepped out into the morning sun.

The bird had stopped his crowing and silence washed over him. It was so quiet, he wondered if he was really awake.

He stood on a patio of stone and brick. Several large fruit trees, he saw oranges and maybe lemons, were spaced among the pavers. A rather ornate, stone railing stretched along the edge of the space before him. Beyond that, was a sky-filled panorama broken by tall mountain peaks, jagged and wild.

He heard a sound then; a soft wisp of noise, a rhythmic swishing, back and forth, to a determined cadence. He moved toward the sound which came from beyond the balustrade before him.

When he reached the railing, he saw, spread before him, a beautiful lake. The water was a vivid cobalt blue, still and serene. Surrounded by dense forests of dark green trees and the mountains beyond, it was a breathtaking spectacle of beauty.

The sound that had drawn him to the railing had stopped and below the balustrade he saw a man, at least it looked like a man, staring back at him.

The man, an oddity no more than three feet tall and as white as snow, was standing on another patio holding a broom. The handle was taller than he was. He was smiling.

"Good Morning, Alex. How do you feel this fine day?" the man said in a voice surprisingly baritone for one so small.

Alex tried to speak but his voice cracked and croaked, and he realized how dry his mouth was.

"Ah, one moment, Alex!" the little man said putting down his broom and, at an astonishing speed, dashing up the set of stairs to where Alex stood.

He took Alex's hand, pulling him to a wooden table under the branches of an orange tree, pulled a chair back from the table and said, "Sit here for a moment. I shall return with something for your voice."

Alex did as he was told.

Less than a minute later, the little man was back at Alex's side, with a tea-pot and a tea-cup. He poured until the cup was half full and then said, "Now, go ahead and drink. I promise you your voice will be as good as new."

Alex stared at the little man for a moment a feeling of *déjà vu* giving him chills. The man stared back, his brilliant smile firmly in place. Alex raised the cup and took a drink.

The liquid, whatever it was, brought an instant smile to Alex's face, which resulted in an exclamation of pleasure and a bout of laughter from the little man.

"See! Now, finish your tea and we will try out your voice."

Alex drained the cup and set it down on the table. Swallowing, he realized his mouth and throat were no longer dry. Tentatively he spoke, "Who are you?"

"Excellent. Your voice sounds wonderful," the little man responded. "I am Sabatticus."

Alex frowned and he repeated the man's name, "Sabatticus? I feel like I've heard that name before and somehow I know you. But I know we've never met before. That, I'd remember."

Sabatticus smiled a sly grin and poured more tea into Alex's cup. "Oh, we've met. But I understand if you do not remember our first meeting. You were pre-disposed, as it were."

Confused, Alex began to ask what Sabatticus meant when the little man interrupted him, "You've been under my care for these many weeks. I watched over you while you slept, read to you, told you stories--I am a great story teller--and nursed you back to health. Of course, I was not alone in this endeavor."

Thoroughly confused now, Alex said, "I have no idea what you're talking about. Where am I and what's happened to me?"

"I have no doubt you're confused after what you've been through. Tell me, what's the last thing you remember?"

Alex thought for a moment and realized he remembered nothing before the crowing of the rooster. A feeling of panic began to take hold before Sabatticus laid his tiny hand on his and said, "Easy, Alex. Don't be afraid or surprised. It will all come back to you in due course. For now, come with me. I hear the goats and they need to be let out into the meadow."

Sabatticus pulled Alex out of the chair and led the way across the patio. Alex was now able to get a glimpse of the building he had exited and was surprised by its size. It was massive, at least four stories tall with balconies and windows spread across its length. Constructed of stone, the bottom courses were made of huge boulders which looked as if they'd been in place for centuries. The ancient manor house exuded age and nobility. Like the rest of his surroundings, it was beautiful.

"My Master's home, Alex," Sabatticus said. "It was built in 1335. Of course, it's been added to and expanded over the years, but it's much as it was then."

Alex looked at the little man in surprise. He looked back at the mansion, or was it a castle? Either way it was awesome and looked to be in perfect condition. Like the window in the room he'd woken in, none of the other windows had glass in them. They all had heavy wooden shutters, held back by metal hooks on the outside, and slatted shutters on the inside.

"My Master does not care for glass windows. He prefers to feel the breezes through the house. It's wonderful for the most part although it does get a bit drafty in the winter. Luckily we depart for warmer climes during those times and--."

"Wait a minute," Alex interrupted. "That's the second time you've done that."

"Done what, my friend?"

"Well, if I didn't know any better I'd say you're reading my mind."

Sabatticus laughed as if Alex had told a good joke. "How on earth could I ever do such a thing?"

Alex started to say something, but they'd reached the end of the patio and stood looking out over an expanse of grassy meadow which stretched down a sloping grade to the edge of the lake. An amazing variety of wildflowers dotted the landscape, and again Alex was struck by the beauty of this place.

Sabatticus walked a short distance to a small corral. He opened a gate and stood aside as at least twenty goats, with long, white, flowing hair, raced out and into the field. The little man clapped his hands chasing after a few stragglers, then closed the gate.

Suddenly, Alex went deathly still. He knew without turning, someone was behind him. Slowly, he turned and almost jumped back in surprise and shock.

"Malamek!" Sabatticus said. "Why do you insist on sneaking up on people like this? Don't you know Mr. Alex has not fully wakened yet?"

Standing before Alex, was a...well, it was a giant. It was a man at least two feet taller than Alex and twice as wide. He was dressed in a simple, but elegant light brown robe. His feet, like Alex's, were clad in sandals. His eyes were locked on Alex and his face was stern and forbidding, not a trace of a smile. In his hands was a tray of food.

"I swear sometimes you do that just to showoff," Sabatticus continued. "Ah, I see you have breakfast ready. You get used to Malamek slinking around and once you partake of his culinary wonders, you forgive him his little games."

Alex was still staring into Malamek's eyes when those eyes broke their hold, swiveling off over Alex's shoulder into the distance. For a moment, Alex thought he saw the twitching of a smile at the corners of the giant's mouth.

Alex turned to see what he was looking at to find Sabatticus, as well, staring off across the meadow. The little man turned back to Alex and with a knowing smile pointed toward the lake. "Our master approaches," he whispered.

Alex peered into the distance, in the direction Sabatticus pointed. He squinted for a moment, and then made out a man on horseback riding toward them.

Drawn forward, Alex found himself moving into the field. The rider drew closer. The horse was slowly cantering through the meadow. Something about the horse's pace and gait seemed hypnotic and Alex realized his heart was pounding.

As he drew nearer, Alex could make out the rider more clearly. He rode with grace and an easy bearing, giving Alex the impression the man was part of the animal beneath him.

As the horse drew closer, Alex realized it was huge, a massive black beast with a long mane blowing in the breeze. The rider wore a dark hat and a white shirt very much like the one Alex himself wore. Black pants were stuffed into the tops of a pair of knee high boots.

As the horse drew closer, Alex felt the rider's eyes boring into him. Once more, a sense of *déjà vu* assailed him.

The horse was so close now he could hear its snorting breath. Alex stood, rooted to the ground, and just when he thought the horse might run him down the rider reined him in, the horse coming to a sliding stop beside him.

Alex found himself staring into the rider's face; he was smiling.

"I see you have decided to rejoin us, Alex. Good! It has been some time," the rider said in a voice Alex knew he had heard before. But where?

Alex felt a movement behind him and turned to find the giant striding up to the horse. He took the horse's bridle in a massive hand and the man swung off the horse in a fluid, graceful movement.

Taking his hat from his head, he spun it through the air, straight into the hands of Sabatticus, who stood smiling a short distance away.

"So, how do you feel? Did Sabatticus give you some of his tea?" the stranger asked.

Alex stared at the man, unable to speak. He knew this man! He studied him, trying to coax something, anything, up from wherever his memories had gone. What was happening to him? Nothing made sense.

The man was the same height as Alex and the closer he looked at him the more he realized how much alike they were. He couldn't quite pin down the man's age but he felt somehow it was close to his own. He face was tanned, as though he spent most of his days under the sun, but it was devoid of lines or creases. His hair, like Alex's, was brown, but longer, hanging well below the collar of his shirt.

It was his eyes though that held him. They were dark, almost black and they radiated age; unfathomable age and knowledge.

And just as he finished thinking those things a voice, Alex knew it was the stranger's, spoke to him within his mind, "Do not be afraid Alex. I am your friend. Take my hand."

The man's smile hadn't wavered, his lips never moved. Alex looked down to see the man holding out his hand. A hand crisscrossed by a web of scars and welts.

Alex raised his hand, and slowly, took the stranger's outstretched hand. The grip was strong, the hand calloused and rough. Once more, Alex locked eyes with the smiling stranger.

"Hello, Alex Donovan. I was your grandfather's friend and now I am yours. I am, Gaspar de Rouse."

In an avalanche of memories, which assaulted his mind with the force of a hurricane, he remembered everything; every story, every page of the book, all that had happened.

In the end, his mind had not healed enough to handle the burden of his memories and the black, like a funeral veil, slid down over his mind and he collapsed into the arms of Gaspar.

EPILOGUE

Somewhere in the Alps, Switzerland, August 2010

Dominicus Bureau sat in a comfortable old leather chair under the shade of a large pine tree. The sun beat down out of a cloudless sky but this high up in the Alps, the air still had a hint of a chill to it. He stared off into the distance, in the direction of a line of jagged snow capped peaks. A shiny black cane spun lazily back and forth from one hand to another.

He saw neither the beautiful scenery before him, nor did he seem to feel the chill in the air. What he did see was in his mind and what he heard was a voice inside his head.

He had been sitting in this chair everyday for the last two months replaying the scene from Zurich, the battle with Cassandra, and his confrontation with Gaspar.

Was that the right word, confrontation? If Gaspar had wanted to, he obviously could have allowed Dominicus to die. His doctors, at this hidden and very discreet hospital, had made it very clear his injuries should have killed him. Why they hadn't the physicians couldn't say.

Dominicus knew. He knew Gaspar had saved him. The question swirling within his mind, which tormented him, was why? Gaspar knew Dominicus searched for him and in fact wished him ill. Why?

The Arimathean's words haunted him, *"Is what you seek worth all the blood you have spilled? Perhaps what you seek is not what you believe it to be."*

This was in fact the first time doubt had clouded his vision. Others had doubted. He had removed some of those doubters from the land of the living himself. Now, he sat here confronted by the fact the man he had searched for all these years existed in the flesh. He was no longer some phantom, a wraith dancing through time and space always a step ahead of his pursuit. He had looked into his eyes and seen the centuries there. He had felt his hand on his face and been frozen in...not fear. Wonder.

He had spared him and given him a warning, given him a way out. Was it real or a trick? His whole life had been spent pursuing what Gaspar guarded. His soul was heavy with the weight of the blood he had shed in his quest. Hundreds, thousands before him had pursued the same treasure.

In the end it was too much. He had to know. He had to see it with his own eyes. The Arimathean had tried to warn him away. It had to exist and he would be the one to finally place his hands upon it.

He reached over to a small table next to the chair and retrieved the satphone which had laid there for two months. He dialed a Paris number. After two short rings a voice answered, "Dominicus?"

"I'm ready. I'll be leaving tomorrow."

"Where are you going?" the voice asked.

"To find Alex Donovan."

The End

ABOUT THE AUTHOR:

Husband and father, voracious reader and entrepreneur, Vernon finally found the courage to put soul to paper. **Slow Boat To Purgatory** is his first novel.

He lives with his wife and children on the coast of Maine and in the panhandle of Florida. Occasionally, when the need arises, he travels to Venice to see an old friend...a very old friend.

Made in the USA
Charleston, SC
23 June 2013